THE DANGER GAME

THE DANGER GAME

KEVIN BROOKS

TRAVIS DELANEY

MACMILLAN CHILDREN'S BOOKS

First published 2014 by Macmillan Children's Books
a division of Macmillan Publishers Limited
20 New Wharf Road, London N1 9RR
Basingstoke and Oxford
Associated companies throughout the world
www.panmacmillan.com

ISBN 978-1-4472-3897-3

3 5 7 9 8 6 4 2

A CIP catalogue record for this book is available from
the British Library.

Printed and bound by CPI Group (UK) Ltd, Croydon CR0 4YY

For Teeny – you have a special place in my heart.

1

It was just gone three thirty on a cold and wet Friday afternoon when Kendal Price came up to me and said he'd like a quiet word. I'd just finished a double period of PE – half an hour's fitness training, another half-hour of football practice, followed by two twenty-minute seven-a-side games. I was covered in mud, tired out, and although I was still dripping with sweat, the icy wind blowing across the playing fields was beginning to bite into my bones. So all I wanted to do just then was get into the changing rooms, get out of my muddy football gear, and have a quick shower. And that's exactly what I told Kendal when he caught up with me just outside the changing rooms and said he wanted to talk to me about something.

'Just let me get changed first, OK?' I told him, rubbing my arms. 'It's freezing out here.'

'Now would be better,' he said.

'I'll only be ten minutes. Can't it wait?'

'No,' he said simply, 'it can't.'

If it had been anyone else, I probably would have stood my ground. 'If you want to talk to me,' I would have said, 'you'll just have to wait.' But this wasn't anyone else, this was Kendal Price.

Kendal is the kind of kid that every school has – the

all-round superstar who's naturally brilliant at everything. Captain of the school football and cricket teams, a straight-A student, sophisticated, popular, attractive. The teachers all love him, and constantly hold him up as a 'shining example' to the rest of us. The girls all love him because he's tall, blond, and handsome. And the boys all love him (or envy him, at least) because he's not only really good at football and cricket, but he's tough and courageous too, both on and off the field. So even though he's a straight-A student who's loved by all the teachers – which normally might make him a prime target for bullying – no one ever messes with Kendal Price. Not if they know what's good for them anyway. In fact, Kendal's such an all-round superhero that even the genuinely hard kids – the ones who claim to hate his guts – go weak at the knees in his presence.

Personally I've never really had any strong feelings about him either way. I don't worship the ground he walks on, but I don't despise him or envy him either. He is what he is, and he does what he does, and as long as that doesn't affect me, I'm really not that bothered. Mind you, having said that, I'm pretty sure that if Kendal had come up to me last term and asked if he could have a quiet word with me, I probably would have been just a tiny bit thrilled.

But a lot can change in a few short months, and so much had happened to me during the summer holidays that I was a completely different person now. My world had been turned upside down, my outlook on life changed for ever, and I'd found out the hard way that most of the stuff we spend our time worrying about doesn't actually mean anything at all.

So when Kendal approached me that afternoon, I wasn't thrilled or overawed or flattered. I didn't care that merely by talking to me he was boosting my reputation and making me look cool. I couldn't have cared less about 'looking cool'. That kind of stuff just didn't mean anything to me any more.

So why didn't I tell Kendal that if he wanted to talk to me he'd just have to wait?

Because I was curious, that's why. And curiosity was one of the things that still meant something to me.

Questions: Why on earth did the almighty Kendal Price want to talk to me? What could he possibly want? And why was he so insistent on talking to me *before* I went into the changing rooms?

Questions had kept me going through my recent summer of hell, and I wasn't going to stop asking them now.

2

'I'm sorry about your mum and dad,' Kendal said. 'It must have been really hard for you.'

It had been four months since my parents had died in a car crash, and I'd got so used to condolences now that my response had become automatic – a nod of acknowledgement, and a look that said, 'Thanks, I appreciate your kindness.'

Kendal's initial reaction was the same as most people's – a sombre nod back, followed by an awkward silence. I let the silence hang in the air and gazed out over the playing fields. We'd crossed over to a bench at the edge of the little car park in front of the changing rooms, and from where we were sitting I could see all the way across to the girls' changing rooms on the other side of the school grounds. There were three full-size football pitches, another area marked out for five- and seven-a-side games, and a running track that wouldn't be used now until next year. A fine November rain was drifting across the fields, and a few kids in wet and muddy football gear were hurrying back to the changing rooms, desperate to get out of the cold.

Kendal was still wearing his football kit too – he'd just finished playing for the Under-15s in a match against a visiting French school – but although he was just as sodden and caked in mud as everyone else, it didn't seem to bother him at all. Or if it did, he was really good at hiding it.

'You're not living at your old place in Kell Cross any more, are you?' he asked casually.

I looked at him, slightly surprised that he hadn't changed the subject. Most people, once they've offered their condolences, quickly start talking about something else. But, as I've already said, Kendal wasn't like most people.

'I live with my nan and grandad now,' I told him.

'How's that going?'

'It's good.'

He nodded thoughtfully, giving the impression that he was genuinely interested in my welfare, but it wasn't hard to see through him. I might possibly have believed him and been grateful for his care and concern if he'd offered it four months ago, but he'd barely even looked at me before today, let alone spoken to me or shown any interest in my personal circumstances, so I was pretty sure he had an ulterior motive. His pretence didn't actually bother me that much. I was just intrigued to find out what he was *really* after.

'Your parents were private investigators, weren't they?' he asked, as if the thought had just occurred to him.

'Yeah,' I said. 'My mum and dad ran a private investigation business called Delaney & Co.'

'What's happened to the business now?'

'My grandad's taken it over.'

'Right . . .' Kendal said, doing some more thoughtful nodding. 'So you're still involved in the investigation business yourself?'

I sighed. I'd had enough of this now. I looked him straight in the eye and said, 'Are you going to tell me what this is about, Kendal? Because I don't know about you, but I'm getting *really* cold out here.'

He was momentarily taken aback by my frankness, but he quickly recovered his composure. 'All right, look,' he said, 'before I tell you anything, I need you to promise me that you'll keep it to yourself. It's really important that none of this goes any further.'

I shook my head. 'I can't promise anything.'

'Why not?'

'I don't know what you're going to tell me, do I? I mean, for all I know, you might want to confess to a murder or something.'

Kendal smiled. 'That's not very likely, is it?'

'Even superstars are capable of murder,' I said, grinning at him.

I thought he might take offence at that – he probably wasn't used to being mocked about his status – but, to his credit, he took it pretty well. I don't think he liked it very much, but he didn't make a big deal of it or anything. He just gave me one of those condescending looks that adults use when they think you're being childish. Which might sound a bit odd, given that Kendal wasn't an adult.

But although we were both the same age – fourteen years old – there was no doubt that in lots of ways Kendal was years ahead of me. He was much taller than me, for a start – at least five feet ten – and he was also a *lot* hairier. Hairy legs, hairy arms, hairy upper lip, sideburns. His voice was deep, his face rugged and knowing, and he had an air of self-confidence about him that I could only dream about.

Compared to Kendal, I *was* just a child.

Which was the kind of thing that used to bother the hell out of me.

But not any more.

'All right,' Kendal said in a businesslike manner, 'how about this – you give me your word that you'll keep quiet about this conversation *unless* I tell you something that puts you in a legally compromising position. Is that acceptable?'

'Perfectly.'

He gave me a look, making sure I was taking him seriously, and then he finally started telling me what it was all about.

3

The petty thieving from the boys' changing rooms had started in October, Kendal explained. The first time it had happened was at an Under-14 football match between our school – Kell Cross Secondary – and Barton Grammar, our biggest rivals. Then a couple of weeks later it had happened again during an Under-15 game against Seaton College.

'To be honest, we didn't take it very seriously at the time,' Kendal said. 'Partly because the items that went missing didn't have any great value, and partly because the kids who owned them weren't even sure they *had* been stolen.'

'What kind of stuff was going missing?' I asked.

Kendal frowned. 'Well, that's the weird thing. The first time it was a graphic novel, and the next time it was a hat . . . you know, like a baseball cap. That was it. No money was taken, no mobiles or watches or anything. Just a comic book and a hat. So, like I said, we didn't really give it much thought—'

'Who's "we"?'

'Mr Jago and me. I mean, the kids reported it to Mr Jago first, of course, and then he told me about it.'

John Jago was the senior PE teacher. As well as being in charge of all the school's sporting activities, he personally coached the football and cricket teams from Under-14 level upwards. He was obsessed with the sporting reputation of the school, and he spent a lot of time working with the most gifted athletes. Kendal was one of his protégés, and he treated him like a trusted lieutenant.

'Anyway,' Kendal went on, 'when the thieving started again straight after the half-term break, and it quickly became more frequent, we realised we had to do something.'

'Was the same kind of stuff being taken?'

He nodded. 'A book, a scarf, another hat . . . it still happens mostly when we're playing another school, but earlier this week a kid's belt went missing during a normal games period.'

'Any thefts from the girls' changing rooms?'

'Nothing's been reported.'

'The changing rooms are locked when they're not being used though, aren't they? I mean, we can't get in until someone's keyed in the entry code.'

'Yeah, and the code's changed every day.'

'What about the door inside that connects the home and away dressing rooms?'

'Unless there's any reason for it to be opened, it's always kept locked. Mr Jago has a key, and there's a spare one in the headmaster's secretary's office.'

'Any signs of forced entry?'

'We haven't found any.'

'No broken windows or forced latches?'

'No.'

'Have the police been informed?'

'Not yet.'

'Why not?'

Kendal just looked at me, as if the answer was obvious.

'The Twin Town Cup?' I said.

'Exactly.'

The Twin Town Cup is a school football tournament that takes place every two years. Four teams from Barton – the town where I live – take on four teams from the two towns that Barton is twinned with: Wetzlar in Germany and Rennes in France. The venue for the tournament changes each time it's played, and this year Kell Cross was hosting it for the first time. It was a pretty big deal for the school, with all kinds of sponsorship and press coverage and stuff, and the teachers and administration staff had been working on all the travel and accommodation arrangements for months. The tournament lasts for almost two weeks. In the first week, the eight teams are split into two groups of four and each team in the group plays the other three once. The top two teams in each group then progress to the knockout stage – which, in effect, are the semi-finals – and the winners of the semi-finals go on to play each other in the final.

Today's matches had been the concluding games in

the group stages. The semi-finals were being played on Monday, and the final was on Wednesday. By beating the French team this afternoon, Kell Cross had finished top of their group and were playing the runners-up from the other group in the semi-final.

'We don't know who's responsible for these thefts,' Kendal told me. 'It could be a pupil at Kell Cross, it could be someone from outside the school. Until we know for sure, we'd prefer to deal with it ourselves rather than calling in the police.' He looked at me. 'I mean, imagine how embarrassing it would be for the school if the police showed up and arrested someone in the middle of a Twin Town Cup game. We'd never live it down.'

'Why don't you just put a guard on the changing-room doors?' I suggested. 'Two teachers, or two Year 12s, one on each door at all times. Then no one can get in.'

'That's precisely what we've been doing. But it hasn't made any difference.'

'Stuff's still going missing?'

'Yeah.'

'How the hell are they getting in?'

'That's what we want you to find out.'

4

I was planning on going round to Delaney & Co's office as soon as I'd got changed anyway, so I started telling Kendal that I'd talk to my grandad and his partner, Courtney Lane, about the changing-room thefts when I got there.

'I don't know how busy they are at the moment,' I said, 'so I can't promise they'll be able to do anything straight away—'

'That's not what we want,' Kendal said.

'What do you mean?'

'We want to keep this as quiet as possible. If we hire anyone on an official basis, it's bound to get out sooner or later.'

'So what *do* you want?'

'We were hoping that you could do it.'

'Me?'

'You said you were still involved with the investigation business, didn't you?'

'Well, yeah . . .'

'Do you know enough about it to look into the thefts yourself?'

I thought about that for a while, mulling over what the job might entail and whether I was capable of doing it myself or not. It didn't take me long to reach a decision.

'Yeah,' I told Kendal. 'I don't see any reason why I can't do it.'

'And you'd be OK with a verbal contract?'

I shrugged. 'If that's what you want.'

'Confidentiality guaranteed?'

'I'd need to discuss the job with my grandad and his partner.'

'But no one else?'

'No.'

'What about payment? We'd prefer to keep any financial transactions off the books, but I'm sure we can work something out.'

'I don't want any money,' I said.

'Really? Well, that's very good of you—'

'All I want is a written promise from all my teachers that I'll get excellent grades this year.'

Kendal looked at me, his eyes narrowed in disbelief.

'Joke,' I said, grinning.

He sighed, shaking his head. 'Yeah, very funny.'

I was beginning to realise that despite his all-round magnificence, the one thing Kendal didn't have was a sense of humour.

'Have you discussed with Mr Jago how you want me to go about it?' I asked him.

'We decided it was best to leave the practical details to you, but Mr Jago thinks it'd be a good idea to include you in the Under-15 team for next week's matches. That way you'll always be around when the games are taking place, which should make it easier for you to keep an eye on things.'

'He wants *me* to play for the Under-15s?'

'What's the matter?' Kendal said, amused by the look of disbelief on my face. 'Don't you think you're good enough?'

'I *know* I'm not good enough.'

I wasn't being modest or anything, I was simply telling the truth. I mean, I like football – both playing it and watching it – but I'm not really any good at it. The only sport I *am* pretty good at is boxing, but that's something I do in my own time.

'You've played in goal for the reserves a couple of times, haven't you?' Kendal said.

'Well, yeah, but only because the regular keeper was injured. I'm nowhere near good enough for the first team.'

'Don't worry about it,' Kendal said. 'You wouldn't actually be *in* the team, you'd just be part of the squad.'

'As a substitute?'

'That's right.'

'How many's in the squad?'

'Sixteen.'

'So it's pretty unlikely that I'd have to play.'

'Highly unlikely.'

I nodded. There was no doubt it made sense to include me in the squad as a non-playing substitute. Investigation-wise, it gave me the perfect cover story, and football-wise it didn't jeopardise the team's chances. There was also no doubt at all that I genuinely wasn't good enough to get in the team. I knew that. But even so, I still couldn't help feeling just a little bit disappointed that I wasn't going to get to play.

'Have you got any ideas how you're going to catch the thief?' Kendal asked.

'Hidden surveillance cameras should do it,' I said, putting the irrational feelings of disappointment from my mind. 'One in each dressing room. I can link them up to my mobile phone—'

'That's out of the question,' Kendal said.

'Why?'

'Think about it.'

I thought about it, and almost immediately realised what a ridiculously stupid idea it was. Hidden surveillance cameras in a school changing room? Yeah, right. That wasn't asking for trouble, was it?

'No cameras then,' I said, somewhat sheepishly.

'No cameras,' Kendal agreed.

'In that case, it'll have to be some kind of motion sensor device, ideally with a Wi-Fi link to my mobile.' I paused, thinking about the practicalities. 'I'm not sure what equipment we've got in the office at the moment. I might have to customise one of the bugs we usually use.' I glanced at my watch. 'I'll talk to my grandad and see what he thinks, and I'll get back to you as soon as possible.'

'I'll give you my mobile number.'

'I'll probably need access to the changing rooms over the weekend.'

'No problem. I'll let Mr Jago know. Is there anything else you need?'

'Who else knows about the thefts apart from you and Mr Jago?'

'Well, the kids whose stuff was taken obviously know, and no doubt they'll have been talking to their mates about it, but there's nothing we can do about that. The teachers who've been guarding the doors know what's been happening – Mr Wells and Mr Ayres. But that's about it, I think.'

'What about the Year 12s who've been watching the doors?'

Kendal shook his head. 'They were just told that it was a new security procedure.'

'Does anyone else know you've asked me to investigate the thefts?'

'No.'

'Not even the headmaster?'

'He's aware that Mr Jago's dealing with it – he *told* him to deal with it – but he didn't want to know any details himself.'

'So if anything goes wrong, it's nothing to do with him.'

Kendal said nothing, which told me I was right. The headmaster wasn't just looking after the school's reputation, he was looking after his own as well.

'Right,' I said, getting to my feet and rubbing my arms again. 'I'm going to get changed now before I freeze to death.'

Kendal stood up. 'I'll get you my mobile number.'

As we walked together back to the changing rooms, I could see a few kids watching us and muttering among themselves. I guessed the rumours would soon start spreading – Delaney's in with Kendal now . . . Kendal's got a new best buddy . . .

I couldn't help smiling quietly to myself.

5

Barton is about five kilometres from Kell Cross, and by the time I'd had a shower and got dressed and cycled into town, it was getting on for five o'clock. Delaney & Co's office is situated in North Walk, a pedestrianised street at the quiet end of town. A lot of the small shops and businesses were either closed or closing up as I wheeled my bike along the pavement towards the office, and the street had that strangely muted end-of-the-day kind of feel to it. The sky was dark, the street lights glowing orange. The footsteps of office workers going home echoed dully around the streets, and there was a sense of weariness to the air. It was almost as if the town itself was winding down after a long hard day. In a couple of hours' time the night-shift would begin, and the town would come back to life again, but until then it was going to sit down for a while, put its feet up, and take a much-needed rest.

Delaney & Co shares a small office building with two other businesses. We're on the ground floor, Tantastic Tanning are on the first floor, and Jakes and Mortimer, Solicitors are on the second floor.

I opened the main door and wheeled my bike along the corridor. As I leaned it against the wall outside Delaney & Co's office, I heard footsteps coming down the stairs.

The tanning salon usually closes at four, so I guessed it was someone coming down from Jakes and Mortimer. I instinctively looked up to see who it was, but just as a pair of legs appeared on the stairs, the handlebars of my bike slipped off the wall, the front wheel jerked outwards, and the bike kind of lurched forward and began sliding down to the floor. As I lunged after it, stooping down to try and get hold of it before it hit the ground, I somehow cracked my shin against the front sprocket. It wasn't a really hard whack or anything, but it caught me right on that bony spot, and it hurt like *hell*. I let out a sharp yelp of pain and a few choice words, and immediately bent down and rolled up my trouser leg to examine the damage.

'Are you all right?' I heard someone say.

I looked up and saw a girl in high-heeled boots standing on the stairs just above me. I guessed she was about sixteen or seventeen. She had short blonde hair, heavily made-up eyes, and she was stunningly pretty. As well as the high-heeled boots, she was wearing a short black skirt and a little black jacket, and she was carrying a handbag and an armful of post.

'I'm Bianca,' she said, smiling at me, 'Mr Mortimer's new secretary. I started last week.'

'Oh, right . . .' I muttered, rolling down my trouser leg and straightening up. 'I'm Travis . . . Travis Delaney.' I stupidly waved my hand at the office door, as if that explained everything.

'Is your leg all right?' Bianca asked.

'Yeah . . . yeah, it's nothing . . .'

She grinned. 'It didn't sound like nothing.'

I just stared at her, unable to think of a single thing to say. My mind was utterly empty. And as if that wasn't bad enough, I could feel myself blushing. My face felt as if it was on fire. I lowered my eyes, looking down at the floor in a vain effort to compose myself, and that's when I realised that I hadn't rolled down my trouser leg properly. So, basically, I was standing there with a bright red face and a half-rolled-up trouser leg, mumbling incoherently and waving my hand around, with my bike lying on the floor at my feet.

Way to go, Travis, I told myself. *You certainly know how to impress the ladies, don't you?*

'Well,' Bianca said, 'I'd better get going before the post office shuts. It was nice meeting you, Travis.'

I looked up, desperately trying to think of something cool to say to rescue the situation, but as Bianca headed gracefully towards the door, glancing back at me with an easy smile, all I could manage was a dopey-looking grin and another idiotic wave of my hand.

I watched her go out and close the door, and then I just shook my head, let out a sigh, and bent down to pick up my bike.

6

Before setting up Delaney & Co on his own in 1994, my grandad had spent five years in the Royal Military Police and twelve years as an officer in the Army Intelligence Corps. My mum and dad had started working with Grandad straight after leaving university, and when Grandad retired from the business about ten years ago, they carried on running the agency together. So Delaney & Co had always been a huge part of my life, and I'd pretty much grown up with the business – hanging around the office all the time, helping out Mum and Dad whenever they'd let me. But like so many other things that we take for granted, it wasn't until after my parents' fatal car crash that I'd realised how much Delaney & Co meant to me. The business, to me, *was* Mum and Dad. It was us, our life. And the idea of it not being there any more was almost too much to bear.

I'm not quite sure how I'd persuaded Grandad to come out of retirement and re-open Delaney & Co – in fact, I'm not even sure it was down to me at all – but whatever it was that had convinced him to do it, it meant everything to me that he had.

Although he was tougher and smarter than most men half his age, there was no getting away from the fact that Grandad wasn't as active and healthy as he used to be, which was why he'd asked Courtney Lane to be his partner. Courtney had been Mum and Dad's assistant. She was still in her early twenties, and as well as being super-athletic and incredibly intelligent – both academically and street-wise – she was rapidly becoming a really good private investigator.

Courtney had carried on dealing with all the secretarial and administrative stuff for the first couple of months after Grandad had re-opened the business, but eventually – just over two weeks ago – Grandad had taken on a new assistant. The person he'd hired was an old acquaintance of his from his Army Intelligence days, a woman called Gloria Nightingale. I didn't know exactly how old Gloria was, but I assumed she was about the same age as Grandad, around sixty-two or sixty-three. Not *ancient*, but certainly not young.

When I went into the office that afternoon, still blushing from my encounter with Bianca, Gloria was sitting at her desk in the main office, tapping away at her laptop.

'Hello, Travis,' she said, looking up and smiling at me. 'Are you all right? You look a bit hot.'

'I just got off my bike,' I told her, trying to sound casual.

'Oh, I see.' She glanced over at the window. 'Was that Bianca I saw just now leaving with the post?'

'I think so, yeah.'

Gloria looked back at me. 'She seems like a nice girl, doesn't she?'

I shrugged. 'I suppose so . . .'

I could tell from the teasing glint in Gloria's eyes that she knew perfectly well why I was blushing, and that she was just having a bit of fun at my expense. I knew she didn't mean anything bad by it though, and if it had been anyone else I probably wouldn't have minded. But it wasn't anyone else, it was Gloria, and the way I felt about Gloria Nightingale was complicated, to say the least.

About a week after Gloria had started working for us, I was in the sitting room at home one night and I'd overheard Grandad and Nan talking about Gloria in the kitchen. I'd thought at first they were just chatting about how she was getting on in her new job, but it soon became apparent that Grandad was actually telling Nan, for the very first time, that he'd hired Gloria as his assistant. I was really quite shocked, to be honest. Grandad always discusses everything with Nan, and I'd taken it for granted that he'd consulted her about employing Gloria, and I couldn't understand why he hadn't.

Nan didn't sound very pleased at all when he told her, which I assumed was simply because he hadn't talked to her before hiring Gloria, but then Grandad had said something like, 'Look, I'm sorry, love, I understand how you feel, but—'

And Nan had blown her top. 'Do you?' she'd snapped. 'Do you *really*? Is that why you didn't *ask* me if I *minded* you employing your old girlfriend?'

Nan had stormed off in a huff then, leaving Grandad on his own in the kitchen, and me in a state of utter bewilderment. Old girlfriend? Old *girlfriend*? Gloria Nightingale was Grandad's old *girlfriend*?

I simply *had* to find out what that was all about, and I knew just the right person to tell me. My great-grandmother, Granny Nora, shares the house with us. She's eighty-six years old and suffers from chronic arthritis, so she spends most of her time in her room upstairs, which is fitted out like a self-contained little flat. She's Grandad's mum, so obviously she knows more about him than anyone else, and I was sure she'd have some answers for me.

Granny's usually more than happy to talk to me for hours – about everything and anything – but when I'd gone in to see her that night, her arthritis was really playing up and she was in a lot of pain, so I didn't stay very long. When I'd told her what Nan had said about Gloria, and asked her what she'd meant by it, Granny had smiled her devilish smile and told me that it was a long and convoluted story, which she'd tell me all about when she was feeling better, but the essence of it was that Gloria Nightingale had indeed been Grandad's girlfriend for a short while before he'd met and married Nan.

'Nan doesn't like her, does she?' I'd said.

Granny had chuckled. 'Show me a woman who claims to get along with her husband's ex-girlfriends and I'll show you a liar.'

So that was the situation with Gloria. It felt really awkward, knowing that she was Grandad's ex-girlfriend, and I wasn't quite sure how to deal with it. Since my parents had died, I'd come to think of Nan and Grandad as sort of substitute parents. They could never replace Mum and Dad, of course – that was *unthinkable* – and they weren't my entire world in the way that Mum and Dad had been, but I felt I belonged with Nan and Grandad now. They were *mine* – my guardians, my family, my everything. So although Grandad wasn't my dad, and Nan wasn't my mum, this whole business with Grandad and Gloria still felt how I imagined it would feel if you found out that one of your parents was spending a lot of time with someone they used to go out with.

Like I said, it felt really awkward.

Not quite right.

Kind of *icky*, if you know what I mean.

I just didn't like it, basically. And that's mostly why I didn't feel very comfortable around Gloria.

Another reason, at least initially, was the overall impression she gave of being a bit stuck-up and old-fashioned. She was one of those well-groomed elderly women who always dress quite formally – tweedy skirts, sensible shoes, cardigans, blouses, pearl necklaces – and she had an almost aristocratic air about her that was quite intimidating at first. But, as my mum once told me, you have to be very careful about judging people by their appearance, and the more I'd got to know Gloria, the more I'd realised she wasn't just a 'stuck-up old posh lady'. She *was* posh, there was no denying that, but there was nothing stuck-up about her. She was perfectly friendly, quite funny at times, and – perhaps most surprising of all – she knew more about modern technology than anyone I'd ever met. Computers, phones, cyberspace, surveillance equipment . . . she knew almost everything there was to know about everything.

I had to admit that in lots of ways Gloria was a pretty cool old lady, and if I hadn't known about her history with Grandad, and how Nan felt about her, I'm fairly sure that having her around the place would have been OK.

But I *did* know about her and Grandad.

And it wasn't OK.

I kept trying to tell myself that it was what it was, that these things happen, and that it wasn't up to me to judge anyone.

Unfortunately, that wasn't always as easy as it sounds.

'So what's been going on?' I asked Gloria that afternoon after she'd finished teasing me about Bianca. 'Anything exciting?'

'Your grandad's been in his office all afternoon,' she

told me, looking over at the door to what used to be Mum and Dad's private office, 'and Courtney's out working on that tanning salon case.'

I went over to the coat rack on the wall next to Gloria's desk and hung up my parka. 'What about you?' I asked, turning to her and glancing idly at the screen of her laptop. 'Are you working on anything interesting?'

'Never you mind, nosy-boots,' she said, quickly closing her laptop.

Even though she did it in a light-hearted manner, it was still a slightly odd thing to do. In fact, to be honest, it kind of annoyed me. Delaney & Co was *my* grandad's business, and until a few months ago it had been *my* mum and dad's business. So surely it wasn't right for someone who'd only been working here for a couple of weeks to hide anything about the business from me?

Then again, I thought, maybe I was just overreacting, being too sensitive. As Grandad's secretary, Gloria had to deal with a lot of confidential information, and maybe she was just taking her responsibilities a bit too far. Or perhaps it was something else she didn't want me to see, something personal – her Facebook page, a private email . . . it could have been anything really.

The office door opened then, and when I turned round and saw Courtney Lane coming in, I quickly forgot all about Gloria. Courtney always looks pretty spectacular, and today she was even more eye-catching than usual. One side of her head was shaved, the hair on the other side swept up into a striking platinum-blonde wave. Her eyes were darkened with smoky-black eyeliner, her lips were a bright glossy pink, and she was wearing short denim shorts, yellow-and-red striped tights, and a black leather biker jacket over a cropped white vest.

'Hey, Travis,' she said, her familiar smile lighting up her face. 'How's it going?'

'Excellent, thanks,' I said.

'Good.' She grinned. 'Do you want to see what I've been up to?'

7

The tanning salon case that Courtney had been working on was a supposedly straightforward injury compensation claim. Jakes and Mortimer, the solicitors on the top floor, were acting on behalf of a young woman who'd allegedly suffered serious eye damage as a result of visiting a local tanning salon called Tanga Tans. According to this woman, she hadn't been provided with any protective eyewear, the timing mechanism on the sunbed she'd used was faulty, and the staff at the salon were both negligent and unprofessional. Jakes and Mortimer had taken on her case, and they'd contracted Delaney & Co to investigate Tanga Tans and gather evidence to back up their client's claim. So that afternoon Courtney had visited the salon wearing a hidden miniature surveillance camera, and now she was back with the results.

She shared the private office with Grandad now, and as we went in there to watch her surveillance video, I was half expecting Gloria to come in with us. But as I followed Courtney over to her desk, Grandad went out into the main office and spoke quietly to Gloria for a moment or two, and when he came back she wasn't with him. I had no idea what that meant, if anything, and Grandad had his blank face on, so I knew there was no point in asking him. It wasn't the first time he'd done something like that though – sidling off for a quiet word with Gloria – and it was beginning to get on my nerves a bit.

'So what's Tanga Tans like?' he asked Courtney as she sat down at her desk and began connecting the miniature camera to her laptop. 'I mean, what's your overall impression of the place?'

'Well, it's not exactly a high-class establishment,' she said. 'It's in one of those rough little side streets just off Slade Lane, not far from the estate. There's a fried chicken place on one side of it and a minicab office on the other side. I'm not being snotty or anything, but it's not the kind of place I'd go to if I wanted to top up my tan.'

I knew what she meant. The Slade Lane estate *is* a pretty rough area, and the people who live there don't take kindly to strangers. Even if you know people who live there, which I do, you've still got to watch your step.

'Right,' Courtney said, tapping at the keyboard of her laptop, 'here we go.'

I watched as the video footage appeared on the screen. It was kind of jumpy at first, and I couldn't work out what I was looking at, but then Courtney said, 'The salon's on the first floor. That's me going up the stairs.'

The video settled down then, and we watched as Courtney entered the salon and went up to the reception desk. From what we could see of the salon, it didn't look as if a lot of money had been spent on it. There was a poky little waiting area in front of the reception desk, with a couple of cheap-looking settees and a shabby little coffee table with a pile of old magazines on it, and the room itself looked as if it had been decorated in a hurry by someone who'd never used a paintbrush before.

The woman behind the desk had shortish dark hair and light-olive skin, and she was dressed in a plain blue T-shirt and jeans. There was a simple prettiness to her face that vaguely reminded me of someone, but I couldn't for the life of me think who. Although she wasn't that old – around thirty-five, I guessed – the woman's prettiness was already fading, her face weighed down with sadness and worry.

The video played on: Courtney asking about prices, the woman wearily answering her questions . . . then Courtney being shown into a booth and the woman pointing out how everything worked. She sounded bored out of her mind.

'No mention of protective goggles?' Grandad asked Courtney.

'Not a word.'

'Was anyone else there? Any other staff?'

'Someone comes in later,' Courtney said, 'which I think you'll find interesting. But at that point, Lisa was on her own.'

'Lisa?' Grandad said.

'I asked her what her name was when I left.'

'Just Lisa?'

'It would have been a bit suspicious if I'd asked for her full name, wouldn't it?'

Grandad grinned. 'Just checking.'

Courtney tapped the keyboard and fast-forwarded the video. 'Nothing happens for the next ten minutes or so,' she explained.

'Did you actually get on the sunbed?' I asked.

Courtney frowned at me. 'That's a bit personal, isn't it?'

'Sorry,' I muttered, immediately feeling my face go red, 'I only meant—'

'You never learn, do you?' Courtney said, smiling at me. 'You're so easy to wind up it's almost no fun.'

I looked at her, trying to think of something smart to say, but I couldn't come up with anything.

Courtney gave me another quick grin, then turned her attention back to the laptop. She hit a key and the fast-forwarding stopped. 'This is where the sunbed timer goes off,' she told us, starting the video again.

'It wasn't faulty then?' Grandad said.

'No.'

'And this is definitely the same booth that Jakes and Mortimer's client used?'

'Yeah, I checked with them before I went. There are three booths, and their client used the one nearest the door. That's the one I'm in.'

'Maybe the timer's been fixed since their client used it,' Grandad suggested.

'Listen to this,' Courtney said, turning up the volume.

The muffled sound of raised voices crackled from the laptop speaker – a man's voice, shouting . . . then Lisa's voice yelling in reply.

'I'm still in the booth at this point,' Courtney said, 'but as soon as I heard the ruckus outside . . . well, as you can see, I went out to see what was going on.'

The viewpoint from the camera showed Courtney opening the door and going out into the reception area. Over at the desk, a mean-looking guy in an expensive-looking suit was shouting at Lisa and angrily jabbing his finger towards her face. He was a bit younger than Lisa – in his mid- to late twenties – but there was no doubt that he was in charge.

'You're supposed to be *running* the place,' he was yelling at her. 'It's not *difficult*, for Christ's sake.'

'I'm doing my best,' Lisa told him.

'Yeah, well it's not good enough, is it?' He glared at her. 'You know what'll happen to you if anything comes of this, don't you?'

'It's not my fault, Dee Dee,' Lisa said. 'All I do is take their money and tell them which booth to use.'

The guy called Dee Dee turned towards the camera then, suddenly aware of Courtney's presence. 'Yeah?' he snarled at her. 'What are you looking at?'

'Sorry,' Courtney said hesitantly, 'I was just . . . I didn't mean to interrupt . . .'

Now that Dee Dee was looking straight at the camera,

it was clear that he wasn't just mean-*looking* – he was a lot more than that. He was, without doubt, the scariest-looking man I'd ever seen. Physically he wasn't anything special – medium size, medium weight, not overly muscle-bound or anything – but there was a dead-eyed menace about him that even the hardest of tough guys don't have. He didn't just look mean and hard, he looked as if he could kill you without blinking.

He'd turned away from Courtney now and was staring at Lisa again.

'I haven't finished with you,' he said to her.

She nodded.

He glanced briefly at Courtney again, then strode off and disappeared through a door at the back of the salon.

'Nice guy, eh?' Courtney said, turning off the tape.

'I think I know who he is,' I said quietly.

Grandad and Courtney both looked at me.

'Lisa called him Dee Dee,' I explained. 'Dee Dee's the street-name of a guy called Drew Devon.'

'And who's this Drew Devon?' Grandad asked.

'He runs the Slade Lane estate.'

8

I'd heard about Dee Dee from a friend of mine called Mason Yusuf. Mason's a couple of years older than me. He lives on the Slade, and he knows pretty much everything that goes on there. He knows most of the gang kids, and he knows what they get up to, and I'd be very surprised if he isn't involved in at least some of it himself. Mason's no angel, that's for sure. But he's been a true friend to me ever since I helped out his younger sister once, and I'll always be in his debt for the help he gave me in solving the case my parents were working on when they died.

'When you say that this Dee Dee character *runs* the Slade Lane estate,' Grandad said to me, 'what does that actually mean?'

'He runs the biggest gang on the Slade,' I said. 'And it's the gangs that control the estate. It was Dee Dee who organised the riot in North Walk just after Mum and Dad died, remember?'

Grandad nodded. The riot had been arranged to cover up a break-in at Delaney & Co's office. A secretive organisation known as Omega were searching for material relating to the case my parents had been working on at the time, and they'd paid Dee Dee to get a load of kids from the Slade to go on a rampage and smash up all the shops and offices in North Walk so that the break-in at our office didn't arouse any suspicion.

'According to my friend Mason,' I continued, 'Dee Dee's a *very* powerful man.'

'So what's he doing in a rundown tanning salon?'

'Maybe he owns it,' Courtney suggested.

'Why would someone so powerful own a shabby little place like that?' Grandad said to her. 'Were there any other customers around when you were there?'

'No.'

'Did it *look* like a profitable business to you?'

She shook her head. 'I paid five pounds for a ten-minute session. I was in the salon for about fifteen or twenty minutes altogether, and I hung around outside for twenty minutes or so before I went in. When I left I spent another twenty minutes in the fried chicken place next door. I didn't see anyone going in or out of the salon the whole time.'

'So in the hour that you were there, Tanga Tans made a grand total of five pounds,' Grandad concluded. 'It's not exactly big money, is it?' He got up and began pacing around the office. 'I don't suppose it really matters though, does it?' he mused. 'We're not being paid to question the ownership of the place, or why a big-shot local gangster is threatening the woman who works there. That's not *our* concern, is it?'

He wasn't really asking us the question – he was pretty much talking to himself – so neither of us bothered answering him.

'We've done what we were paid to do,' he went on. 'We've got the video evidence that Jakes and Mortimer wanted. It's up to them what they do with it.'

He stopped pacing, thought deeply for a moment, then looked over at us. 'What do you think?'

'I wouldn't mind looking into it a bit more,' Courtney said. 'For curiosity's sake if nothing else. I mean, it's not as if we're working on anything else at the moment, is it?'

Grandad looked at me, asking for my opinion.

'I could have a word with Mason, if you want,' I told him. 'See if he knows anything about the salon.'

Grandad nodded. 'I suppose I could ask Gloria to do a bit of digging into Tanga Tans' financial records. She might find something that sheds a bit of light on things.' He turned to Courtney. 'Like you said, we're not exactly rushed off our feet at the moment, so it's not as if we haven't got the time to take a closer look at Tanga Tans.'

'It'll show how incredibly efficient we are,' Courtney said.

'That's true. And if another job comes up in the meantime, we can stop being "incredibly efficient" and get back to doing some proper work.'

'Sounds good to me,' Courtney said.

'Travis?' Grandad said, turning to me.

I nodded.

'Right,' Grandad said, 'so that's agreed then. We'll carry on looking into it for a few more days and then . . . well, we'll just see what happens, OK?'

*

When I told them about the school changing-room thefts, and that I'd been hired to look into them, they were both genuinely pleased for me.

'Congratulations,' Grandad said. 'Your very first solo investigation. I'm impressed.'

'Yeah, well done, Trav,' Courtney added. 'That's fantastic. You'll be taking over from me if I don't watch out.'

'Thanks,' I told them. 'But I didn't really do anything. Kendal just came up and asked me if I'd do it.'

'A job's a job,' Grandad said. 'It doesn't matter how you get it.'

'What equipment do you think I should use?' I asked him. 'I was thinking of some kind of motion sensor device.'

'Let me see what we've got,' he said, getting up and going over to a cupboard by the window. He opened it up and pulled out what he called his 'gadget case'. It was a large aluminium briefcase, about the size of a small suitcase, in which he kept all the tracking and surveillance equipment. 'How much are you charging them for this job?' he asked, bringing the case over to his desk.

'I think I said I'd do it for nothing.'

'You *think*?'

'Well, Kendal told me they wanted to keep it unofficial, and I made a joke about getting paid with good grades,

38

and then . . . I don't know. The question of payment kind of got forgotten.'

'We're not a charity, Travis,' Grandad said, sitting down and opening the gadget case. 'We're professional investigators. We don't work for nothing, OK?'

'Not even for friends?'

'Especially not for friends.'

'Sorry. I just thought—'

'It's all right,' he said, rummaging around in the case. 'Don't worry about it. Just make sure you get paid next time, OK?'

I leaned over his desk and looked at the bewildering array of electronic surveillance equipment inside the case – cameras, trackers, recorders, bugs, cables.

'I think these are your best bet,' he said, fishing out a couple of small metal cylinders. 'They're simple motion sensor devices, no video or audio capability. These particular models use ultrasonic waves to detect movement. You can link them up to your mobile with a Wi-Fi connection, and set whatever type of alert you want – sound, flashing lights, vibration. All you need to do is work out a way to hide them.'

I reached into the gadget case and pulled out what looked like a stick-on air freshener. It was actually a disguised miniature surveillance camera. 'Could we take the cameras out of these and replace them with the motion sensors?' I asked.

'I don't see why not,' Grandad said. He looked

across at Courtney. 'What do you think?'

'Here, let me have a look,' she said, getting up and coming over to us.

I passed her the air-freshener camera. She took a small Swiss Army knife from her pocket, opened up a screwdriver attachment, and began taking the air freshener apart.

'As long as the camera isn't permanently fixed inside,' she said, 'it shouldn't be a problem.'

I watched her working – her eyes narrowed in concentration, her delicate fingers carefully dismantling the plastic device – and then I glanced at Grandad. He'd put his reading glasses on and was studying the back of a packet he'd taken out of the gadget case.

'Have you seen these, Trav?' he said, passing me the packet. 'I ordered them last week and they've just come in.'

The packet contained two small silver discs. They were about the size of a 5p coin, but thicker. They looked a bit like hearing-aid batteries.

'They're GPS tracking devices,' Grandad said, tapping at his laptop. 'There's a magnetic strip on one side, so you can easily fix them to a vehicle or anything metallic, or you can just plant them in someone's pocket or handbag or whatever. All you have to do to activate them is go to this website, enter the code specific to each device, put in your mobile number, and that's it. The device sends a signal to your phone, and you can follow its location on whatever kind of map you want – road map, street view, satellite view. You just choose the option from a menu on your phone.'

'What's the range?'

'Well, it's supposed to be up to five kilometres, but I'd imagine it's a lot less in built-up areas. Do you want to give it a go?'

I took out one of the trackers and read off the code. As Grandad started keying it into the website, I couldn't help smiling at the gleam of excited curiosity in his eyes. He looked like a little kid playing with a brand-new toy. I watched him for a while, then turned my attention to Courtney again, studying her as she worked away on the air-freshener camera. It felt really nice, just sitting there watching them both, and the fact that Gloria wasn't there made it feel even nicer. It was just the three of us, like it used to be, with no one else to complicate things.

As I looked away from Courtney and gazed around the office, I found myself thinking back even further, remembering all the good times I'd spent in here with Mum and Dad, watching them getting on with their work, listening to them talking and joking with each other . . .

It wasn't the same now, of course. Nothing would ever be the same. But being in here with Courtney and Grandad was as close to how it used to be as I could ever hope to get, and despite feeling incredibly sad, I also felt incredibly lucky.

9

It was nearly six o'clock by the time Courtney had finished adapting the air-freshener cams, and by then she was in a hurry to get home. Her house was only five minutes' walk from the office, but she had to get back to take over from the carer who looked after her mum during the day. Her mother has Parkinson's disease.

'When are you going to be putting the sensors into the changing rooms?' she asked me, buttoning up her coat.

'Sometime over the weekend.'

'Give me a call if there's any problems, OK?'

'Thanks.'

'Right, I've got to go. See you later.'

I called Mason Yusuf then and asked him if I could come over and see him about something. He didn't ask me what it was, he just said, 'When?'

'Any time tonight would be good. I could be there in half an hour—'

'I'm kind of tied up with something right now, but I'll be free after seven. Is that OK?'

'Yeah, great.'

'Just ring me when you get to the estate, OK?'

I hadn't eaten anything since lunchtime, so rather than just hanging around before it was time to head off to see Mason, I thought I'd nip into town and get a burger or something. But just as I was fetching my coat, Grandad called out to me from his office.

'Have you got a minute, Trav?'

When I went into his office, he was still sitting at his desk, his laptop open in front of him, his reading glasses halfway down his nose.

'Pull up a seat,' he said, 'I want to show you something.'

I grabbed a chair from the other side of the office, took it over to the desk, and sat down next to him.

'We haven't talked about Omega for a while, have we?' he said.

I looked at him, my heart turning cold.

When my parents were killed in a car crash, they were investigating the disappearance of a young man called Bashir Kamal. At first, there didn't seem to be any connection between the accident and their investigation, and it wasn't until I started looking into the case myself that I began to suspect that the crash might not have been an accident after all. There was a lot more to the case than had first met the eye, and it soon turned out that not only were the CIA and MI5 mixed up in the investigation, but a shadowy organisation known as Omega were involved in it too.

Grandad had told me that he'd first heard the rumours about a rogue security service called Omega back in the 1980s when he was serving with a covert military intelligence squad in Northern Ireland. The story was that a group of intelligence officers from all kinds of backgrounds – MI5, MI6, Special Branch, Army Intelligence – had become so disillusioned with the politics and restrictions of the official national security services that they'd got together and formed their own unofficial security organisation. No one really knew anything about them, Grandad had told me, but it was generally assumed that they undertook the same kind of work as the official security services – counter-intelligence, counter-terrorism, internal and external national security – but they did it on their own terms: no rules, no restrictions, no accountability.

The man we believed to be in charge of Omega – a steely-eyed character who called himself Winston – had put it in much simpler terms. 'We're the good guys, Travis,' he'd told me. 'We do what's right.'

I don't really doubt that he believed what he told me, and in terms of Omega's involvement in the Bashir Kamal case, there's no question that – ultimately – they *were* doing the right thing. But Winston had also told me something else. 'Sometimes we have to make short-term sacrifices for the sake of potential long-term benefits,' he'd said. 'A life risked today might save a thousand lives in years to come.'

I don't know if that amounted to some kind of confession or not, but during my investigation into Bashir Kamal I'd come across evidence to suggest that Omega were responsible – intentionally or not – for the car crash that killed my parents. The evidence was all circumstantial, and Winston and the other Omega men had disappeared back into the shadows before I'd had a chance to question them any further. But I wasn't going to rest until I'd found out what had really happened, and neither was Grandad, and since the day that Winston and his men had slipped away, we'd never stopped searching for the truth. Unfortunately for us, Omega had been operating under the radar for decades, and they were very good at making themselves invisible. As Grandad put it, looking for them was like looking for ghosts in the mist. All we'd found so far was a grainy old black-and-white photograph on the Internet that purportedly showed three special forces operatives in Kuwait, one of whom bore a striking resemblance to a young-looking Winston. According to the website, he was Sergeant Andrew W. Carson, and he'd been 'killed in action' shortly after the picture was taken.

The only other relevant information we'd dug up was that the road traffic accident investigator who'd compiled the report into my parents' crash – which claimed that no other vehicle was involved – had resigned his position quite suddenly and was no longer living in the UK. His whereabouts were still unknown.

So I'd kind of got used to our investigation into Omega not getting anywhere, and when I sat down with Grandad that evening, I just assumed he was going to tell me that nothing much had changed.

But I was wrong.

10

'I don't want to get your hopes up, Travis,' Grandad said to me, 'but I think we might be getting somewhere at last.'

'You've found out something?' I said, my heart quickening.

'Well, actually, most of the credit goes to Gloria.'

'Gloria?' I said, surprised. 'I thought we were keeping this to ourselves.'

'We *are* keeping it to ourselves. Gloria's part of the team now, Trav. She's one of us – me, you, Courtney, Gloria. The four of us are Delaney & Co.' He looked at me. 'You don't have a problem with that, do you?'

'Well, no . . . I suppose not. It's just . . . I mean, it just feels kind of odd, you know, working with someone I don't really know.'

'You'll get to know her. You just have to give it time. But *I* know her, Trav. I've known her for years, and I'd trust her with my life. And you know me pretty well, don't you?'

'I thought I did,' I muttered, almost without thinking.

'What's that supposed to mean?'

I hesitated for a moment, torn between telling him the truth – i.e. that I knew about his history with Gloria – or just avoiding the subject altogether, which was what I'd been doing for the last ten days or so. From the way Grandad was looking at me though – his grizzly old face demanding an explanation for what I'd just said – I knew I couldn't avoid it any longer.

'Why didn't you tell me about Gloria?' I asked him.

'Tell you what?'

'About you and her,' I said awkwardly, not knowing how to phrase it. 'You know, you and her . . . before you met Nan?'

He was too surprised to say anything for a moment, and I could tell by the puzzled look in his eyes that he was wondering how I'd found out.

'I was in the sitting room when you told Nan,' I explained. 'I couldn't help overhearing you.'

'Oh, I see . . .' he said, nodding slowly.

'You should have *told* me, Grandad,' I said, unable to keep the bitterness from my voice. 'And you should have talked to Nan about hiring Gloria. It wasn't fair to just spring it on her like that.'

'I didn't mean to, Travis. Honestly. I know that sounds hard to believe, but it's the God's-honest truth.' He sighed. 'I really *wasn't* trying to hide anything from either of you . . . well, not at first anyway. I didn't plan on hiring Gloria, it just kind of happened—'

'Oh, come *on*,' I said, exasperated.

Grandad looked me in the eye. 'She called me about something else, OK? It was nothing to do with me and her, nothing to do with Delaney & Co, all she wanted

47

was some information about someone I used to know who'd offered her a job. The idea of taking her on as our assistant came to me on the spur of the moment. I suddenly realised how perfect she'd be for the job, and it was obvious she was looking for work, so I just asked her, there and then. If I hadn't, she would have taken this other position she was thinking about. It didn't even occur to me until afterwards, when she'd already agreed to join us, that I hadn't talked it over with you or Nan or Courtney, and it was only then that I realised how awkward it was going to be for Nan.' Grandad paused, looking away from me in embarrassment. 'This thing with me and Gloria . . . it all happened a lifetime ago, before I'd ever met Nan. And even then it didn't last very long. We went out together a couple of times, Trav, that was all. We liked each other a lot, but not in that way . . . you know . . . not as a couple. We realised that we just wanted to be friends.' He shrugged. 'It worked for us, we were much better together as good friends than as a couple. It also made it a lot easier for us when we found ourselves working together some years later. It helped us get through a lot . . . we went through some pretty rough times together.' He went quiet for a moment or two, thinking about something, almost drifting away. Then, after a while, he shook his head and brought himself out of his memories. 'I know I should have told Nan sooner,' he admitted, 'but the truth is, I just got scared. It's not that Nan doesn't trust me or anything, it's just . . . I don't know. Relationships are funny things, Travis. You'll find out yourself when you're older. They don't follow any kind of logic sometimes. Nan *knows* what my relationship with Gloria is. She knows that after those first few dates we've never been anything more than friends and work colleagues, and she also knows I'd never lie to her or cheat on her. But despite all that, despite everything her rational mind tells her, there's just something about Gloria that *gets* to her.'

'Maybe she just doesn't like her,' I suggested.

'Well, whatever it is, I knew Nan wouldn't like it when she found out I'd hired Gloria, so I just kept putting it off . . .'

'And why didn't you tell me about it?'

He sighed again. 'Do you really want to know?'

'Yeah.'

He smiled awkwardly. 'I was embarrassed, simple as that. I'm an old man, Trav. You're my grandson, you're fourteen. I just didn't know how to go about telling you about . . . well, you know . . . *relationship* stuff.'

'I do realise that you *were* a young man once,' I said, grinning at him. 'I mean, I can just about imagine you having a girlfriend back in the day – taking her out in your horse and carriage, twirling your moustache and tipping your top hat to her, all that kind of stuff.'

He laughed. 'You'll be as old as me one day, you know.'

'They'll have cured ageing long before then. I'm planning on living for ever.'

'Well, good luck with that.'

He felt comfortable enough then to tell me a bit more about Gloria – her career in the intelligence services, her knowledge of counter-espionage techniques, her expertise in collecting and analysing information.

'Another really useful thing about her is that she's got a *lot* more up-to-date contacts than me,' he explained, 'which is partly why she's been able to find out a lot more about Omega than me.' He tapped a few keys on his laptop and brought up a photograph of a gaunt-faced man wearing rimless glasses.

'That's one of the Omega men,' I said, staring in amazement at the picture.

'His name's Lance Borstlap,' Grandad said. 'He was a corporal in the South African Special Forces Brigade, went AWOL in 2009, and there's been no official sightings of him since. According to various intelligence reports though, he's developed a very successful career as a mercenary, working for all kinds of organisations and individuals all over the world.'

'Including Omega.'

'So it would seem.'

'Did Gloria find all this out?'

Grandad nodded. 'She tracked him down through the fingerprints we got off your bike.'

One of the first things we'd thought of when we started

trying to find the Omega men was tracing them through their fingerprints. The trouble was, the warehouse they'd used as a base when they were in Barton had been demolished the day after they'd left, so it was impossible to get any prints from there. But then I'd remembered that at one point during the Bashir Kamal investigation, CIA agents had slashed the tyres on my bike, and someone from Omega had replaced the tyres and given the bike back to me. I'd told Grandad about this, and he'd had the bike checked for fingerprints. It turned out that there were a couple of partial prints on the rim of the back wheel that weren't mine. Grandad had passed these on to several of his contacts who'd run them through various databases, but no matches had been found.

'Gloria just extended the search,' Grandad explained. 'Like I said, she's got far more contacts than me, and she eventually struck lucky with someone she knows in the National Intelligence Agency in South Africa.'

'Amazing,' I muttered.

'I told you she was good.'

'So this was the man who fixed my bike,' I said, staring at the face on the laptop screen. 'A corporal in the special forces and a highly regarded mercenary . . . and he mended my bike.'

Grandad shrugged. 'He's a soldier. Soldiers do whatever they're told.'

'Do we know anything else about him?'

'Not yet. But Gloria's working on it.'

'Has she found out anything about any of the others?'

'She's working on that too.'

'Anything else?'

'She's checking up on one of the police officers who was involved in the investigation into your mum and dad's crash, a Detective Inspector Ronnie Bull. She's heard whispers that DI Bull's a dirty cop and that he'll do almost anything for the right price. She's fairly sure that he's not actually *part* of Omega, but she thinks he might have some kind of connection with them.'

'They could have used him to help cover up their involvement in the car crash,' I suggested.

'That's one of the things Gloria's looking into. We've also managed to track down the police officers who were actually present at the scene of the crash. I've already spoken with two of them, and they've told me a couple of things that might be worth following up. In the meantime I'm still trying to arrange to talk to the others.'

'That's really brilliant, Grandad,' I said, feeling freshly encouraged by all this new information. 'We're going to do it, aren't we? We're going to get Omega.'

'There's a long way to go yet,' he said cautiously, 'but, yes . . . we'll get them in the end.'

'Is there anything I can do to help?'

'I don't think so. Not at the moment anyway. But it would make things a lot easier for me if you could try to accept Gloria a little bit more. I know it's not easy, for all kinds of reasons, and I realise I'm asking you to put your faith in someone you don't really know, and maybe don't trust, but just give her a chance, OK? For my sake.'

'All right,' I agreed.

'Thanks, Travis. And listen . . .' He hesitated for a second then, and I thought I saw a flicker of embarrassment in his eyes, a momentary look of shame, or maybe even guilt. I naturally assumed he was still thinking about Gloria, and that he was about to say something else about her, but I was wrong. Or, at least, that's what I thought at the time.

'Listen, Trav,' he said, kind of cryptically, 'whatever happens, right or wrong, never forget that there's more than one way to catch a rat.'

11

It was just gone six thirty when I left the office – too late to get something to eat and still meet Mason at seven – so instead of cycling up into town, I headed straight off to the Slade Lane estate. By the time I'd got there, I'd given up trying to work out what Grandad had meant when he'd said there was more than one way to catch a rat. I supposed it meant the same as the phrase 'more than one way to skin a cat', which I was pretty sure was just another way of saying there's more than one way to achieve something . . . although once I started thinking about that – i.e. the idea of skinning a cat – I got even more confused. What did skinning a cat have to do with anything? And was Grandad intentionally making up his own version of the phrase, or had he just got it wrong? I'd noticed recently that my nan was beginning to get things mixed up more and more often these days – she'd called me Jack a couple of times recently, which was my dad's name – and I guessed it was just something that happens as you get older. So maybe Grandad *had* just got his words muddled up. But even if he had, I assumed he still meant that there was more than one way to do something, and that's what I couldn't work out. More than one way to do *what*?

But, like I said, by the time I got to Slade Lane, I'd had

enough of trying to work it out. And besides, now that I'd reached the estate, I couldn't afford to be thinking about anything else. The Slade Lane estate is as rough as it gets, and although my friendship with Mason Yusuf means that most of the gang kids know who I am and generally leave me alone, I couldn't just assume I was safe. It doesn't matter who you are or who you know when you're on the Slade, you still need all your wits about you. Especially at night.

There's no real beginning or end to the estate, it's just a huge sprawling maze of low-rise blocks and row upon row of slate-grey council houses. Mason lives with his mum and his sister, Jaydie, in a flat in one of the low-rises in the middle of the estate. I'd been to the Slade before with Mason, but although he was forever asking me to come round to his place, I'd never actually been there. I had no idea if Mason was planning on taking me there tonight, or if I was just going to meet him somewhere on the estate. You can never tell with Mason. He likes to keep people guessing.

I'd reached a little square on the edge of the estate now, a drab concrete place with graffiti-scrawled walls and a couple of iron benches bolted to the ground. Tall street lights were dotted around the square, but only one of them was working. I headed over to it, pulled up my bike next to a bench, then took out my mobile and called Mason.

'Hey, Trav,' he answered. 'Where are you?'

I told him where I was.

'Stay there,' he said. 'I'll come and get you. Be there in five.'

As I was putting my mobile back in my pocket, I saw three hooded kids coming across the darkened square towards me. Two of them were about my age, the other one a couple of years older. They were trying to give the impression that they weren't interested in me at all, that all they were doing was just ambling along, casually minding their own business. And if I hadn't known better I might have believed them.

But I did know better.

For a start, I knew that just because they weren't actually looking in my direction, that didn't mean they weren't keeping their eyes on me, thoroughly checking me out. I also knew that the oldest one was probably carrying a weapon, most likely a knife. I'd seen him put his hand in his pocket as soon as he'd entered the square, and now – as the three of them approached me, spreading out in a rough semi-circle – the older kid still had his hand in his pocket.

I'd instinctively glanced around for an escape route from the square as soon as I'd seen them coming – it's always best to weigh up all your options in advance – so I already knew that there were only two ways out. The street up ahead – where the three kids had come from – and the street behind me, where I'd just come from.

I looked quickly at both exits again. Two kids on

bikes had appeared from nowhere and were blocking the street behind me, and as I gazed across the other side of the square I saw a battered old Vauxhall Corsa rolling to a halt at the end of the street.

Both exits blocked, nowhere to run. My options were rapidly running out.

The three kids had stopped in front of me now, the older one slightly ahead of the other two.

'All right?' he said, staring dead-eyed at me. 'How you doing?'

'Pretty good, thanks,' I told him.

He looked to one side, spat through his teeth, then looked back at me. 'You're not from round here, are you?'

'No, I'm a friend of Mason's . . . Mason Yusuf? I'm meeting him here in a minute.'

'Yeah?' the kid said, grinning coldly. 'You his boyfriend or something?'

It was one of those 'what-*you*-looking-at?' kinds of questions, the sort of question that's impossible to answer without getting yourself into trouble. The problem is, if you react to this kind of question by *not* saying anything, that's also going to get you into trouble. It's a lose–lose situation. Which, from the questioner's perspective, is the whole point.

On this occasion, I decided to go for the keeping-my-mouth-shut option, and I just sat there on my bike, staring at the kid as blankly as I could, waiting to see what he'd do next. It was obvious now that my friendship with

Mason didn't hold any sway with these kids, and for a moment or two I found myself wondering why. They clearly knew who he was, and although he'd never been a big name in any of the gangs, his status on the estate had always been recognised and respected. I wondered what had changed.

I quickly stopped thinking about it as the kid in front of me stepped closer. His hand was still in his pocket, and I could see that the muscles in his arm were tensed.

'Give me your mobile,' he said.

'Why?'

'I want to call someone.'

'Haven't you got a phone?'

'Battery's dead.'

'What about your friends? Can't you borrow a phone from one of them?'

'Their batteries are dead too.' He stepped even closer. 'Are you going to give me your phone or not?'

I glanced at his friends, checking their position. They'd moved up behind him, one on his left, the other on his right. They were both smirking at me.

I wished now that I hadn't stayed on my bike when I'd first seen them coming. I'd thought it would give me an advantage – I could ride a lot quicker than they could run – but there was no doubt now that I was going to have to face up to these kids, and sitting on a bike isn't the ideal position to be in when you're about to get into a fight.

I rested my left foot on the bench to steady myself, and reached into my pocket for my phone. I knew that giving it to the kid wouldn't be the end of it. He'd take the phone, then demand something else – my wallet, my watch, my bike – and no matter how much I gave into him, eventually he was going to go for me anyway. So the way I saw it, I might as well go for him first.

I leaned slightly away from him, making it look as if I was just adjusting my balance, then I transferred the phone from my right hand to my left and held it out for him. He grinned at me for a moment, then reached out to take it. By leaning back I'd not only increased the gap between us – which meant that he had to lean in and stretch out his right arm to get the phone – but I'd also put myself in a more balanced position for throwing a punch.

He wasn't expecting me to hit him, so he was completely off guard when I hammered a right uppercut into his chin, and as his eyes rolled and his legs buckled, I knew I'd knocked him out even before he crumpled to the ground.

The kid on his right was the first to react, but he was nowhere near quick enough. By the time he'd realised what had happened – and wasted precious moments gazing down in stunned surprise at his unconscious friend – I'd already jumped off my bike and raced over to him. He looked up at me, anger darkening his eyes, and reached into his back pocket. I slammed my fist into his belly, then hit him again with a vicious left hook to his head as he doubled over in pain. He fell to his knees, groaning and gasping for breath, and I turned to the other kid. He was just standing there staring open-mouthed at me, too petrified to move, and I knew I didn't have to worry about him.

I spun round and saw the two kids on bikes speeding across the square towards me. They looked like they meant business, and as I stepped out to face them, instinctively settling into a boxer's stance – sideways on, left foot in front of the right, with my knees bent slightly and my guard up – I could only hope that they weren't carrying knives or guns. I was pretty sure I could handle them in a fist-fight, but even the best boxer in the world doesn't stand much of a chance against a kid with a gun.

The two kids were about twenty metres away from me now, and they didn't look as if they were slowing down. I braced myself, watching them closely, trying to work out which one to take out first . . .

And then suddenly they both slammed on their brakes and skidded to a halt, and I saw them looking behind me. They hesitated for a second, then one of them said something to the other, and the next thing I knew they'd swung their bikes round and were heading off back the way they'd come.

I watched them go, confused but relieved, then quickly turned round at the sound of approaching footsteps.

'Hey, Trav,' Mason Yusuf said breezily, looking around at the two kids I'd put down. 'Having fun?'

12

Mason rarely goes anywhere without Big Lenny, his devoted friend and minder, and today was no exception. Lenny's a giant of a kid – well over six feet tall, at least eighteen stone of solid muscle, with arms as thick as my waist and a head like a blacksmith's anvil. A lot of people make the mistake of thinking that Lenny's some kind of weirdo. It's an understandable mistake to make. Lenny hardly ever speaks, for one thing, and he has the oddest dress sense of anyone I've ever known. In fact, it's probably fairer to say that he has no dress sense at all. Today, for example, he was wearing an old-fashioned woollen cardigan (with leather buttons) over what appeared to be a striped pyjama top (buttoned up to the neck), together with blue suit trousers and a pair of black elasticated plimsolls. But while he might appear kind of clownish – in a scary sort of way – and he may come across as a little bit strange, there's a sense of serenity and quiet wisdom about Lenny that never fails to amaze me. He's like a big gorilla sitting peacefully in the jungle – perfectly content with himself and his world, but equally ready to stand up and face any threat that comes his way.

We'd left the two injured kids in the square – the other one had run away – and now we were heading through the estate towards Mason's flat. There was no sign of the Vauxhall Corsa I'd seen pulling up at the end of the street, and I guessed they'd either taken off at the sight of Mason and Lenny, or Mason had had a quiet word with them. I didn't bother asking him about it.

There's always an air of tension on the Slade, a sense that, at any moment, anything could happen. But tonight it was even more noticeable than usual. Even though Mason and Lenny appeared quite relaxed, I could tell they were both a bit edgier than normal – constantly on the alert, looking and listening to everything around them – and as Mason started explaining why the kids in the square hadn't left me alone when I'd mentioned his name, I began to understand why the estate felt so uneasy.

'There a lot of gang stuff going on at the moment,' Mason told me. 'You know the Slade kids and the Beacon crew have always hated each other, don't you?'

I nodded. The Beacon Fields estate was about two kilometres from here, at the other end of Slade Lane, and for as long as I could remember the two estates had been sworn enemies.

'There's been talk of a truce,' Mason went on, 'and some of the elders on both sides are actually considering a merger.'

By 'elders' he meant the older members of the gangs, the ones who controlled the business side of things – drug dealing, protection, extortion. They're the bosses, the ones who make all the money, and although they're behind most of the violence on the estates, they don't usually get involved in it themselves. Not on a street level anyway.

'The idea is that if Slade and Beacon get together,' Mason explained, 'the combined operation will have more resources and more manpower, and both crews will save a lot of time and energy by not being constantly at war. Which, in business terms, makes a lot of sense. But for some of the top guys who've been around for years, there's a lot more to it than just business. It's like a family thing for them, it's all about loyalty and tradition. They've been Slade or Beacon all their lives, they've been fighting the other side for decades, they've lost friends and family to them. So, to them, the prospect of joining forces is simply out of the question. It'd be like Arsenal going into partnership with Spurs.'

'Or Millwall teaming up with West Ham,' I suggested.

'Exactly.' Mason paused for a moment, stopping in his tracks as a low-slung car cruised across a junction up ahead of us. Lenny halted next to him and put out his arm to stop me. There were four hooded figures in the car. None of them looked our way as they passed by, but I got the feeling that Mason and Lenny knew who they were. We waited a minute after the car had gone, then we started moving again.

'Anyway,' Mason continued, 'the Slade's pretty much split into two different groups at the moment. There's those who want to join up with the Beacon crew, and those who don't. It's tearing the whole place apart. I mean, it's not actually a civil war situation yet, but it's not far off.'

'Which side are you on?' I asked him.

He sighed. 'I wish I didn't have to be on any side, but unfortunately it doesn't work like that. Staying neutral isn't an option.'

'Why not?'

'Well, it's kind of complicated, but basically it's all about respect. At the moment, everything's in the balance, but it's not going to stay like that for ever. One side's going to come out on top in the end. And if you're not on the right side when that happens, you're going to be nothing. I mean, you'll survive, you'll still be around, and eventually – if you work hard enough – you might get accepted again, but in the meantime you're going to be nothing.' He looked at me. 'It's tough enough being *something* round here. There's no way I'm going to be nothing.'

'So who's going to come out on top?' I asked.

'Money always wins,' he said simply. 'It's a fact of life. If a Slade/Beacon merger brings in more money than the combined profits of both, which it will, then that's what's going to happen.'

'So you're with the group that wants to join forces.'

He nodded. 'I've told you about Dee Dee, haven't I?'

'Yeah.'

'Well, he's the main guy pushing for the merger, and

that's another reason it's going to happen. Dee Dee's not just brutal, he's smart as hell. It's a winning combination all round.' Mason sighed again, and I got the impression that while he accepted that this was how it was, he wished in his heart that it didn't have to be. 'The guy leading the other group is an old hand called Joss Malik,' he went on. 'Malik's been around for ever, so he knows what he's doing, but he's no match for Dee Dee. The kids who came after you in the square were some of Malik's boys.' Mason looked at me. 'That's why they didn't leave you alone.'

We were approaching the block of flats where Mason lived now. It was a squat, grey, rectangular building, three storeys high. Lights were showing in most of the windows, and although it was a cold and miserable night, there were plenty of people hanging around on the cluttered balconies outside the flats at the front. There were quite a few people milling around the block too – young kids on bikes, older ones gathered in groups around cars.

'So anyway,' Mason said, 'enough about my problems. What was it you wanted to see me about?'

'Maybe it'd be better if we wait until we're inside,' I said, glancing at a couple of young kids who were riding along beside us on BMX bikes.

'Don't worry about them,' Mason assured me. 'This is Dee Dee's territory. We're on home ground now.'

I hesitated, wondering if I should just tell him that it was Dee Dee I wanted to see him about. After what he'd

13

Jaydie was a year younger than me, and although she was a great kid and I really liked her a lot, she sometimes made me feel kind of awkward. I don't think she really meant to embarrass me — not most of the time anyway — it was just that she had a bit of a crush on me, and she wasn't one to hide her feelings. She was always giving me hugs and holding my hand and stuff like that. I didn't really mind — in fact, to be honest, it was kind of nice — but I knew she wanted us to be more than just friends, she wanted us to be girlfriend and boyfriend, and I didn't want that. I don't know if it was because I just wasn't ready for that kind of thing in general, or if I simply didn't think of Jaydie in that way. But whatever the reason, it made me feel a bit rotten sometimes. What made it even worse was that Jaydie was so good about it. She didn't get upset or sulky or anything, she didn't lose patience or give up on me, she just kept going. It was almost as if she'd accepted that getting me to be her boyfriend was a long-term project, and she was going to keep working on it no matter how long it took.

When Mason led me into his flat that night, Jaydie's reaction to seeing me was as bubbly and over-the-top as ever. She was sitting on a settee watching TV when we came in, and as soon as she saw me, she jumped up and ran over to me, a big beaming smile on her face, and before I'd had a chance to say hello, she'd thrown her arms round my chest and was squeezing the life out of me.

'I can't breathe, Jaydie,' I mumbled after a while.

'Sorry,' she said, grinning as she let go of me. 'I haven't seen you for *ages*, Trav.'

'Yeah, I know . . .'

She leaned in and kissed me on the cheek. 'I've missed you.'

'Me too,' I muttered.

'You've missed yourself?' she said, smiling.

'No, I meant—'

'I know what you meant.' She stood back and looked me up and down. 'You've got taller since I last saw you. And you've let your hair grow. It looks really nice.'

'So does yours,' I said, admiring her braids.

'You're just saying that.'

'No, honestly,' I told her. 'I like it a lot. It really suits you.'

As I stood there gazing at her, I couldn't help noticing that it wasn't just her hair that looked different, it was everything about her. She was still the same bright-eyed and naturally pretty Jaydie she'd always been, and she was wearing the same plain but stylish clothes she usually wore – black T-shirt and leggings – but there was definitely something different about her. I couldn't quite pin it down, but she somehow seemed a bit more grown-up, a bit more graceful maybe . . .

It was kind of strange, to be honest.

I couldn't take my eyes off her.

'I can go, if you want,' I heard Mason say.

I looked at him. He was grinning.

'Shut up, Mase,' Jaydie said, punching him playfully on the arm. 'Why do you always have to be such a moron?'

'I'm just trying to be tactful,' he said, grinning at me again.

'Just ignore him,' Jaydie said to me. 'He's an idiot.'

I smiled awkwardly at her, trying to think of something to say. But it was one of those moments when your brain seems to disappear and all you can do is stand there looking stupid.

'Is Mum back yet?' Mason asked Jaydie, thankfully changing the subject.

Jaydie shook her head. 'Sit down, Trav,' she said to me, indicating the settee. 'Can I get you anything? A Coke or something? Tea? Coffee?'

'No, I'm all right, thanks,' I told her, going over to the settee and sitting down.

'Do you want something to eat?'

I still hadn't eaten anything since lunchtime, and I was actually really hungry, but for some reason I found myself shaking my head and telling Jaydie I was fine. I think I was probably just too confused and embarrassed to eat.

'I wouldn't mind a sandwich or something,' Mason said.

'Don't let me stop you,' Jaydie told him, sitting down next to me.

He gave her a look, then shrugged, turned off the TV, and sat down in an armchair across from us.

I gazed around the flat. Although I hadn't expected it to be very spacious, I was still surprised at how small and cramped it was. It seemed to consist of one main room, a little kitchen, and a hallway leading off to what I assumed was the bathroom and bedrooms. The main room was about half the size of the front room in my nan and grandad's house, and from what I could see of the kitchen, it was barely big enough to walk around in.

'Right then,' Mason said, settling into the armchair, 'let's hear it, Trav. What can I do for you?'

I was still a bit worried by what he'd told me about his connection with Dee Dee, and it had crossed my mind that maybe it wasn't a good idea to talk to him about the tanning salon after all. But I was here now, I told myself. I might as well give it a go. And besides, what was the worst that could happen? If Mason really didn't want to talk about Dee Dee, all he had to do was tell me. And if that was the case, I'd just say fair enough, and leave it at that.

So, with that in mind, I just got on with it.

'Have you heard of a place called Tanga Tans?' I said to him.

I'd always known that Mason had a scary side to him, and I'd seen the effect he could have on people just by looking at them, but until that moment I'd never experienced it myself. But as his face turned to stone and he fixed me with an ice-cold stare, I suddenly knew exactly how it felt.

It felt damn scary.

14

'What's Tanga Tans got to do with you?' Mason said harshly.

'I'm only asking—'

'I asked you a question, Travis,' he interrupted, his eyes fixed on mine. 'Don't make me ask you again.'

I glanced briefly at Jaydie. She wasn't smiling any more either. I didn't understand what was going on here – why had the mere mention of Tanga Tans caused such a reaction? – but I guessed the only way to find out was to answer Mason's question and then see what he had to say. So, taking a deep breath to gather myself, I began telling Mason and Jaydie about Delaney & Co's investigation into the tanning salon.

Mason didn't say a word while I was explaining the situation, he just sat there listening intently, his face emotionless, his eyes cold and still. It was impossible to tell what he was thinking. When I'd finished telling him everything, he still didn't say or do anything for a while, he just carried on sitting there staring at me. It was a really uncomfortable and confusing situation. Eventually – after what seemed like an hour, but was probably only a minute – he took a breath, let out a long sigh, and said, 'Who's your client?'

'I'm sorry, Mase, you know I can't tell you that.'

'Why not?'

'Client confidentiality.'

He nodded. 'Why did you come to me about this? What do you want from me?'

'I just thought you might know something about Dee Dee's connection with the salon, that's all. I mean, it's not important or anything . . .' I leaned forward and looked at him, trying to get through to the Mason I knew, the Mason who was my friend. 'Listen, Mase,' I said, 'I'm really sorry if I've offended you in any way, OK? If I've crossed some kind of barrier here, just tell me, and I promise I won't say another word about it.'

His face remained cold and blank.

'Come on, Mason,' I sighed. 'Talk to me, for God's sake. Don't just sit there—'

'Tell your grandad to drop the case,' he said.

'What?'

'You heard me. Tell him to drop it.'

I was beginning to lose patience now. I just couldn't understand why he was acting like this. I turned to Jaydie.

'Can you tell me what's going on here?' I asked her.

'It's complicated, Trav. It's not just—'

'Shut up, Jay,' Mason told her. 'This hasn't got anything to do with him.'

'Don't tell me to shut up,' she said, glaring angrily at her brother. 'If I want to talk to Travis about it, I will. It's just as much about me as it is about you.'

Mason's face softened slightly. 'I know it is.'

'You can't keep running away from it, Mase.'

'I'm not running away from anything. I'm just . . .'

'What?' Jaydie said bitterly. 'You're just what?'

As the two of them sat there scowling at each other, I decided it was probably best if I left. There was obviously something serious going on here, some kind of family thing, and I didn't want to get caught up in the middle of it. But then, just as I was about to get up, a key rattled in the front door, and when the door swung open and a dark-haired woman let herself in, everything suddenly made sense.

'Hey, Mum,' Jaydie said. 'This is Travis.'

'Hello, Travis,' the woman said. 'Nice to finally meet you.'

'Hi, Mrs Yusuf,' I muttered, trying not to stare at her.

'Please,' she said, 'call me Lisa.'

I just nodded.

Lisa.

Mrs Yusuf – Mason and Jaydie's mum – was Lisa from Tanga Tans.

15

Now that his mum was back, Mason's demeanour changed from streetwise tough guy to caring and protective son, and although it was obvious that his mum didn't have any problems with me being there, Mason couldn't get me out of the flat fast enough.

'Please don't go on my account, Travis,' she said as Mason bundled me towards the door.

'He's got to get going, Mum,' Mason told her.

'Oh, well,' she said, taking off her coat, 'maybe next time you can stay a bit longer.'

'Yeah, I'd like that,' I said.

As Mason opened the door and ushered me out, he leaned in close and whispered in my ear, '*Please* leave this alone, Travis, OK? I'm asking you as a friend. If me and Jaydie mean anything to you, stay away from Tanga Tans.'

I'd never heard him sound so desperate before, and as I looked into his eyes I saw something that until then I'd never have believed. He was frightened. Not for himself, but for someone else. He was frightened for his mum.

'Listen, Mason—' I started to say.

'Lenny will see you off the estate,' he said, and without another word he shut the door.

I'd left my bike in the corridor outside the flat, and as I

looked over at it now I saw Big Lenny standing beside it. He nodded at me. I stood there for a moment, wondering if I should go back in and try talking to Mason again, but as Lenny wheeled my bike over to me, I decided it was best to leave it for now and give myself time to think things through.

'All right?' Lenny said to me in his big deep voice.

I looked up at him. He passed me my bike.

'Stay close,' he said simply.

He walked off along the corridor, and – with a confused heart – I followed him.

We'd just reached the edge of the square surrounding the block of flats, and were about to head off into a narrow street, when I heard someone calling out my name. I turned round and saw Jaydie hurrying out of the block towards us. She wasn't wearing a coat or a jacket, and all she had on her feet was a pair of clog-style slippers. As she ran towards me, she kept glancing over her shoulder, looking back at the window of her flat. It was pretty obvious that she'd slipped out without telling Mason.

Lenny had stopped at the sound of her voice and was just standing there scanning the square, looking out for any sign of trouble. If he was conflicted in any way about seeing Jaydie, he didn't show it.

Jaydie slowed down as she approached us, and I could see her breath misting in the cold night air. She looked back at the flats again, then turned to me.

'but Mum occasionally talks to me about him. It's funny really. I mean, considering what he did to her, you wouldn't expect her to have anything good to say about him. But although she quite often ends up crying her eyes out when she's telling me stuff about him, it sometimes makes her really happy too. From what she's told me, he sounds like one of those men who never really grow up – you know, they just carry on being kids all their lives, and all they ever think about is themselves . . .' Jaydie paused for a moment, waiting for a group of kids to pass by. Once they'd gone, she continued. 'Anyway, Mum's always done all right bringing us up on her own, but a couple of years ago she went through a bit of a bad patch and it really messed her up. It started when she lost her job, and then a really good friend of hers got caught up in some stupid gang thing and ended up getting stabbed . . .' Jaydie shook her head. 'Mum took it really hard, and she just . . . well, she used to have a lot of problems with drugs when she was younger, but she sorted herself out when she was pregnant with Mason, and she hadn't touched anything since. But when her friend was killed and she lost her job, she just kind of fell back into it again. It was pretty bad for a while, and without Mason's help it might have got even worse. Mase was brilliant, Travis. I mean, he was only about thirteen when all this was going on, but he took control of everything – looking after me, helping Mum get off the drugs, sorting out all the bills and shopping and stuff. It was amazing really. He never complained about anything, never blamed Mum for getting herself into a mess, he just got stuck in and did what had to be done.'

'Did your mum get off the drugs again?' I asked.

Jaydie nodded. 'She's been clean ever since. The trouble was, because she didn't have a job at the time, there wasn't much cash coming in, and once she'd run out of stuff to sell or hock to get the money to pay for her drugs, she started borrowing from a loan shark. By the time Mason found out about it, she owed thousands. Mason couldn't believe it. That was the only time I've ever seen him lose his temper with her. It wasn't even the fact that she'd spent so much money on drugs that made him angry, it was that she hadn't come to him for it. But by then it was already too late.'

'What do you mean?'

'Do you know how illegal money-lending works?'

'Not really,' I admitted. 'But I don't suppose it's like borrowing from a bank.'

'Not unless your bank has like a 10,000% interest rate,' Jaydie said ruefully. 'Mum's first loan was for a hundred pounds. A week later, when she hadn't paid it back, she owed just over three hundred. So then she borrowed another five hundred to pay off the three hundred and have another two hundred for drugs, and after that she just carried on borrowing more and more. By the time Mason found out what she'd been doing, she owed almost ten thousand pounds, and even Mason couldn't help her out with that kind of money.' Jaydie looked at me. 'Another difference between a loan shark and a bank is that if you get behind with your payments to the loan shark, you don't just get a phone call or a sternly worded reminder, you get a couple of bone-headed psychopaths hammering on your door, threatening to set their pitbulls on you.'

I just looked at her for a moment, unable to think of anything meaningful to say.

I've always known that life on the Slade is a world away from the life I know, but it never ceases to amaze me just *how* different it is. Whether or not my awareness of the way other people live makes any difference to the way I try to live, I'm not really sure. But it certainly helps to put things into perspective. Before I knew Mason and Jaydie, for example, I used to worry about all kinds of stupid little things – something some kid at school had said about me, whether I'd bought the right trainers or not, what people were saying about me on Facebook. These days though, when I find myself worrying about stuff like that, I just try to remind myself how lucky I am. *You think you've got problems?* I tell myself. *Well, imagine what it's like living on the Slade. Imagine what it's like to walk home every day wondering if you're going to get stabbed or shot. Now* that's *a problem.* It doesn't always work, of course. Just because you know there are bigger problems in the world than yours, that doesn't necessarily make yours any easier to deal with. But sometimes it helps.

'Are you all right, Trav?' Jaydie said.

'Yeah, sorry . . . I was just thinking about something.' I looked at her. 'So what happened to your mum? I mean, what did she do about all the money she owed?'

'Well, that's the thing. She's still paying it off, and that's why Mason got so uptight with you about Tanga Tans.'

16

Although Jaydie didn't know for sure why Dee Dee had taken over her mum's debt, she was fairly sure that Mason had something to do with it.

'When I asked Mase if he'd made some kind of deal with Dee Dee,' she told me, 'he didn't actually *say* that he had, but he didn't deny it either.'

'What kind of deal are you talking about?' I asked.

'Well, I don't really know the details, but basically Dee Dee took over Mum's loan – he probably paid it off at a huge discount – and in return Mum agreed to run Tanga Tans for him.'

'Does Dee Dee own the salon?'

'I don't know if he owns it officially. I mean, the ownership's probably in someone else's name. But, yeah, it's his business.'

'Does your mum know anything about running a tanning salon? Is she trained or anything?'

'No.'

'Does she get paid for working there?'

'Yeah, but Dee Dee keeps most of it to pay off her debt. With what's left after he's taken his share, plus her benefit money, we've just about got enough to live on.'

'How long's it going to take to pay off the debt?'

'As long as Dee Dee says.'

It was clear now why Mason had reacted the way he did. If Jakes and Mortimer went ahead with their client's compensation claim against Tanga Tans, Mason's mum was going to be in a whole lot of trouble. Even if the claim wasn't successful, it was bound to come out that Lisa Yusuf wasn't qualified to run a tanning salon, or even legally employed, so at the very least she'd lose her job, and she'd still be in debt to Dee Dee. And if Dee Dee ended up paying compensation, or even losing his business, Lisa wasn't going to be his favourite person, to say the least.

No wonder Mason wanted Delaney & Co to drop the case.

'Why didn't Mason tell me about this himself?' I asked Jaydie.

'I think he's just really mixed up about it. He wants to look after Mum, and he thinks he can do it all on his own. He's too proud to admit he needs help. I'm not sure he knows what to do about Dee Dee either. He knows Dee Dee's taking advantage of Mum and treating her like dirt, but he also knows that if it wasn't for Dee Dee, Mum might have ended up in even worse trouble. And now there's all this gang stuff going on too.' She looked at me. 'Did Mase tell you about that?'

'Yeah.'

'So you know he's committed himself to Dee Dee's side in this merger thing?'

I nodded. 'The question is, how far does that commitment go?'

'What do you mean?'

'Well, now that Mason knows about the investigation into Tanga Tans, it puts him in a really difficult position, doesn't it? I mean, what does he do? Tell your mum about it? Tell Dee Dee? Don't tell anyone? Whatever he does, I can't see it having a happy ending.'

'Couldn't you ask your grandad to drop the case?'

'It wouldn't make any difference. We've already done our part of the job, the rest of it is up to Jakes and Mortimer and their client. If they want to go ahead with the claim, there's nothing we can do about it.'

'Can't you at least try?' Jaydie asked. 'I mean, if it all starts going wrong for Mum again . . .'

Her voice trailed off, and I could see she was struggling to keep her emotions under control.

'I'm sorry, Jaydie,' I said quietly. 'If there was anything I could do to help, anything at all, I wouldn't hesitate for a second. But I honestly can't think of anything . . .'

'It's all right,' she muttered. 'It's not your fault, is it?'

'Look, I'll talk to my grandad, OK? He'll probably say the same as me, but you never know . . . maybe he can talk to the solicitors or something. I doubt if it'll do any good, but it's worth a try.'

'Thanks, Trav,' she said, smiling sadly. She glanced over at the flats. 'I'd better be getting back before Mason starts wondering where I am.' She got to her feet, took off my jacket and gave it back to me, then leaned down and kissed me on the cheek. 'Call me soon, OK?'

I nodded.

She started heading back to the flats.

'Does Mason like Dee Dee?' I said to her.

She stopped and turned round. 'What?'

'Does Mason actually *like* Dee Dee?'

The look she gave me was the look of a kindly teacher trying to explain something blatantly obvious to a very naive and dim-witted kid. 'You don't like or dislike people like Dee Dee,' she said. 'They are what they are, and that's all there is to it. You don't *feel* anything about them at all.'

17

Nan and Grandad's house is a nice old three-bedroomed place on Long Barton Road, the main road between Kell Cross and Barton. I still really miss my old house in Kell Cross. I was born and raised there, and it holds all kinds of special memories for me, but it's been sold now – it's become someone else's home – and I try not to think about it too much any more. And besides, I pretty much think of Nan and Grandad's place as my home now.

When I got back that night, Granny Nora was upstairs in her room as usual, and Nan and Grandad were watching TV in the front room.

'How's Granny today?' I asked Nan. 'Is her arthritis still really bad?'

'No, she's a lot better now,' Nan said. 'She's been asking about you actually. Something about a story she was going to tell you?'

There was a question in Nan's voice – *what story is this then?* – but I pretended not to hear it, and Nan didn't push it any further. She was trying her best to be OK, but I knew she was still a long way from being her usual bright and chirpy self, and it was clear from her attitude towards Grandad – polite but distant – that she hadn't forgiven him yet.

The two of them had already had their dinner, and

despite my protestations that I needed to talk to Grandad about something *immediately*, Nan insisted that I sat down at the table and had a proper meal before I did anything else.

'You might think you're all grown-up and independent now that you're fourteen,' she said, half jokingly, 'but as long as you're living here, you're going to eat something reasonably healthy at least once a day. Understood?'

'Yes, ma'am,' I said, grinning at her.

Her face broke into a fragile smile and she ruffled my hair.

'How does beans on toast sound?' she asked.

'You'll probably find out after I've eaten them,' I said.

It was getting on for ten o'clock by the time I got round to telling Grandad what I'd found out about Tanga Tans. We were in my room – me sitting at my desk, Grandad relaxed in the old armchair in the corner – and through the window I could see a fine wintry rain misting in the darkness.

'I don't really see what we can do to help Lisa Yusuf,' Grandad said thoughtfully. 'I'm perfectly happy to ask Jakes and Mortimer if they'd consider dropping the case, but I can't think of any reason why they would. Their only responsibility is to their client. They're not going to back off just because Lisa Yusuf is your friends' mum.' Grandad looked at me. 'Sorry, Trav, but that's just the way it is.'

'Yeah, I know,' I sighed. 'That's pretty much what I told Jaydie myself. What do you think will happen to her mum if the compensation claim goes ahead?'

Grandad shrugged. 'It's hard to tell. If the claim's successful, I'd imagine the salon itself will take most of the blame. Whoever the official owner is, they'll have to pay the compensation and probably a fine as well, but I doubt very much if Lisa Yusuf will get away without some kind of punishment, especially if she's not qualified or legally employed.'

'I think Mason's more concerned with what Dee Dee has in mind for her,' I said.

Grandad frowned, stroking his chin. 'Did Mason tell you anything else about Tanga Tans?'

'Like what?'

'How long Dee Dee's run the business, when he took it over . . . anything like that?'

'No. Why?'

'I've been trying to figure out why a man like him would want anything to do with a crummy little tanning salon in the first place. I mean, if he was trying to boost his reputation as a businessman, I would have thought he'd buy into a nightclub or a bar, not a tanning salon. Unless . . .' Grandad paused, thinking about something.

'Unless what?' I asked him.

'I need to wait and see what Gloria comes up with,' he said, avoiding a direct answer. 'I called her earlier this evening. She's going to do some digging into Tanga Tans' financial records over the weekend. If there *is* anything to find out, Gloria will find it.'

I waited for him to go on, hoping he'd tell me what he thought Gloria might discover, but after thinking quietly to himself for a few moments, he turned to me and said, 'So, Travis, how are you feeling about your debut investigation? Excited? Nervous? Scared?'

I didn't know what he was talking about for a second – I'd kind of forgotten about the thefts from the school changing rooms – and even when I finally realised what he meant, I can't honestly say that I felt very much about it at all. In comparison to what Mason and Jaydie and their mum were going through, a bit of petty thieving at school seemed to pale into insignificance. I'd told Kendal I'd look into it though, and – as my dad once told me – a man is only as good as his word. Mind you, strictly speaking, I hadn't actually given Kendal my word, I'd just told him I'd do it. But still, it wouldn't be right to back out of it now just because it didn't seem very important any more.

'Yeah,' I told Grandad, trying to summon up some enthusiasm, 'I'm looking forward to it. The next cup game's on Monday afternoon, so I'll probably install the motion sensors on Sunday and then double-check them on Monday morning . . .'

We didn't spend a lot of time discussing the case. Grandad asked me some questions about the thefts, and after I'd explained exactly what had been going on, he gave me a few tips about installing the sensors, and some practical advice about thieving in general and what kinds of things I needed to look out for, and that was pretty much it. I got the impression that he probably had a lot more to say, but he didn't want me to think he was intruding too much into my case.

After he'd gone back downstairs, I waited five minutes or so, then I went to see Granny Nora.

18

Granny Nora quite often sleeps during the day and stays up late into the night, so although it was gone eleven o'clock when I went in to see her, she was wide awake and more than happy to talk to me. She was sitting in her usual place – in her ancient armchair by the window – and the table beside her was piled up with all her usual stuff: dozens of paperback crime novels, her iPhone, her iPod, her brand-new iPad. Her binoculars were on the windowsill right next to her, and she was fiddling with the controls of her latest online purchase, an infrared night-vision scope. Granny Nora likes to keep herself busy, and although she can't get around very much any more, she still likes to know what's going on. So when she's not reading or listening to music or messing about online, she's perfectly content just sitting by the window watching the world go by.

'Is it any good?' I asked her, glancing at the night-vision scope as I sat down in the cushioned wicker chair opposite her.

'Is it what?' she said, turning her good ear towards me.

She's completely deaf in one ear and losing her hearing in the other, but despite having a perfectly good hearing aid, she's always forgetting – or *pretending* to forget – to turn it on. And even when she does turn it on, she 'forgets' to turn up the volume. I know she does it on purpose, and I also know that she knows I know. She still does it though. She's got a wicked sense of humour, my gran.

'The scope,' I said, raising my voice, 'is it any good?'

'Ah, I don't know,' she replied, putting it down on the table. 'I think maybe the street lights are too bright for it to work properly. Everything looks kind of glarey.'

I smiled, enjoying the familiar sound of her voice. Granny Nora's from Dublin, and she has a lovely thick Irish accent that I never get tired of hearing. I don't know why I like it so much, but it just seems to make me want to listen to every word she says.

'Maybe you could ring the council,' I suggested. 'Ask them to turn off the street lights for you.'

She grinned. 'I was thinking of buying myself an air rifle. I could turn off the lights myself then.'

She raised an imaginary rifle and mimed taking a potshot out of the window. I knew she was only joking, but I also knew that if she *did* have an air rifle, and she really did want to shoot out the street lights, she wouldn't think twice about doing it.

'So, Travis,' she said, turning back to me, 'how's everything going?'

'Not too bad, thanks.'

'School OK?'

I shrugged. 'Same as ever.'

'And what about you?' she asked quietly, her kindly

old eyes looking deeply into mine. 'How are *you* doing?'

I knew what she meant – how was I feeling about Mum and Dad – and I knew she was only asking because she cared so much for me. But even if I'd wanted to, I couldn't have given her much of an answer. How was I doing? I didn't *know* how I was doing. I didn't know if all the stuff I was going through was the kind of stuff you're *meant* to go through when both your parents die suddenly. I didn't know if it was normal to sometimes feel OK, and then hate yourself for feeling OK. I didn't know if I was supposed to cry myself to sleep every night and then get up in the morning and go to school and just carry on as if everything was perfectly normal. I didn't know if it was OK to sometimes realise for a terrifying moment that I couldn't picture what my mum and dad looked like . . .

'I honestly don't know how I'm doing, Gran,' I muttered. 'I just . . . I just don't know.'

'You don't *have* to know, Travis,' she said gently. 'If there's one thing I've learned as I've got older, it's that it's perfectly all right to have doubts and uncertainties – about yourself, about the world, about everything. There are so many things that none of us will ever understand, things that simply don't have any answers, but the trick is to realise that we don't *have* to know all the answers. We live in a mysterious universe that has no purpose or reason. We don't *have* to feel frightened of not knowing things.'

'Do you really believe that?' I said, looking at her.

She smiled. 'I don't know.'

We talked about Grandad for a while then. He'd always been prone to very dark moods, and he often suffered flashbacks and nightmares about the terrors he'd been through during his army career, especially the time he'd almost lost his life in a car-bomb explosion in Northern Ireland. But Granny had noticed that since he'd started running Delaney & Co again, his depressive moods had become far less frequent and debilitating, and he seemed to be actually enjoying life again.

'I know he still comes across as being a grizzly old grump most of the time,' she said, smiling, 'but I know my son, and I can tell he's got his lust for life back again. Everything about him is different now, even the way he walks. He doesn't mope around with his shoulders slumped any more, he struts around the place, his chest out, his head held high . . . it's a wonderful thing to see. And I've got you to thank for that, Travis. If it wasn't for you, he never would have gone back to work.'

'I needed Delaney & Co as much as he did,' I said. 'We're both helping each other really.'

'Well, that's as maybe, but I'm still eternally grateful to you. You gave your grandad his life back.'

After we'd carried on talking about nothing in particular for a while, we finally got round to the unfinished story of Grandad and Gloria Nightingale, or as Granny called her, the mysterious Ms Nightingale.

'Who says she's mysterious?' I said.

'I do.'

'Why?'

'Because she is.'

I sighed. 'Are you going to tell me the story or not?'

Granny just looked at me for a moment or two, her eyes twinkling with the impish delight of a gossip, then she leaned back in her chair and began telling me the story.

Gloria's surname was Hanson when Grandad first met her, Granny told me. She couldn't remember the exact year they met, but it was sometime in the early 1970s, shortly after Grandad had joined the army.

'Gloria was at Cambridge University at the time,' Gran explained. 'I don't know how or where she met your grandad, but as I told you before, they went out together a few times, maybe over a period of a month or so, but it all fizzled out fairly quickly. They still kept in touch though, and from what I can gather they became very good friends.' Granny looked at me. 'That's a rare thing, Travis, I can tell you. A very rare thing. Lots of couples promise each other they'll stay friends when they break up, but they're almost always empty words. Your grandfather actually meant it.'

'I bet Nan wishes he hadn't,' I said.

Granny nodded. 'It was difficult for her. When she married your grandad she didn't want to break up his friendship with Gloria, but it was only natural that she didn't want him spending *too* much time with her. And to your grandad's credit he realised how your nan felt, and although he still kept in contact with Gloria, they stopped meeting up on a regular basis.'

'Grandad worked with Gloria though, didn't he?' I said. 'That's what he told me anyway.'

'That was about ten years later, sometime in the early 1980s. Gloria was working for MI6 by then – she'd been recruited while she was still studying at Cambridge – and your grandad was an officer in the Army Intelligence Corps. I don't know if their friendship had anything to do with them being teamed up to work together, or if it was just a coincidence, but either way they ended up working with each other on a joint-services undercover operation in Czechoslovakia. I've no idea what it involved – there were all kinds of shadowy Cold War operations going on back then – and your grandad's always refused to talk about it, so I can only tell you what I've heard over the years, and I'm sure that most of that has been embellished to some extent. But what's not in any doubt is that whatever your grandad and Gloria were working on, it all went terribly wrong for some reason, and they were both captured by the KGB, the Soviet Intelligence Agency, and held on charges of espionage somewhere in Czechoslovakia.'

It sounded just like something out of an old spy film – KGB agents in long black trench coats interrogating

British spies in underground prisons, shining lights in their eyes, beating them up, and worse . . .

'What happened to them?' I asked breathlessly.

'Well,' Granny said thoughtfully, 'that's where it all starts getting a bit mysterious. For about six weeks or so, neither MI6 nor Army Intelligence heard anything about your grandad or Gloria. They didn't know where they were, whether they were still in Czechoslovakia or had been moved somewhere else. They didn't know what the Soviets were doing with them. They didn't even know if they were still alive. And then suddenly, completely out of the blue, Army Intelligence HQ received a call from the US Embassy in Prague saying that your grandad was safe and well and that arrangements were being made to fly him back to the UK.'

'Was he OK?'

'Physically he wasn't *too* bad. He'd lost a lot of weight and was suffering from a severe chest infection, but apart from that, and a few cuts and bruises, there wasn't anything seriously wrong with him. Psychologically though . . . well, like I said, he's never talked about it, so we can only guess how the experience affected him.' Granny went quiet for a moment, her eyes filled with sadness for the pain her son had suffered. 'Anyway,' she said after a while, 'it turned out that some kind of exchange deal had been made between the Soviets and the CIA. The KGB released your grandad, and in return the CIA released a Soviet spy.'

'What was Grandad's connection with the CIA?' I asked.

Granny shrugged. 'Who knows? There were rumours that the Army Intelligence Corps had something the CIA wanted – information about something – and getting Grandad released gave the CIA the bargaining tool they needed.'

'What happened to Gloria?'

'No one knows. She wasn't released with your grandad, and the CIA claimed they had no information about her at all. Your grandad hadn't seen her since they'd been captured. MI6 had no idea where she was or whether she'd talked or not. After two years had passed without any news, it was assumed that she was either dead or that she'd been turned by the Soviets and was working for them.'

'*Was* she working for them?'

'Again, no one knows for sure. The mystery deepened when all of a sudden, two and half years after she'd disappeared, Gloria resurfaced in London.' Granny shook her head. 'No one seems to know what happened to her, whether she somehow escaped, or was recaptured by MI6, or released for some reason . . . it's anyone's guess really. She just came back. And that's when all the rumours started.'

'What kind of rumours?'

'She was a double agent, working for the Soviets. She'd been brainwashed. She'd been a double agent all along, and it was her who'd tipped off the KGB about the undercover operation in Czechoslovakia in the first place . . . even now, no one really knows the truth.'

'Not even Grandad?'

Granny Nora smiled. 'You'll have to ask him about that.'

'Did Gloria carry on working for MI6?'

'She was officially retired shortly after her return. She disappeared off the radar for a few years after that, and at some point she got married, but apparently it only lasted a few months. Some people say she moved into the private sector and made a small fortune working for multinational financial corporations, but others maintain that she never actually stopped working for MI6 at all, she just went deep, *deep* undercover. There are also those who think she was working for the Soviets all along, that she's never stopped working for them, and that even now her true loyalties lie with the Russian intelligence services.' Granny looked at me. 'And that's just about it really. End of story.'

'Just about?'

'Well,' Granny said hesitantly, 'there is one more thing you should know . . . but like so much of this story, it's nothing more than hearsay and rumour.' She paused for a moment, then sighed and went on. 'There was a lot of talk going around that Gloria and your grandad weren't *just* working together when they were in Czechoslovakia.'

'You mean they were having an affair?'

'Some people thought so, yes.'

I stared at Granny, doing some quick mental calculations. 'Dad would have been born by then, wouldn't he? He would have been about five or six years old.'

Granny nodded. 'It was *just* talk, Travis. There's no proof that your grandad and Gloria got back together. And while you can never rule out *any*thing when it comes to matters of the heart, I'd bet my life that my son never cheated on Nancy. He just wouldn't do something like that. He's not that kind of man.'

Nancy is my nan's name, and Granny loves her as if she were her own daughter. From the look in Granny's eyes just now, if she thought that Grandad *had* cheated on Nan, there was no doubt whose side she'd be on.

'Does Nan know about these rumours?' I asked her.

Granny nodded. 'She's known about them for years.'

'Is that why she's so annoyed with Grandad for hiring Gloria?'

Granny shook her head. 'There a lot more to it than just that. There's no doubt that Nan doesn't *like* Gloria, but that's mostly down to the fact that she just doesn't like her as a person.' Granny looked at me. 'Your nan trusts Grandad. She doesn't believe any of the rumours about him having an affair with Gloria. That's not the main reason she's so upset with him for hiring her.'

'What is it then?'

'Well, the fact that he didn't talk it over with her first

has something to do with it, but the thing that's really bothering her . . . well, I think she's just worried that he's putting too much trust in Gloria.'

I frowned at Gran. 'I don't get it.'

'It all goes back to what happened in Czechoslovakia. If Gloria *was* working for the Soviets as a double agent, if it *was* her who tipped them off about the undercover operation . . . well, who's to say she won't betray your grandad again?'

'Why would she do that? And who would she betray him *to*?'

'I don't know. I'm just saying that that's how I think your nan sees it. Once a traitor, always a traitor.'

'Do *you* trust Gloria?' I asked her.

'I honestly don't know, Travis. I've never met the woman. I don't know enough about her to form a valid judgement.'

'All right, but what's your gut feeling about her?'

'What's yours?'

'You're not answering my question, Gran.'

'You're not answering mine.'

We looked at each other for a few moments then, waiting to see who'd make the next move. I'm pretty good at waiting, and after a while I think Granny realised that it was up to her to speak first.

'Your grandad trusts Gloria,' she said. 'He wouldn't have hired her if he didn't. And while my son might have his faults, I'd never doubt his judgement of character.'

Granny shrugged. 'If *he* thinks Gloria's OK, that's good enough for me.' She smiled at me. 'Does that answer your question?'

I nodded. 'It's good enough for me.'

19

At two o'clock on Monday afternoon I was sitting on the bench with the rest of the substitutes watching the semi-final of the Twin Town Cup. Kell Cross Under-15s were playing a German team from a place called Steindorf, which apparently is somewhere near Wetzlar. The German side weren't bad, but they were no match for Kell Cross, and although the game had only been going for fifteen minutes, Steindorf were already 1–0 down.

It was another cold and drizzly day, and on top of my football kit I was wearing a tracksuit and a parka (with the hood up) and a beanie hat pulled down over my ears. If I had to sit here doing nothing for the next eighty minutes or so (U-15 matches are forty minutes each way), the least I could do was keep warm.

The other semi-final was taking place on the adjacent pitch – Slade Lane Comprehensive v Saint-Jacques-de-la-Lande. I didn't know if the French team were any good or not, but even without having seen them play I doubted they'd have much chance against Slade Comp. Slade's team had an almost unbeatable combination of exceptional skill and savage brutality. They not only had half a dozen really top-class players, they also had three or four who were both reasonably skilful and frighteningly vicious. So even if Slade did come up against a side who were as good as them football-wise – which very rarely happened – they always had a Plan B to fall back on, which basically was to kick the other team off the park.

Despite the miserable weather, there were pretty decent crowds watching both games. A lot of them were pupils, of course – anyone who didn't have exams coming up was free to watch the semi-finals – and there were quite a few parents and teachers on the sidelines too. There were also one or two reporters and photographers from the local newspapers, a handful of representatives from various sponsors, and I'd even heard rumours that a couple of scouts from professional clubs had been spotted watching the games.

As I mentioned before, the Twin Town Cup was a big deal for the school, and as I gazed around now – taking everything in, soaking up the atmosphere – I had to admit that it was actually pretty exciting. It would have been even more exciting if I'd thought there was a chance I might get to play, but that wasn't why I was here, I reminded myself. I was here to catch a thief.

A muted roar went up, and as I looked across the pitch I saw Kendal Price trotting back to the centre circle, modestly accepting the congratulatory hugs and pats from his teammates. I hadn't actually seen him score, but Kendal's one of those big tall centre backs who always lumber upfield for corner kicks, and I'd be willing to bet that he'd just hit the net with another of his trademark towering headers.

Steindorf were 2–0 down now, and as the game kicked off again, it was obvious from their body language that most of their players were already resigned to getting beaten. Which was kind of untypical for a German team, as they're usually renowned for never giving up. 'You can never write off the Germans', the football pundits always say. Well, you could write off this lot, no trouble.

I glanced over at the changing rooms. They were housed in an L-shaped building, with the away dressing room in the shorter side of the L and the home side in the longer part. The car park in front was jam-packed with cars and buses, blocking my view of most of the building, but I'd taken care to position myself so that I could still see both doors. Mr Ayres, who taught history and PE, was standing guard outside the away dressing room, and Mr Wells – English and drama – was by the other door.

When I'd met up with Mr Jago and Kendal at school on Sunday afternoon to install the motion sensors, I'd asked Mr Jago if he was going to tell the teachers who'd be guarding the doors about the sensors.

'No,' he'd said. 'All I've told them is that once the teams have left the changing rooms, they're to lock the doors and not let anyone back in without asking me first. Unless there's a really good reason for anyone to go back in – a serious injury, say – then the changing rooms stay locked until half-time.' He glanced at the air-freshener sensor in my hand. 'Are you going to be able to switch that on and off when necessary?'

'They're remotely connected to my mobile,' I'd explained. 'I can either turn them on and off whenever you tell me, or you could just leave it to me. As long as I can see the changing-room doors, I'll know when everyone's left and the doors are locked, so I can just turn them on then.'

'And turn them off again at half-time?'

'Yeah. Then I'll put them back on again when the second half starts and the doors are locked again. So you'll only have to contact me if someone needs to get into the changing rooms unexpectedly.'

'Right. And you'll let me know immediately if the sensors pick up anything.'

I nodded. 'It's probably easiest if we keep in touch by text.'

I'd installed the sensors on the wall above each door, and with Kendal's help I'd double-checked to make sure they covered every inch of the changing rooms. I'd also spent an hour or so having a really good look round the changing rooms, both inside and out, searching for anything that might indicate where and how the thief had got in. As far as I could tell, there were no signs of forced entry anywhere. The windows were all safe and intact, there were no telltale marks on the doors, and I'd even climbed up a ladder and had a quick look at the roof, but it was just a flat slab of solid concrete, and there was no way that anyone could have got through it.

I couldn't help being intrigued as to how on earth the

thief had got in, and despite my earlier lack of enthusiasm for the case, I found myself thinking more and more about it. By the time Monday morning had come along – and I'd gone into school early to check everything out one more time – I was actually feeling quite nervous and excited.

Now though, as I glanced at my mobile again, making sure I hadn't missed an alert from one of the sensors (I hadn't), I was beginning to wonder if anything was going to happen after all. Maybe the thief had somehow found out what we were doing, or maybe they hadn't actually found out but had just seen or heard something that made them wary. Or perhaps, despite all my double- and triple-checking, I hadn't installed the sensors properly. Or I'd made a mistake setting up the Wi-Fi . . .

I shook my head. I knew I hadn't made any mistakes. I knew it beyond doubt. But now that the thought was in my head, I just couldn't get rid of it, and I started going over everything I'd done, replaying in my mind every stage of the installation, every step of the connection process, everything I could have possibly done wrong . . .

And then my mobile buzzed.

To keep things as discreet as possible, I'd set the sensor alarm to vibrate, and I'd put my mobile in my trackpants pocket so there was no chance of missing the alarm if it went off.

I quickly dug into my pocket and pulled out my mobile. The alarm was still buzzing, and the sensor icon was flashing red. There was a letter H inside the icon, which told me that it was the sensor in the home dressing room that had been activated. I'd set a forty-minute timer on my mobile to help me keep track of the match-time, and as I quickly checked it now I saw that there was still almost ten minutes of the first half to go. My heart quickened as I glanced over at the changing rooms. I could see Mr Ayres standing outside the away dressing room, but my view of the other door was blocked by a bus that for some reason was reversing out of its parking slot. I couldn't see the home dressing-room door or Mr Wells.

I texted Mr Jago, using the simple signal we'd agreed on over the weekend – *AAH*. Alarm Activated, Home dressing room. I looked over at him. He was standing near the touchline at the far end of the subs bench, waving his hands around and yelling out instructions. He stopped suddenly, pulling out his mobile and glancing over at me at the same time. I saw him open the text and read my message, and then – after a quick word with one of the subs on the bench (a regular first-team player called John Cohen, who was being rested for this game) – Mr Jago headed off towards the changing rooms.

I realised then that we hadn't actually discussed what I was supposed to do if the alarm went off, so I wasn't sure whether to follow Mr Jago or stay where I was and wait to see what happened.

I looked over at the changing rooms again. The bus

was parked right in front of the building now, and I still couldn't see the door. I could see Mr Jago though, and as I watched him marching sternly across the car park, his face a picture of grim determination, I almost felt sorry for whoever it was he was about to surprise.

I watched Mr Jago disappear round the back of the bus and then I looked at the timer on my mobile again. There were five minutes to go until half-time. I turned to the kid sitting next to me, a nippy little striker called Mosh Akram. He was leaning forward on the bench, his eyes fixed intently on the match.

'I'm just going to the toilet, Mosh,' I said, getting to my feet.

'Have one for me while you're there,' he replied, without so much as a glance at me.

I stuffed my hands in my parka pockets and hurried off to the changing rooms.

20

The changing-room door was open when I got there, and as I moved towards the doorway I could hear Mr Jago talking angrily to someone inside. He wasn't shouting or anything, and he didn't have that scolding-teacher tone to his voice, but he definitely wasn't happy.

It's not difficult, *for Christ's sake*, I heard him say. *I mean, how many times do I have to tell you what to do? Just stay outside the door and don't go inside. It's not bloody rocket science, Ralph.*

I knew who he was talking to now. Ralph was Mr Wells's first name.

I'm sorry, John, Mr Wells said wearily. *But like I told you, I thought I heard someone in here, so I just came in to take a look.*

Jago sighed. *We already talked about this, Ralph. If you see or hear anything suspicious, you call me. We* agreed *on that, remember?*

I just thought—

Don't think, *Ralph*, Mr Jago said dismissively. *Just stick to the plan, OK?*

Although I couldn't see him, I could hear the condescending sneer in Jago's voice, and knowing Mr Wells, it wasn't hard to imagine how he was taking it. I could picture him standing there, with Mr Jago towering over him, his shoulders stooped, his eyes lowered, unable or unwilling to stand up for himself . . .

Mr Wells was a nice man. Too nice for his own good, probably. He was also a very troubled man. And whatever he'd done wrong now, whatever silly mistake he'd made, he didn't deserve to be treated like dirt.

I decided then that it was best if they didn't know I'd overheard them, and as I began backing away from the changing-room door, I realised that my fists were clenched and my heart was filled with hate.

Mr Wells's son Peter had been two years older than me, so although I used to see him around at school, I didn't actually know him personally. I used to hear lots of rumours and gossip about him though, so I had a rough idea at the time of what he was going through, but it wasn't until afterwards that I found out the details of what had happened to him and his father.

Peter was the spitting image of his dad – kind of swotty-looking, a bit weedy, wire-rimmed glasses, an old-fashioned haircut – and he had the same kind of personality as his dad as well. Quiet, harmless, a bit of a loner. He was nice too, just like his dad. But there are all kinds of 'nice', and his was the kind that doesn't go down very well with some kids. It was the kind of 'unmanly' niceness that attracts derision and mockery, especially from so-called tough boys, and Peter was forever having to put up with teasing and name-calling – Gay Boy, Pete the Poof . . . pathetic stuff like that. Which would have been bad enough in itself, but Peter had the extra burden of being the son of a teacher, which made everything a hundred times worse for him. I remember seeing him in his dad's car once, the two of them leaving school together at the end of the day, driving out of the teachers' car park through a throng of boisterous kids. Some of the kids were deliberately dawdling along in the middle of the road, getting in the way of Mr Wells's car, and as he beeped his horn and waved them out of the way, and they laughed and joked around – pretending to be startled, jumping out of the way – poor Peter just sat there in the passenger seat with his eyes lowered, his shoulders drooped, his face bright red with embarrassment. I remember thinking to myself at the time that he looked like the loneliest kid in the world.

I don't know what I would have done if I'd been in his position. I'm lucky really, in that I've never been seriously bullied or picked on or anything. I've never been 'in' with any of the tough kids, but I've hardly ever had any trouble with them either. I'm not sure if they generally leave me alone purely because they know I can look after myself, but there's no question that that's a big part of it. My dad started teaching me how to box when I was just a little kid, and I've been going to my boxing club every Tuesday night since I was ten years old, so I know how to box, and I know I'm pretty good at it. I also know how to fight dirty – I've got my grandad to thank for that – so, all in all, when it comes to any kind of physical conflict, I'm more than capable of holding my own. And whether you like it or not, the ugly truth is that sometimes violence *is* the only answer. It's all well and good saying that you should 'turn the other cheek' or that 'the pen is mightier than the sword', but if you're trapped in a dead-end alley in the middle of the night with a twenty-stone psychopath coming at you with a samurai sword, a pen isn't going to do you much good, is it? Not unless you're James Bond and your pen has a hidden button that turns it into a flamethrower or something.

Anyway, all I'm trying to say is that it was different for Peter Wells. He wasn't a fighter. He couldn't stand up for himself. He couldn't physically fight back against the kids who made his life a misery. He couldn't beat them at their own game. And I suppose that's why he decided to join them. Or at least, that's what he tried to do.

It was a fairly gradual process, and it started off with relatively minor changes in Peter's behaviour. He began getting average marks for his written work – Bs and Cs instead of A*s – and when he was in the classroom he no longer put his hand up to answer questions. He just sat there, looking bored out of his mind. If the teacher asked him a question, or asked for his opinion about something, he just shrugged. It was more a case of a bad attitude than actual bad behaviour, but over time it got worse and worse, and Peter progressed from being a slightly sullen but essentially harmless boy to being a kid with serious behavioural problems. He was reported for swearing at a female teacher, and it wasn't just the everyday kind of swearing, it was the *really* unpleasant stuff. He started missing classes, on one occasion just getting up and walking out halfway through a lesson, and it was suspected – but never proved – that he stole over a hundred pounds from a charity collection box for kids with leukaemia.

Although his self-styled transformation from nice-quiet-swotty kid to socially-disruptive-serious-problem kid didn't actually win him any friends, the kids who used to make his life a misery did actually start leaving him alone. I don't think it was because they began to admire or accept him though, I think it was because they thought he was crazy, and it wasn't the kind of craziness they liked to laugh at either. It was the kind of craziness that actually frightened them a bit. That's my opinion anyway. I remember passing Peter in the corridor once. He was just standing there staring at the wall, a weird kind of smile on his face, and when he turned and stared at me, the look in his eyes sent a shiver down my spine. It was like looking into the eyes of something from another world.

It was a pretty tough situation for Mr Wells to deal with, of course. Peter wasn't just his son, he was one of his pupils too, so he didn't just have to cope with it on a personal level – which must have been hard enough in itself – he had his responsibilities as a teacher to consider as well. So I suppose it was kind of understandable that when Peter was caught shoplifting one day, and Mr Wells was called out of school to go down to the police station to sort it all out, he was so exasperated and embarrassed by his son's behaviour that when he got him home he really let rip at him. There were no witnesses to this outburst, of course – it only came out later because Mr Wells admitted it himself – so no one knows what was said or what really happened, but two days later Peter's body, or what was left of it, was found on the mainline railway track just a kilometre or so from his house.

21

Although the official verdict of the coroner's inquest into Peter's death was death by misadventure, most people thought that he'd taken his own life. Mr Wells certainly did, and as far as he was concerned it was all his fault. He blamed himself for his son's death. If he hadn't been so hard on him that day, he thought, if he hadn't lost his temper with him, if he'd only been a little more compassionate and shown him how much he loved him, Peter would still be alive.

I don't suppose it really mattered whether he was right or not, it was what Mr Wells believed.

For the first couple of weeks after Peter's death, Mr Wells seemed to be coping fairly well. He was only off school for a week, and when he came back it was almost as if nothing had happened. He was just the same old nice Mr Wells. A bit sadder than usual, perhaps. A bit quieter. But essentially the same person.

But then gradually – in a strangely similar fashion to Peter's gradual change – Mr Wells began falling apart. He started coming into school looking like he hadn't slept or washed or changed his clothes for days – his face unshaven, his eyes bloodshot and ringed with dark circles, his normally pristine suit all crumpled and stained. And when he got close to you, he smelled really bad, all sour and sweaty, and his breath absolutely stank. Then the drinking started. At first, it was only apparent in afternoon lessons, when he'd obviously had a few drinks at lunchtime. He wasn't incapable or anything, but everyone in the classroom could tell he'd been drinking – his words were slurred, his eyes were glazed, he was slightly unsteady on his feet. It didn't happen every day, but over time it became more and more frequent, and eventually it got to the stage where Mr Wells was pretty much drunk all the time, and that's when he *did* become incapable. He'd fall asleep in the middle of a lesson. He'd start talking to the class about Peter, and then he'd end up sitting at his desk crying his eyes out. And he started talking *to* Peter as well. You'd see him walking along the corridor, his head down, his eyes fixed to the floor, and when he went past, you could hear him muttering under his breath, and if you listened closely you'd realise that he was having a discussion with his dead son.

Eventually the headmaster insisted that he take three months' compassionate leave, and although he wasn't given an official ultimatum, I think he was basically told that if he didn't seek professional help and get himself sorted out, he wouldn't be coming back.

I don't know if Mr Wells did get professional help or not – alcohol rehabilitation, grief counselling, stuff like that – but whatever he did, when he returned to school at the beginning of the autumn term, he was at least halfway back to himself again. He'd lost a lot of weight, and his wife had left him, and whenever I saw him I got the sense that a light had been switched off in his heart. But he was sober again, and he no longer talked to himself or his son, and after the initial surprise that he'd actually come back to school – which no one had really believed would happen – the gossip and the whispering about him gradually faded away and he simply became Mr Wells again: English and drama teacher, a nice but troubled man.

He was really good to me when my mum and dad died. Most of the teachers were pretty good, to be honest – offering their condolences, asking me if there was anything they could do to help, telling me not to worry about homework and stuff. But Mr Wells was the only one who took the time and trouble to actually sit down and *talk* to me about my parents' death. He didn't just offer his sympathy and heartfelt condolences either, he talked to me about the practicalities of my situation – who are you living with now? are you happy with your nan and grandad? are they financially secure enough to look after you? They were the kind of questions that no one else had bothered to ask me, and although I *was* perfectly happy living with Nan and Grandad, and there weren't any practical problems, I really appreciated the fact that Mr Wells had thought to ask. It was also really good talking to him because he knew exactly what it was like to lose someone you love. He knew from personal experience what it can do to you, and he knew better than most that whatever grief does to you, you can't really control it.

'It's as if something gets inside you,' he said to me once, 'something that's you, but *not* you. And whatever it wants you to do, there's nothing you can do to stop it.' He smiled sadly at me. 'That probably doesn't make a lot of sense, does it?'

'It makes perfect sense to me,' I told him.

All of that was on my mind as I backed away from the dressing-room door that afternoon – Peter Wells's troubled life and death, the hell Mr Wells had been through, the way he'd come through it, and his kindness to me – it all flashed through my mind in a matter of moments, and I couldn't help but despise Mr Jago for the way he'd just treated Mr Wells.

I was about ten metres away from the door when Jago came out of the dressing room, followed closely by Mr Wells. Jago saw me, glanced at his watch, and just as he looked back at me and was about to say something, the referee in charge of the Slade Lane game blew his whistle for half-time.

Jago turned to Mr Wells. 'You might as well wait inside till the start of the second half now.'

Mr Wells nodded, smiled at me, then went back into the changing rooms.

As Mr Jago came over to me, the ref in the Kell Cross match blew for half-time, and when I looked out over the playing fields I could see that a few players were already ambling over towards the changing rooms.

Half-time in school games isn't like half-time in Premier League matches. We don't get fifteen minutes in the dressing room with a limitless supply of energy drinks and massages from physios and tactical team-talks from the manager, we usually get a five-minute break at the side of the pitch with a plate of sliced oranges and a litre-bottle of tap water. But because this was the Twin Town Cup, half-time had been stretched to ten minutes and allowances had been made to let players back into the changing rooms if they needed to use the toilet or change their studs or their kit or whatever.

'It was a false alarm,' Mr Jago said irritably, stopping in front of me.

I couldn't help glaring at him.

'What?' he said, frowning at me.

I shook my head. There was no point in saying anything to him about Mr Wells. 'I've turned off the sensors,' I told him. 'I'll reset them and put them back on again when the second half starts.'

'Right.' He sighed. 'Hopefully a certain member of staff will remember what he's supposed to do now.'

'We all make mistakes,' I said.

'You can say that again.'

He gave me a look then – a kind of man-to-man, you-know-what-I'm-talking-about kind of look – and it was pretty obvious that he wasn't just referring to Mr Wells's mistake in opening the door. He was, in effect, sharing with me his opinion of Mr Wells in general. And not only that, he was assuming that I'd agree with him too.

As he turned round and began strutting back across the playing fields, his chest puffed out like a tracksuited pigeon, I had to force myself not to run after him and punch him in the back of his head.

22

As the second half of the semi-final began, and I resumed my place on the subs bench, I couldn't help wondering what I was still doing here. It was freezing cold, the rain was bucketing down, soaking me to the skin, and – thanks to Mr Jago – my enthusiasm for the case had virtually disappeared again. His despicable treatment of Mr Wells had ruined everything for me, and the fact that *he* was the only reason I was sitting here was almost too much to take.

I looked over at him now, standing on the touchline, bawling out stupid instructions – 'PUSH UP, KELL CROSS! COME *ON*, KENDAL, GET THEM PUSHED *UP*! PRESS, PRESS, *PRESS*!'

'Idiot,' I muttered.

'You what?'

I'd forgotten that Mosh Akram was sitting next to me.

'Nothing,' I said, shaking my head.

Mosh glanced at Mr Jago, then turned back to me. 'He thinks he's Arsène Wenger.'

'More like Arse*hole* Wenger.'

Mosh grinned. 'No offence, Trav, but how come he picked you as a sub?'

'I'm his secret weapon.'

'Yeah?'

I nodded. 'I'm so useless that when he brings me on, everyone on the other side breaks down in hysterics, and while they're laughing themselves stupid, we stroll upfield and score.'

Mosh laughed. 'That's Jago's master plan, is it?'

'Yeah.'

'Maybe he's not such an idiot after all.'

'No,' I said, 'he's definitely an idiot.'

I felt a bit better after that, and although I still hated the idea of having anything to do with Mr Jago, I found that if I kept reminding myself that I wasn't actually working for him, I was working for the school, that made things just about tolerable.

Even so, I would have been perfectly happy to get through the rest of the day without the motion-sensor alarm going off again. But something told me that wasn't going to happen. In fact, I was so sure it *was* going to happen that when it finally did I felt a strange sense of almost pleasant relief.

It was just gone three o'clock by then, about midway through the second half, and Kell Cross were 3–0 up and cruising to an easy victory. I took out my phone and checked the screen. This time the letter A was showing inside the flashing alarm icon, which meant the sensor in the away dressing room had been activated. Before doing anything else, I looked over at the changing rooms. The bus that had previously blocked my view wasn't there any more, and I could clearly see both doors. Mr Ayres was still outside the away dressing room, and – more importantly – Mr Wells was definitely outside the home dressing room. Both doors were shut, presumably locked. There shouldn't have been anyone inside. But someone or something was in the away dressing room, and as my alarm went off again and I saw the letter H inside the flashing icon, I knew that someone or something had activated the other alarm now too. Unless there was something wrong with the sensors, that could only mean that someone had been in the away dressing room and had now got through the connecting door into the home dressing room.

I glanced over at the changing rooms again, saw that Mr Wells was still there, then texted Mr Jago – *AAA+AAH*. Alarm Activated, Away and Home dressing rooms. Just like before, Jago immediately stopped yelling out instructions, pulled out his mobile, read the message, then headed off towards the changing rooms.

Unlike before, I didn't follow him.

I'd seen how he'd dealt with an innocent intruder. I didn't want to be anywhere near him when he got hold of a genuine thief.

I turned my attention back to the match. A chorus of boos and jeers had just gone up, and there was a scuffle going on in our penalty area.

'What's going on?' I asked Mosh.

'The German number nine just got booked for simulation.'

'He dived?'

Mosh shook his head. 'Kendal brought him down, but he made sure the ref didn't see it. When the German kid appealed for a penalty, Kendal started yelling at him, calling him a cheat, then everyone else joined in, accusing the kid of diving, and the ref fell for it.'

'No wonder they call it the beautiful game,' I said.

Mosh shrugged. 'It's all about winning, Trav. That's all that matters in the end.'

My phone buzzed again, this time alerting me to a text. It was from Mr Jago. *Target apprehended*, it read. *Come now.*

'Idiot,' I muttered, getting to my feet.

'You got the squits or something?' Mosh asked, assuming that I was going to the toilet again.

I couldn't be bothered to think up a better excuse, so I just said 'Yeah,' and trudged off to see who Mr Jago had 'apprehended'.

23

As I approached the changing rooms, I saw Mr Jago come out of the home dressing room and say something to Mr Wells. Mr Wells hesitated for a moment, then Jago gave him a stern look and spoke to him again. Mr Wells nodded sheepishly and walked off round the front of the changing rooms. He stopped and said something to Mr Ayres, Mr Ayres frowned and looked over at Mr Jago, then he shrugged his shoulders and the two of them walked off together towards the playing fields.

Mr Jago waited in the doorway, watching them go, then he turned and beckoned me over, gesturing at me to hurry up. As I headed towards him, I wondered if he thought he was being subtle, but was just really bad at it, or if he was simply too stupid to realise how unsubtle his actions were.

'Come *on*, Delaney,' he said in a loud whisper, 'we haven't got all day.'

I followed him into the dressing room, and he closed the door behind us. A kid I'd never seen before was sitting on a bench across the room. He looked about fourteen or fifteen. He had pale skin, close-cropped hair, and was dressed in a green bomber jacket and black jeans. He was staring silently at the floor.

'He had these on him,' Mr Jago said, holding out his

hand to show me an iPhone, an iPod, and two wallets.

I looked over at the connecting door. It was open. The lock had been forced. I glanced over at the kid again.

'Do you know him?' Mr Jago asked me.

I shook my head. 'Haven't you asked him who he is?'

'He won't say a word to me. He just sits there staring at the floor.'

'Hey,' I said to the kid. '*Wie heißt du?*'

He looked up and sneered at me. '*Hau ab!*'

'What did he say?' Mr Jago asked.

'I asked him what his name was. He told me to get lost.'

'He's German?'

Duh, I thought.

'Yeah,' I said. 'He must be with the team from Steindorf. Maybe a non-playing reserve or a first-team player with an injury or something. He was probably in the dressing room next door with his teammates at half-time, and when they went back out for the second half, he hid somewhere, waited for Mr Ayres to lock the door, then forced the lock on the connecting door and started nicking stuff from in here.'

'Do you think he's the one we're looking for?' Jago said.

I couldn't believe he really meant it at first. I stared at him, waiting for him to realise that of *course* this wasn't the thief we were looking for, but he just looked back at me, waiting in all seriousness for me to answer him.

'No,' I said, barely able to keep the disbelief from my voice. 'This isn't our thief.'

'What makes you so sure?'

'Well, firstly, our thief doesn't force his way in. Secondly, ours doesn't take valuables. And thirdly, this kid wasn't even in the country when our thief first started stealing stuff.'

Mr Jago nodded thoughtfully. 'So it seems we're back to square one.'

'Looks like it,' I agreed.

'Damn. I was hoping to get this all sorted out before the final.' He looked over at the German kid. 'And now I'm going to have to work out what to do about him as well.'

'Why don't you just report him to his teachers?'

'If only it were that simple.'

I guessed he was referring to the diplomatic complexities of the situation. Steindorf were guests of the school, and the school represented both the town and the tournament sponsors. If news got out that a Kell Cross teacher was accusing a Steindorf pupil of theft, the repercussions could be seriously damaging.

Luckily for me, that wasn't my problem.

All I had to do – once Mr Jago had made arrangements for the connecting door to be fixed and then escorted the German kid from the changing rooms – was reset the sensors, go back to the subs bench, and watch the rest of the game.

The final score was 4–0 to Kell Cross. As the full-time whistle blew, and the players celebrated to the cheers and applause of the home crowd, I got to my feet, pulled out my mobile, and turned off the motion sensors. The other semi-final hadn't finished yet, and as I wandered over to catch the last few minutes, I spotted someone I recognised watching from the sidelines. Her name was Evie Johnson. She was a year or two older than me, and I'd met her at her boxing club when I was investigating my parents' last case in the summer. Together with Mason and Lenny, she'd helped me out when I'd confronted the men from Omega, and although we'd only spent a short time together, we'd become pretty close. I hadn't seen her since then though, but I'd thought about her quite a lot, and I'd often thought about calling or texting her, but for some reason I kept chickening out. I wasn't sure what it was that had held me back, but whatever it was, I was suddenly feeling it again now.

Evie hadn't seen me yet, and as I carried on walking towards her, I couldn't keep my eyes off her. She looked even more amazing than I remembered. Those deep dark eyes, that beautiful light-brown skin, that strangely intriguing face . . . I felt exactly the same now as I'd felt when I'd first set eyes on her – weirdly confused. It was like I *wanted* to talk to her, but I *didn't* want to talk to her. I wanted to be with her, but I also wanted to run away.

Good and bad at the same time.

Very confusing.

She turned my way then, almost as if she'd sensed me looking at her, and when she saw me her face lit up and she waved and called out to me.

'Travis! Hey, Travis!'

As I smiled and raised my hand and headed over to her, I saw her put her hand on the shoulder of a young man standing next to her. I guessed he was about seventeen, and it was obvious from the way Evie leant in close to him, lovingly gripping his arm as she pointed me out to him, that he was her boyfriend.

I couldn't help feeling a tiny pang of disappointment and jealousy. I knew it was totally irrational. I hardly knew Evie really, and there was never any realistic chance of us being anything more than just friends. I'd only just turned fourteen. She was at least fifteen, more likely sixteen. And the boy she was with was a big handsome black guy who no doubt had a car and a job and was to all intents and purposes a fully grown man . . .

It made me feel kind of stupid, to be honest. Seeing Evie with her grown-up boyfriend was like a sudden – and embarrassing – reality check. I was just a kid. I went to school, I rode a bike, I lived with my nan and grandad. Why on earth would a beautiful sixteen-year-old girl want anything to do with *me*?

I really wished the ground would open up and swallow me then, and for a moment or two I seriously considered just turning around and walking away, but Evie was still smiling at me, still watching me as I headed over towards her, and I knew I had to go through with it.

'Hey, Travis,' she said again as I went up to her. 'It's *really* good to see you.'

'Hi, Evie,' I said.

She broke away from her boyfriend and came over to me then, and to my surprise she threw her arms around me and gave me a hug.

'How've you been?' she said. 'How's your grandad and Courtney?'

'Yeah . . . good, thanks,' I told her. 'Everything's pretty good. How about you? What have you been up to?'

'Same as ever, you know. This and that.' She took me by the arm and led me over to the boy she was with. 'This is Daniel,' she told me.

I nodded hello to him.

'You remember Travis, don't you?' Evie said to him.

'Yeah,' he said smiling. 'How could I forget?'

I gave Evie a questioning look. I was pretty sure I'd never met Daniel before, so how come he seemed to know me?

'Daniel was at the gym that day when I challenged you to a fight,' Evie explained.

'Oh, right.'

Evie had been quite belligerent towards me when I'd first met her, and we'd ended up getting into the boxing ring together. She's an excellent fighter, strong and aggressive, with a really hard punch, but I'm a better boxer than her, and after a bruising few minutes I'd finally knocked her out.

'You've got a good right hand,' Daniel said to me now. 'She never saw it coming.'

'He just got lucky,' Evie retorted, punching him playfully on the arm. 'I was off balance, that's all.'

'Yeah, right,' Daniel said, grinning at her.

The final whistle blew then, and as the watching crowd cheered and clapped, and some of them started to leave, I saw Daniel looking around, as if he was trying to find someone.

'Listen, babe,' he said to Evie, 'I've just got to go and see Royce about something. I won't be long, OK?'

'I'll wait here,' she told him.

He gave her a quick kiss, then headed off through the throng of spectators.

Evie turned back to me. 'Were you watching the other game?'

'Yeah. I was on the subs bench.'

'Really?'

I nodded. 'We won 4–0.'

'It's us against you in the final then.'

I looked out at the celebrating Slade Lane players. 'What was the score?'

'5–2.'

I knew Evie lived on the Slade Lane estate, but I wasn't sure if she went to Slade Comp or not.

'Are you here with the school?' I asked her.

She shook her head. 'My brother's in the team.' She looked across the pitch and pointed out a young kid who was clearly the centre of attention. He was surrounded by other kids, and there were also a couple of men in suits trying to talk to him. 'He scored a hat-trick today,' Evie said proudly.

'That's Quade Wilson,' I said.

'Yeah.'

'He's your brother?'

'Well, half-brother . . . he uses his dad's surname.'

I didn't know Quade Wilson personally, but I knew *of* him. Everyone who had any interest in football knew about Quade Wilson. He was easily the best young player in Essex, possibly one of the best in the country, and it was rumoured that three or four Premier League teams were interested in signing him. He was still only thirteen, but he not only played for Slade Lane Under-15s, he'd also played for the England schoolboys Under-15 side.

'Who are those men in suits?' I asked Evie.

'One of them's from Arsenal, the other one's an agent.'

'So it's true the big clubs are after him?'

'There's a lot of interest, yeah. The only trouble is . . .'

'What?'

'Well, they all know how *good* he is, and there's no doubt he's got the skill to make it to the top. And he really *wants* it, you know? Football's his whole life. Being a pro is all he's ever wanted. But it's just . . .' Evie sighed. 'He gets kind of anxious sometimes. I mean *really* anxious.'

'Panic attacks?'

'Not exactly . . . it's more like a lack of belief in himself. Most of the time he's perfectly OK, and outwardly you'd never guess he had any problems. It's just every now and then, when he's under a lot of pressure, he finds it really hard to cope.'

'Do the clubs who want to sign him know about it?'

She nodded. 'He's already had schoolboy contracts with a couple of Championship clubs, one when he was nine and another two years later, but with both clubs he just . . .' She sighed. 'Well, you know, he just couldn't deal with it. And for anyone else that probably would have been their last chance, but Quade's *so* good that the big clubs still haven't given up on him, despite his problems. That's why they're watching him all the time – they want to see how he copes when he's put under *real* pressure.'

'What about seeing a counsellor or a doctor?' I suggested. 'I mean, there's all kinds of help you can get for anxiety and stuff.'

'Quade's from the Slade,' Evie said. 'If it got out that he was seeing a counsellor, he'd never live it down.'

I gazed over at him again. He was smiling and joking, talking to everyone around him. Evie was dead right, you'd never guess from looking at him that he had any problems at all.

I was just about to say something else to Evie when

I spotted Daniel talking to someone on the far side of the pitch. The man he was talking to – who I assumed was Royce – was a really nasty-looking guy with heavily tattooed arms. A girl was at his side, her arm looped through his. She was staring up at him with adoring eyes, as if he was some kind of superhero or something. She had short blonde hair and heavily made-up eyes.

It was Bianca, the new secretary at Jakes and Mortimer.

'Who's that guy Daniel's talking to?' I asked Evie.

She looked over at him. 'That's Royce. Royce Devon.'

'Devon?' I said. 'Is he related to Drew Devon?'

'Yeah,' Evie said. 'Royce is Dee Dee's brother.'

A stream of questions suddenly burst into my head. What was Bianca doing with Dee Dee's brother? Did he know that she worked for the solicitors who were currently investigating Dee Dee's tanning salon? Was that why he was with her? Why wasn't she at work? And what about Daniel, Evie's boyfriend? What was his connection with Dee Dee's brother?

It *could* all be perfectly innocent, I told myself. It could be just a series of meaningless coincidences.

Yeah, I thought, and Millwall *could* buy Lionel Messi and Cristiano Ronaldo in the January transfer window and get promoted to the Premier League.

My mobile rang then. I took it out of my pocket, hoping it wasn't Mr Jago. It wasn't. It was Grandad.

'Hi, Grandad,' I said.

'Where are you, Travis?' His voice sounded urgent and serious.

'Is something the matter?' I asked.

'Where are you?' he repeated.

'I'm still at school. Is something wrong?'

'It's Courtney,' he said. 'She's been attacked.'

'*What?*'

'It's all right,' he said quickly, 'she's not *too* seriously hurt. But she's taken a pretty bad beating.'

'Who did it?'

'We're at the hospital. Get yourself down here as soon as you can, OK? I'll explain everything when you get here.'

'I'm on my way.'

I ended the call.

'Is everything all right?' Evie asked me.

'Courtney's in hospital. Someone beat her up.'

'Oh, no!'

'I need to get to the hospital as quickly as possible. I could go on my bike, but—'

'Daniel will drive you,' Evie said without hesitation. 'That's his car over there.' She pointed towards the car park. 'The green BMW 640.' She took out her phone and hit a speed-dial button. 'Daniel? Travis needs a lift to the hospital . . . yeah, right now.' She looked at me. 'Go . . . he'll meet you at the car.'

24

At eleven o'clock that morning Courtney had had a meeting with Jakes and Mortimer, ostensibly to give Mr Mortimer her report on the Tanga Tans investigation and to ask him if there was anything else he wanted Delaney & Co to do. Gloria had accompanied her to the meeting.

I don't know much about Graham Mortimer, but he's always seemed a nice enough man to me. I'd guess he's in his mid-fifties. He's the kind of man who always wears a suit and always looks a bit weary and bored, as if he's not particularly happy with his life, but has long since accepted there's not much he can do about it.

At eleven o'clock on the dot, he'd invited Courtney and Gloria into his office, shaken their hands, and asked them if they wanted tea or coffee. They'd politely declined his offer, and then they'd all sat down at his desk and got on with the business in hand.

It was clear to Courtney and Gloria that Mr Mortimer had no real interest in the case, but he was courteous enough to go through the motions of dealing with it professionally and efficiently – opening the relevant file on his laptop, asking a few straightforward questions, occasionally remembering to jot down a few notes. As Gloria said later, it was as if he was just cruising along on automatic pilot – doing and saying all the right things, performing his job perfectly adequately, but at the same time giving the impression that he wasn't actually *there*. His mind and his heart were worlds away.

Which, for the purposes of Courtney's plan, was ideal.

At a pre-arranged signal, Gloria had stood up, picked up the written report, and said to Mr Mortimer, 'There's a couple of things I'd like to point out to you, if that's OK?'

'Of course,' he'd said, smiling vaguely.

According to Courtney, Gloria's performance as a slightly doddery old lady was perfect. As she'd moved round the desk towards him, walking with a slight limp and stooped shoulders, the report 'accidentally' slipped out of her hand, and as she stopped to pick it up she seemingly lost her balance and toppled backwards to the floor, letting out a frail yelp of pain. Mr Mortimer immediately jumped to his feet and hurried over to help her. There was no doubt he was genuinely concerned, and it was equally clear that Gloria's apparent mishap had sparked some life into him, focusing his mind by suddenly giving him something vaguely interesting to deal with.

'Oh, I'm *so* sorry,' Gloria said, wincing with pain. 'I'm such an old fool sometimes.'

'Don't be silly,' Mr Mortimer said, bending over her. 'Are you all right? Have you hurt yourself? No, don't try to get up yet . . . just stay where you are, get your breath back . . .'

While Mr Mortimer was tending to Gloria, Courtney quickly leant across the desk, spun his laptop round, and scanned the Tanga Tans file for the name and address of the client.

Half an hour later, after a few phone calls and a quick look at some databases (which, officially, she shouldn't have had access to), Gloria had already compiled a potted biography of Jakes and Mortimer's client.

'Raisa Ferris,' she announced, reading from her notes. 'Twenty-six years old, single, no children, presently unemployed. She's lived on or around the Slade Lane estate all her life, but she's only been at her present address for six months. She's been in trouble with the police since she was fourteen, mostly minor offences, and she has a string of convictions for petty fraud – false benefit claims, insurance scams, identity theft. She's known to be associated with several high-ranking gang members, and she's been arrested on numerous occasions, but never charged, with intent to supply class-A drugs.'

'She's not exactly Snow White then,' Courtney said.

'Apparently not.'

'Right,' Courtney said, getting her coat, 'well, I think it's time to go and see Miss Ferris and find out what she's really up to.'

'Be careful,' Grandad told her.

'I'm always careful.'

*

The block of flats where Raisa Ferris lived was no more than a hundred metres away from Mason and Jaydie's block, and it looked exactly the same – a squat, grey, rectangular building, three storeys high, with little balconies outside the windows. Raisa's flat was on the second floor. Although Courtney's presence certainly hadn't gone unnoticed on the estate – strangers never go unnoticed on the Slade – the only hint of trouble she'd come across as she'd made her way to Raisa's block of flats was a few intimidating looks and a fair bit of staring. The staring didn't bother her in the slightest. Because of her striking appearance, she tends to get stared at wherever she goes, so she's used to it. And although she didn't *like* the more intimidating kinds of looks, she didn't think they were anything much to worry about, and by the time she got to Raisa's flat she was beginning to wonder if the Slade's reputation as a no-go area was something of an exaggeration.

She told me later that in hindsight she realised how stupid she'd been to venture into the estate on her own, and that in the future, no matter how safe she *felt*, she'd never let herself get lulled into a false sense of security again.

It was around two o'clock when she got to Raisa's flat. The first thing she noticed was that the front door was ajar, and the second thing she noticed was that the frame of the door was cracked and broken. The door had been forced open, probably kicked in. Courtney didn't do anything for a while, she just waited outside the door, listening for any sign of life inside. She didn't hear anything. She looked up and down the corridor, but there was no one around.

'Raisa?' she called out. 'Hello? Are you in there?'

There was no reply.

She cautiously pushed the door open and called out again. 'Hello? Is anyone there? Raisa? Miss Ferris?'

Still no reply.

She thought about leaving then. It was probably the sensible thing to do, she thought. Go back to the office, talk it over with Gloria and Grandad, maybe call the police. But Courtney knew in her heart that she wasn't going to do that. Somebody had obviously broken into Raisa's flat. They might have attacked her, hurt her. She could be lying on the floor, in desperate need of help, and Courtney wasn't the kind of person to turn her back on someone in need of help. And if she was wrong, if Raisa hadn't been attacked, or if she wasn't even in the flat, what was the point in calling the police? All it would do was make her look foolish and attract unnecessary and unwanted attention.

She went into the flat, leaving the front door open.

'Raisa? Can you hear me?'

No reply.

She went down the hallway, looked in the kitchen. It was empty. She went into the front room. There was no one there. She went back out into the hallway. The front door was closed now, and two men were standing at the far end of the hallway. They were both wearing hoods, their faces covered by scarves.

Courtney's pretty tough. She's strong and fit, she's won a couple of kick-boxing competitions, and she's learned a few street-fighting tricks from Grandad. So she's a lot better at looking after herself than most people. And from what I can gather, she put up a hell of a fight against the two thugs who attacked her in Raisa's flat. I heard afterwards that she kicked one of them so hard between the legs that he eventually ended up in hospital, and the other one didn't escape without injury either. But there were two of them, and they were both bigger and stronger than her, and no matter how hard she fought, there was only ever going to be one outcome.

The second-to-last thing she remembered before she passed out, she told me, was being literally thrown across the room by one of the men, and then a sudden searing *crack* as she smashed head first into a solid stone mantelpiece. And the very last thing she remembered was the sound of the front door crashing open, then footsteps running down the hall, and someone yelling out, '*Get your stinking hands off her!*'

25

Courtney was in a private room at the hospital, and when I eventually found my way there, Grandad was waiting for me outside her door. I was desperate to go in and see her straight away, but Grandad assured me that she was OK, and insisted on sitting me down and explaining what had happened before I went in to see her.

'I should never have let her go on her own,' he said after he'd told me everything he knew. He shook his head. 'I don't know what I was thinking.'

'There's nothing you could have done to stop her, Grandad,' I told him. 'You know what she's like when she sets her mind on something.'

'That's no excuse. I should have done something.'

'Like what? You couldn't have forced her not to go, could you?'

'Well, no, I suppose not . . .'

'Can I go in and see her now?'

He nodded. 'She looks pretty bad,' he warned me. 'But she's been thoroughly examined and the doctor's assured me that most of her injuries are superficial. She's got a couple of broken ribs and a fractured finger, lots of cuts and bruises, and she took a really bad whack to the back of her head which the doctors are still a bit worried about. So far though, they're fairly confident that there's no permanent damage. She's quite heavily sedated at the moment, so don't expect too much from her, OK?'

Despite Grandad's warnings, I was still shocked to the core when he led me into the room and I saw for myself the state Courtney was in. She was lying in bed with all manner of tubes and drips and wires fixed to various parts of her body. Her right eye was completely shut, just a swollen mass of purple and black bruising, and her lips were all bloodied and puffed up. She had numerous stitched-up cuts all over her face, a particularly nasty-looking one above her left eye, and she had a bandage wrapped tightly around her head.

As I stood there looking at her, her poor face battered and broken, I'd never felt so sickened and angry in all my life.

'Hey, Travis,' she mumbled thickly, her voice barely understandable. 'Don't you know it's rude to stare?'

My legs were unsteady as I went over and sat down in a chair beside her bed, and as she tried her best to smile at me, my heart felt as if it was going to explode. I reached out and gently took her hand. She squeezed it weakly.

'Don't look so glum, Trav,' she mumbled, 'it's not as bad as it looks.'

'We'll get them,' I promised her through gritted teeth. 'Whoever did this to you, we'll get them.'

'I didn't get a look at them . . . but one of them's going to be limping badly, and I'm pretty sure the other one's going to look like he's been in a fight.' She paused for a moment, staring at nothing, and I could see the pain and fear in her eyes. 'I did my best, Trav,' she muttered quietly. 'I didn't give up . . . but they were just too strong for me . . . they were like . . . like *animals* . . .'

'Hey,' I said softly, 'it's OK now. You're safe.'

She shook her head. 'If the others hadn't turned up when they did . . .'

'Did you get a look at the guys who saved you?' I asked.

'I was barely conscious. I heard them come in, and I vaguely remember one of them shouting . . . but that was it. The next thing I knew, I was waking up in here.'

'Did you recognise the shouting voice?'

'No,' she mumbled dopily, trying to keep her eyes open. 'What about Raisa? We need to find out what happened to her. She might be . . .'

As her voice trailed off and her eyes began to close, the door opened and a white-coated doctor carrying a clipboard came in.

'This is Dr Adams,' Grandad told me. 'He's been looking after Courtney.'

'You must be Travis,' Dr Adams said, quickly shaking my hand. 'Your grandad's told me about you.'

Without waiting for a reply, he went over to the bed and started checking the readings of the various monitors surrounding Courtney.

'Is it OK if I stay with her tonight, Doctor?' Grandad asked him.

'Well, strictly speaking,' he said, carefully examining Courtney's eyes, 'overnight visitors should be immediate family only, but I'm given to understand that Ms Lane's mother is all the family she has, and as she's not in any condition to visit . . .' He paused, jotting down some figures on his clipboard, then looked over at Grandad. 'I don't have any trouble with you staying, Mr Delaney.'

'Thank you,' Grandad said.

'But for the next couple of hours it's crucial that Ms Lane gets some rest.'

'I won't say a word,' Grandad promised.

Dr Adams shook his head. 'She needs *complete* peace and quiet. You can come back later, but right now she needs to be left alone.'

'I'd rather stay, if you don't mind.'

'I'm not *asking* you, Mr Delaney,' Dr Adams said firmly, but not unpleasantly, 'I'm telling you.'

'Yes, but—'

'Do you want her to get better or not?'

'Of course I do.'

Dr Adams smiled. 'See you later then.'

26

I could tell that Grandad was really unhappy about leaving Courtney, and I was pretty sure it was because he felt responsible for what had happened to her and was desperate to make up for it by not letting her out of his sight again. I thought about telling him again that it wasn't his fault, and that he didn't need to feel guilty, but in the end I decided to leave it for the moment and hope that he'd eventually see sense and realise that he wasn't to blame and he didn't have to punish himself.

On the way out to the hospital car park, he told me that whoever it was who'd rescued Courtney, they hadn't called the police.

'They called emergency services and requested an ambulance,' he explained, 'but they refused to give their name, and by the time the ambulance arrived they'd already disappeared. They'd left Courtney in the care of two middle-aged women who lived on the same floor as Raisa. The women claimed not to know what had happened to her.'

'The paramedics must have called the police though,' I said.

Grandad nodded. 'Two uniformed PCs came to the hospital. Dr Adams wouldn't let them talk to her, so they asked me what had happened.'

'How much did you tell them?'

'I gave them my name, told them I was a PI and that Courtney was my partner, and I said she was visiting Raisa Ferris with regard to an ongoing investigation. They wanted a lot more details, of course, but that was all they got.' Grandad shrugged. 'They told me they'd be back when Courtney was feeling better, and that CID officers would be in touch with me later. To be honest though, I'd be very surprised if we hear from them again. I know it sounds cynical, but if the police launched a CID investigation every time someone got beaten up on the Slade, they'd never have time to do anything else.'

It did sound cynical, but unfortunately it was true.

Just as we got to his car, Grandad got a phone call from Gloria. After updating her on Courtney's condition, he spent the next few minutes just standing there, leaning against his car with the phone to his ear, listening to what Gloria was saying. It was impossible to work out what she was telling him, because he was barely saying anything in reply, just the occasional *uh-huh*, *right*, *I see*. Even when he finally ended the call, he still didn't say anything for a minute or two, he just stood there, staring into the distance, lost in thought.

'Hello?' I said to him after a while. 'Earth to Grandad . . . is anyone there?'

He turned and looked at me. 'Sorry, Trav,' he said. 'I was thinking about what Gloria just told me.'

'Any chance of sharing it with me?'

'Yes, of course, sorry.' He opened the car door. 'I'll tell you all about it on the way back to the office.'

The first thing Gloria had found out, he told me, was that the GP who'd provided written verification to back up Raisa Ferris's injury claim was currently under investigation by the General Medical Council for unethical behaviour and forging prescriptions.

'He runs a surgery near Beacon Fields,' Grandad said. 'Apparently it's an open secret that if you've got enough money you can get whatever you want from him – prescriptions, sick notes, false medical reports.'

'So there's probably nothing wrong with Raisa Ferris's eyes,' I said.

Grandad nodded. 'Not that it matters now anyway. She's dropped her claim.'

'Since when?'

'About an hour ago. She called Jakes and Mortimer and told them she no longer wishes to pursue her compensation claim against Tanga Tans.'

'Did she give a reason?'

'No.'

'She's been scared off,' I said. 'Dee Dee's boys must have paid her a visit. They're probably the same ones who beat up Courtney.'

'Almost certainly,' Grandad agreed. 'And from what Gloria just told me, I'm fairly sure now why Dee Dee is so keen to avoid an investigation into Tanga Tans.'

He glanced across at me. 'Do you know what the term "money-laundering" means?'

'Not exactly,' I admitted. 'I mean, I've heard of it, and I think it's got something to do with criminal gangs, but I don't really understand it.'

'It's basically a way of turning criminal profits into money that appears to be legitimate,' Grandad explained. 'You see, the problem criminals face when they make huge amounts of money is that most of it is usually in cash, which makes it really difficult to account for. You can't just stick millions of pounds of cash into a bank account without explaining where it came from, and if they were to buy everything with cash, the tax people and the police would soon start asking questions. I mean, it's all right if you're just spending a few thousand in cash here and there, but big-time criminals want to invest in property and businesses, and you can't buy a legitimate business with a sackful of fifty-pound notes. So the criminals and gangsters have to find a way of 'cleaning' their money, making it look like it's legitimate. There are lots of different ways of doing it, but one of the easiest and most common methods is to set up a business through which the dirty money can be channelled. The criminals usually pick some kind of service-based company – taxi firms, betting shops, clubs, bars – anything that deals mainly in cash, which makes it difficult for the authorities to keep tabs on how much the business is really earning. Then all the criminals have to do is siphon their drug profits or whatever into the business, mix it up with the legitimate earnings, and then – hey presto – everything's suddenly nice and clean.'

'So Tanga Tans is just a front?' I said.

'Well, it's a legitimate company, and I'm sure it makes *some* money from genuine customers. But Gloria managed to get hold of their accounts, and in the last financial year they showed a turnover of between five and ten thousand pounds a week. There's no way they made that much from genuine customers.'

'Right,' I said, thinking it through. 'So Dee Dee uses the tanning salon to launder his criminal profits, and it looks like Raisa just chose the wrong company to scam.'

'Unless she was put up to it by one of Dee Dee's rivals,' Grandad said. 'If a rival gang knew he was using Tanga Tans to launder his money, it's possible they set the whole thing up. If Tanga Tans ended up in court, the money-laundering scheme would be revealed, and Dee Dee's business would take a hit.'

'Maybe,' I said. 'But either way, whether Raisa was put up to it by someone or she was working on her own, Dee Dee found out and put a stop to it.'

'That's what I can't figure out,' Grandad said, frowning. 'How the hell *did* he find out?'

'His brother told him.'

'What?'

'His brother, Royce. I saw him at the Twin Town Cup semi-finals this afternoon. He was with Bianca.'

'Jakes and Mortimer's new secretary?'

'Yeah, she was all over him.'

'Are you *sure* it was her?'

'Positive.'

Grandad glanced across at me. 'You're absolutely certain?'

I took out my phone. 'What's Jakes and Mortimer's number?'

Grandad told me. I rang it. A man's voice answered. It sounded like Mr Jakes himself.

'Good afternoon,' he said. 'Jakes and Mortimer. How can I help you?'

'Could I speak to Bianca, please?'

'I'm afraid Miss Spencer isn't in today. Can I help you?'

'Will she be back tomorrow?'

Mr Jakes sighed. 'She's off sick today. I don't know when she'll be back. Now, if this is a personal call—'

I hung up.

'She called in sick today,' I told Grandad. 'Do you believe me now?'

'Damn it,' he said. 'If she's been leaking information to Dee Dee's brother . . .'

'That's how Dee Dee found out about Raisa. He sent his boys round to scare her off, and they must have hung around her flat waiting to see if anyone else showed up. If Bianca told Royce about Raisa, she probably told him that Jakes and Mortimer hired us to investigate Tanga

Tans too. She might even have given Royce a description of Courtney.' I looked at Grandad. 'Dee Dee's not just scaring off Raisa, he's trying to make sure that we leave the case alone too.'

'He's made a big mistake then, hasn't he?' Grandad said with quiet determination. 'This isn't just business any more. This is personal.'

27

The rain was coming down heavily when we reached the North Road roundabout, and as the nearest parking to Delaney & Co's office is a backstreet at the rear of the office, a couple of minutes' walk away, Grandad dropped me off at the end of North Walk.

'There's no point in both of us getting soaked,' he said. 'I'll see you in a few minutes, OK?'

It was dark and miserable as I hurried along to the office, keeping in close to the buildings to avoid the worst of the rain. There were no lights showing in the upper two floors of the office building when I got there, so I guessed Tantastic and Jakes and Mortimer had already closed up for the day. It was getting on for six o'clock now, and Gloria normally goes home at around five, but this wasn't a normal day, so I was expecting to see her at her desk when I entered the office. But although all the lights were on, the main office was empty. *She's probably in the bathroom*, I thought to myself, taking off my coat and hanging it up. But then, to my surprise, the door to Grandad's private office opened and Gloria came out. She was studying a document file, totally oblivious to my presence, and when I said to her, 'What are you doing?' she almost jumped out of her skin.

'Bloody hell, Travis!' she gasped, clutching her chest,

'you nearly gave me a heart attack!'

'What are you doing in Grandad's office?' I repeated.

'What do you think I'm doing?' she said, frowning at me.

'I don't know. That's why I'm asking.'

'I'm doing my job, Travis,' she said, crossing over to her desk and putting down the file. 'Your grandad asked me to see what I could find out about Drew Devon.' She sighed and picked up the file again. 'This is my report. I put it on his desk an hour ago, and I've just realised there are a couple of things that need adding to it.' She stared at me, an unreadable look on her face. 'Is that all right with you?' She held out the file towards me. 'Do you want to have a look, make sure I'm telling the truth?'

I have to admit I felt pretty stupid and ashamed of myself then. There was no reason Gloria shouldn't have been in Grandad's office – she was his assistant after all – and I had no right to question what she was doing anyway. It was just that when I'd seen her coming out of Grandad's office I'd suddenly remembered Granny Nora's words – *once a traitor, always a traitor* – and I'd jumped to the totally irrational conclusion that Gloria was up to no good. But now I'd had time to think, and time to recall what Grandad had said about Gloria – *I'd trust her with my life* – and I realised then that I'd taken Granny Nora's words out of context anyway. She'd never said that Gloria *was* a traitor, all she'd said was that Nan might *think* she was.

The trouble was, I'd heard so many different opinions about Gloria over the last few days that they were all getting mixed up in my head.

'I'm sorry,' I said to her, genuinely regretful. 'I don't know what I was thinking. I just . . . I don't know. I really *am* sorry.'

She put the file back on her desk. 'Look, I don't know what you've heard about me, Travis,' she said calmly. 'I mean, I know there are all kinds of rumours milling around about my past, and maybe you've heard some old stories or read some of the rubbish that people with nothing better to do put on the Internet. And if you have, well I don't really blame you for finding it hard to trust me. But all I ask is that you take me at face value, OK? You're perfectly entitled to make judgements about me, but for goodness sake base them on what you know, not on what other people *think* they know.' She smiled at me. 'Does that sound fair?'

'Yeah,' I said. 'More than fair.'

'Good.' She glanced over at Grandad's office, then looked back at me. 'So how's Courtney doing? Did you get to see her?'

I was just about to reply when the main office door opened and Grandad came in. From the look on his face I could tell straight away that something was wrong, and a moment later I knew what it was. Grandad wasn't alone. As he came through the door, three young men followed him in. Two of them were big muscle-bound guys in hoods and tracksuits, their faces all cut up and bruised. One of them was limping badly. The third one was Dee Dee. He was dressed the same as he'd been in Courtney's surveillance video – designer suit and T-shirt, brand-new trainers – and as he sauntered into the office like he owned the place, sniffing disdainfully and scratching the underside of his chin, there was an almost tangible aura about him that said, this is a man you *really* don't want to mess with.

As one of his thugs closed the office door, Dee Dee looked over at me and said, 'You must be Travis. I've heard about you.'

'Yeah?' I said, clearing my throat. 'I've heard a few things about you too.'

He smiled coldly. 'You ain't heard nothing yet.'

28

'You're Joseph Delaney, right?' Dee Dee said to Grandad.

Grandad just nodded. He hadn't said a word so far, and he hadn't taken his eyes off Dee Dee either. He wasn't trying to look tough or scare him or anything, he was just studying him silently, weighing him up, waiting to see what he had to say.

'You own this place, yeah?' Dee Dee said.

Another nod from Grandad.

Dee Dee grinned at him. 'You don't say much, do you?'

'Just get on with it, boy,' Grandad said.

Dee Dee didn't like that, and just for a moment he almost lost his cool. But the flash of anger that crossed his eyes was so brief it was almost unnoticeable, and within half a second he was back to himself again.

'Delaney & Co, Private Investigation Services,' he said, staring at Grandad. 'You were recently contracted by Jakes and Mortimer to investigate Tanga Tans on behalf of a woman called Raisa Ferris who claims her eyes were damaged by faulty equipment and negligent staff at the salon. Last Friday, a *very* nice-looking girl called Courtney Lane, who I believe is your partner, paid a visit to Tanga Tans in order to gather evidence to back up Raisa Ferris's compensation claim.' Dee Dee paused to light a cigarette. He took a drag on it and tapped some ash on the floor. 'Now,' he went on, 'those are the facts as you know them, and I don't hold it against you for doing your job. We've all got to earn a living, haven't we? This is what you do. I don't have a problem with that.' He shrugged. 'And I don't blame you for getting dragged into a cheap little ruse either. You weren't to know that Raisa was paid by a competitor of mine to try and get my business closed down. You were just a tool in the operation, an unwilling dupe, if you will.' He smiled, seemingly pleased with his turn of phrase. 'However,' he continued, 'the fact that it's not your fault doesn't change the fact that you *were* involved, and unfortunately that means you're going to have to deal with the consequences.'

'What have you done with Raisa?' Grandad said.

'Done with her?' Dee Dee said innocently. 'We haven't *done* anything with her. She's been made aware of her mistake and she's rectified it. She's withdrawn her compensation claim, the case is closed. Simple as that.'

'And what about Courtney?' Grandad asked, glaring at the two bruisers who were standing by the door. 'Did you tell these two pig-ignorant thugs to make Courtney "aware of her mistake"?'

'Don't push it, old man,' Dee Dee said. 'I'm doing my best to be reasonable here.' He looked over at Gloria, glanced at me, then turned back to Grandad. 'It's up to you how this goes,' he said calmly. 'Do you understand what I'm saying? If you listen to me and do as I say, we can all walk out of here tonight in one piece. But if you start making things awkward . . . well, you know what's going to happen, don't you?'

Grandad just stared at him. 'What do you want from me?'

'That's better.' He dropped his cigarette to the floor and stepped on it. The carpet smouldered. He ground his foot into the blackened patch of carpet and the smouldering stopped. 'Right,' he said, 'this is what I want. Number one, I want the original surveillance video that your girl recorded in Tanga Tans.' He paused, looking at Grandad.

'You want it right now?' Grandad asked.

'No, there's no hurry,' Dee Dee said sarcastically. 'I'll come round and pick it up sometime next week.' He shook his head. 'Of course I want it now.'

Grandad turned to me. 'It's in a small white envelope in the top right-hand drawer of my desk.'

'I know where it is,' Gloria said, getting to her feet. 'I'll get it.'

'You stay where you are,' Dee Dee told her. He looked at me. 'What are you waiting for?'

I went into Grandad's office, opened his desk drawer, and took out the envelope he'd described. I looked inside and made sure the micro memory card was there, and I was just about to go back into the main office when I noticed that Grandad's laptop was open, and when I saw what was on the screen, I realised why Gloria had been so keen to come in here and get the memory card. The picture on the laptop was the photograph of Lance Borstlap that Grandad had shown me a few days ago. Lance Borstlap, one of the Omega men. The menu strip at the bottom of the screen showed two more open files. I clicked on one of them and the grainy old photograph of the three special forces operatives in Kuwait came up, the one that showed Sergeant Andrew W. Carson, who we thought might be Winston, the man in charge of Omega.

'Hey, kid,' I heard Dee Dee call out. 'What the hell are you doing in there?'

I quickly opened the other file. It was a copy of the traffic accident report into my parents' car crash.

There was no way that Grandad would have left these files open, and the only other person who'd been in here was Gloria. She'd lied to me. She hadn't been in here to retrieve her report into Dee Dee, she'd been in here looking through Grandad's files on Omega.

I was suddenly so furious with her, and so angry with myself for being taken in by her lies – and for not listening to what my instincts were telling me – that for a moment or two I just had to close my eyes and breathe slowly in an effort to calm myself down.

Once my heart had stopped pounding, I opened my eyes again, took a deep breath, and let it out slowly. Then I closed the files on the laptop and went back into the main office.

I could see Gloria watching me, trying to work out if I'd seen the open files or not, but I didn't look back at her. I just went over to Dee Dee and handed him the envelope. He glanced inside it, then put the envelope in his pocket.

'How many copies of the video are there?' he said to Grandad.

'I gave one to Jakes and Mortimer, and there's one on my laptop.'

'Delete it,' Dee Dee told him. 'Jakes and Mortimer's copy no longer exists, and the original's going to be burnt. So if I *do* ever see or hear of the video again, I'll know it came from you. Understand?'

'I'll delete it,' Grandad assured him.

'You'll also get rid of everything you've got on Tanga Tans. Computer files, written reports, whatever. Delete it, shred it, destroy it.'

'Anything else?' Grandad said.

Dee Dee stared hard at him. 'You forget all about Tanga Tans, OK? It's nothing to do with you. You forget you ever had anything to do with it. If anyone asks you about the salon or Raisa Ferris, or anything at all about me or my business, you keep your mouth shut.' He looked round at Gloria and me. 'That goes for all of you. You keep out of my business.'

'And if we don't?' Grandad said.

Dee Dee smiled. 'I'm a reasonable man, Mr Delaney. I'm sure you find that hard to believe, and I've no doubt you think I'm just a worthless piece of scum. A drug dealer, a gangster, a mindless thug with a total absence of morality.' He shrugged. 'Of course, you're perfectly entitled to think whatever you like. Your opinion of me – however misguided it may be – is of no interest to me whatsoever. The fact is, I'm a businessman, just like you. I provide a service, just like you. The only real difference between us is that we operate in different worlds. Yours is governed by the laws of the state, mine is governed by the laws of the *e*state.' He grinned, pleased again with his clever use of words. 'In your world, conflicts and wrongdoing are resolved by mostly peaceful means. The police, the courts, the judicial system. But these forces of law simply don't exist in my world. The only justice available in my world is the threat and use of violence. It's not ideal, by any means, but it's all we have.' He stared at Grandad. 'And it *is* very effective, as I'm sure you'll agree.'

'Is there a point to all this?' Grandad said wearily.

Dee Dee's eyes darkened. 'I've told you what I want you to do. If you do it, that's fine. No problem. You won't see or hear from me again. However, if you *don't* do exactly what you've been told, I guarantee that you'll suffer the consequences.' He glanced around the office. 'This place will be burned to the ground, for a start, and I'll do whatever else is necessary to ensure that your business is wiped out. On a personal level, the least the three of you can expect is to be very badly hurt, and on top of that I'll bring pain and suffering to your families too.' He stepped closer to Grandad. 'You wouldn't want anything to happen to Nancy and Nora, would you?'

Grandad said nothing, just stared at him.

Dee Dee turned to Gloria. 'I haven't had you checked out yet, but I'm sure there's *someone* very special in your life – husband, son, daughter. Whoever they are, we'll find them.' He lit another cigarette and turned back to Grandad. 'Oh, and I'll let my two "pig-ignorant thugs" here finish off what they started with the lovely Miss Lane. They'll be only too happy to live up to your insult.'

'Is that it?' Grandad said calmly. 'Are we done now?'

'Yeah, I think that just about covers it. I've made my position quite clear, wouldn't you say?'

'Absolutely.'

'Right, well, unless you've got any questions, or there's anything you'd like to say before we go . . . ?'

'Yeah, I've got a question,' Grandad said, taking a step towards Dee Dee.

'And what might that be?'

'How old are you?'

'What?'

'You heard me. How old are you?'

It wasn't the kind of question Dee Dee was expecting, and I could tell that it threw him off balance a bit.

'I'm twenty-six,' he said, looking and sounding slightly bewildered. 'What the hell's that got to do with anything?'

'Your little lecture about the difference between your world and mine,' Grandad said.

'Yeah? What about it?'

'You were right. They *are* different worlds. But what you need to understand is that I was living in a world like yours before you were even born. I spent over twenty years fighting in real wars, and I've seen and done things that you couldn't imagine in your worst nightmares.'

'Right,' Dee Dee said dismissively, 'and I'm supposed to be impressed by that, am I?'

Grandad shrugged. 'You might want to bear it in mind, that's all.'

Dee Dee grinned. 'Anything else you'd like me to bear in mind?'

'Just this. If you or your thugs so much as lay a finger on any of my family or colleagues, I *will* hunt you down and kill you.'

'Is that a threat, Mr Delaney?'

'It's a stone-cold fact.'

29

After Dee Dee and his two goons had left, the three of us convened in Grandad's office to try to work out what we should do. I kept my eye on Gloria as we went into the office, and although she didn't make it obvious, she definitely glanced at Grandad's laptop. When she saw that the Omega files were closed, a momentary look of realisation crossed her face. She knew that I knew.

As we all sat down – Grandad at his desk, me sitting opposite him, and Gloria at Courtney's desk across the room – the situation between Gloria and me felt really strange. It was as if there was this big mysterious secret hanging over us, but we were both pretending it wasn't there. Also, now that Dee Dee had gone and I'd had a chance to think about it, I didn't understand why Gloria had lied to me in the first place. It wasn't as if she wasn't supposed to know about our investigation into Omega. In fact, as Grandad had told me, it was Gloria herself who'd managed to identify Lance Borstlap. So why didn't she want me to know that she'd been looking at Borstlap's file on Grandad's laptop? It didn't make sense.

For now though, there were more important things to think about, and as Grandad started talking, I turned my mind to the question in hand: what were we going to do about Dee Dee?

'The way I see it,' Grandad said, 'we've got two options. The only sensible course of action is to do exactly what Dee Dee says. We simply wash our hands of the whole case, forget we had anything to do with it, and get on with our lives. The compensation case has been dropped, so Delaney & Co have no responsibility to carry on with the investigation anyway, and whatever we think about the rights and wrongs of how Dee Dee runs his "business", it's not our job to do anything about it.'

'Can we trust him to keep his word?' Gloria said. 'Do you think he really *will* leave us alone if we do what he says?'

Grandad nodded. 'Whatever he is, he's not stupid. I don't doubt for a second that if we don't do what he says he *will* carry out his threats, but as he said, he's a businessman, and he won't want to draw attention to himself if he doesn't have to. I think it's safe to assume he'll stick to his word.'

'What about Courtney?' I said, unable to keep the anger from my voice. 'Are we just going to *forget* what he did to her as well? Wash our hands of *that* and get on with our lives?'

'I didn't say we're *going* to do what Dee Dee wants us to do,' Grandad said calmly. 'All I said was that it's the only sensible course of action.'

'Do you mean we don't *have* to be sensible?'

Grandad smiled. 'It's up to us what we do. The sensible

option isn't always the right one. Sometimes you have to follow your heart.'

'And what's your heart telling you?'

Grandad's smile faded. 'Dee Dee has to pay for what he did to Courtney. It's almost certain that he didn't actually do it himself, but there's no doubt that he was behind it. He ordered his thugs to beat the living daylights out of her, and that makes him just as responsible – if not more so – than the individuals who actually did it. They all have to pay. They're all *going* to pay.'

'Now, hold on a minute,' Gloria said. 'I know how much Courtney means to both of you, and I agree that Dee Dee and his goons shouldn't be allowed to get away with what they did to her. I mean, you know what I'm like, Joe – you know I don't have any qualms about punishing those who deserve it. If I was twenty years younger and I was given five minutes alone with Drew Devon, I'd happily make sure he was incapable of ever hurting anyone again. But we have to be practical about this. *Neither* of us are twenty years younger, are we? I don't know how many men Dee Dee has at his disposal, but it's bound to be at least a few dozen, probably a whole lot more, and they're all going to be young and strong and ready to fight at the drop of a hat. What chance would we have against them? I mean, two old codgers and a fourteen-year-old kid against a small army of streetwise gangsters. It'd all be over in five seconds flat.' She looked into Grandad's eyes. 'And don't forget what Dee Dee said about "bringing pain and suffering" to our families too.'

'So what are you saying?' Grandad asked her. 'We just let him get away with it?'

'I'm saying that if we go up against him and fail – and it's a virtual certainty that we would – all three of us are going to end up in hospital, or worse, and you're going to lose your business. And, if that's not enough, your wife and your mother, and Courtney, are all going to be in danger of getting seriously hurt as well.'

'Maybe there's another option,' I said.

Grandad and Gloria looked at me.

'Dad always told me that when you're in a fight you have to play to your strengths,' I explained. 'As far as I can tell, the only advantage we've got over Dee Dee and his crew is that we're smarter than them.'

'Right . . .' Grandad said, not sounding very confident. 'But even if that's true, and I'm not entirely sure that it is, how exactly is being smart going to help us?'

'We work out a way to get back at Dee Dee without putting ourselves or anyone else in danger.'

'We just "work it out"?' Grandad said.

'Why not? I mean, you two know all about spying and being sneaky and stuff, don't you? You must have been in really tricky positions before when you've had to think your way out of trouble. So that's what we do now. We don't fight with our fists, we fight with our brains.'

Grandad nodded slowly and looked over at Gloria.

'What do you think?' he asked her.

She shrugged. 'Well, there's certainly no harm in trying. Although I have to admit that at the moment I can't see how it can be done.'

'Nothing's impossible if you really put your mind to it,' I said.

She looked at Grandad. 'The optimism of youth.'

'Maybe,' he said, 'but as someone once said, you'll never find a rainbow if you keep looking down.'

Good one, Grandad, I thought, smiling at him.

'All right, look,' he went on, 'there's no rush to decide if we're going to do anything or not, so I think it's best if we all put our thinking caps on and see what we can come up with. And in the meantime, we don't *do* anything, OK?' He gave me a stern look. 'Is that understood, Travis? We don't do anything at all about Drew Devon or Tanga Tans or anything remotely connected to the case. Agreed?'

'Yeah.'

'Right,' he said, standing up, 'well, I'm going back to the hospital now to see how Courtney's getting on. Do you want to come with me, Gloria?'

She glanced at her watch. 'I can't, I'm afraid. Not tonight. But I'll definitely go and see her tomorrow.'

'Just me and you then, Trav,' he said.

I hesitated for a moment, thinking quickly about something, then I looked at my watch, got to my feet and went over to the cupboard. 'I've got to meet Kendal Price

170

at eight o'clock,' I lied, opening the cupboard and taking out Grandad's gadget case. 'We had a problem with one of the motion sensors at the game today. I was going to replace it myself, but Kendal's got to do something at school tonight anyway, so I'm going to give him another sensor and he's going to install it himself.' I opened the case, making sure no one could see what I was doing, and took out the tracking device that Grandad had shown me the other day. 'I won't be long,' I said, checking the code on the tracker to make sure it was the one he'd linked up to my mobile. 'Once I've seen Kendal, I'll get a taxi to the hospital. I should be there by half eight at the latest.'

'Why don't I just give you a lift to wherever you're meeting Kendal?' Grandad suggested. 'I'll wait while you see him, then we can go on to the hospital together.'

I glanced over at Gloria as she got up and went into the main office. I heard her crossing the room and heading towards the little bathroom at the back.

'It's OK, thanks, Grandad,' I said, heading for the main office, 'I'm meeting Kendal at McDonald's in the High Street. There's nowhere to park round there. It's easier if I walk.'

'Well, OK, if you say so,' I heard him say as I went through the door.

I could tell by the sound of his voice that he was slightly puzzled by my behaviour, but I didn't have time to worry about that at the moment. Gloria wouldn't be in the bathroom much longer, and if I was going to plant the tracking device on her, I had to do it now.

To be perfectly honest, I wasn't really sure what I was doing, or why I was doing it. The idea of planting the tracking device on Gloria to see where she went when she left the office had only just occurred to me. I hadn't been planning it or anything – not consciously anyway – it had just suddenly popped into my head. I think it was when Grandad had asked her if she wanted to go to the hospital with him, and she'd looked at her watch and said, 'I can't, I'm afraid. Not tonight.' I don't know why that had aroused my suspicion, there was just something about the way she'd said it that had sparked off an idea in the back of my mind, and the next thing I'd known I was getting the tracker out of the cupboard.

I was at Gloria's desk now, desperately trying to work out what to do with the tracker. Her handbag was hanging on the back of her chair, a big old leather thing with straps and buckles and lots of side pockets. I thought about dropping the tracker into one of the pockets, but it felt too risky. I didn't know what was in the pockets, so I had no way of telling how often she used whatever she kept in them, which in turn meant I had no idea how safe the tracker would be in there . . .

I heard the toilet flush then, and at the same time I heard Grandad's voice.

'Have you seen my car keys, Trav?'

He was coming out into the main office.

I'd run out of time. The bathroom door was opening,

Gloria was coming back, Grandad was walking through the doorway . . . I'd left it too late.

Letting out a sigh, I gave up on the whole idea and went over to the coat rack to get my parka . . .

And then I saw Gloria's raincoat. It was hanging right next to my parka. I didn't stop to think, I just quickly reached up and slipped the tracker into the top pocket, then took her coat off the rack, turned round, and passed it to her.

'Why, thank you, Travis,' she said.

'You're welcome, m'lady,' I replied, bowing my head.

As she put her coat on, and I took my parka off the rack, I just hoped that – like most people – she never actually used the top pocket for anything. Knowing my luck, I thought, she *wasn't* like most people. But there wasn't anything I could do about it now.

'Right,' she said, casually picking up some files off her desk, 'I'll see you both tomorrow then.'

'Don't forget to put your thinking cap on,' I told her.

'Already done,' she said, doffing an imaginary hat. She looked over at Grandad. 'Goodnight, Joseph.'

'Night, Gloria.'

As she left the office and closed the door, I said to Grandad, 'Have you found them?'

'Found what?'

'Your car keys.'

'Oh, yeah . . .' He grinned. 'They were in my pocket. Are you ready?'

'Just a sec,' I said, pretending to be looking through my pockets for something. I was actually waiting to see if Gloria went past the window. She usually did when she was on her way home. I wasn't sure exactly where she lived, but I knew it was off Long Barton Road somewhere, and she always walked to and from the office, so it couldn't be all that far away. If she *was* walking home now, she'd turn right when she left the building and I'd see her passing the window.

'Come on, Trav,' Grandad said. 'Let's get a move on, eh?'

There was no sign of Gloria passing the window, so unless she was walking *really* slowly, she must have turned left, which meant she was heading towards town.

I followed Grandad out of the office, told him I'd see him later, and walked off along North Walk, pulling out my mobile as I went.

30

Following someone on foot is a lot more difficult than it's made out to be in films and TV programmes. It's not so bad if the person you're tailing doesn't know you, or if they have no idea they're being followed anyway, or if they don't know anything about counter-surveillance techniques. But Gloria *did* know me, and even if she didn't, she was an ex-MI6 agent with years of experience, so it was safe to assume that she was fully trained in both spotting and shaking off anyone who might be following her. If I hadn't had the tracker to help me, I'm sure I wouldn't have got anywhere near her without her noticing me. But the beauty of the tracking device was that I didn't *have* to get anywhere near her. I didn't need to keep her in sight. The software that Grandad had downloaded to my mobile the other day was doing all that for me. All I had to do was follow the flashing yellow dot on the screen.

I'd selected the street-map option from the tracker menu. It was pretty much the same as most online map set-ups, with all the usual features – zoom in and out, click and drag, a search facility. I could have added my own location to the map if I'd wanted to, but there was no need. I knew exactly where I was.

Right now, I was about two-thirds of the way down

the High Street, and according to the tracker, Gloria was roughly a hundred metres ahead of me, approaching the High Street entrance to Castle Park. The park is a huge open area on the south side of Barton Castle. The River Barr runs all the way through it, meandering from one side of the park to the other, and on either side of the river there are pathways and rolling fields, picnic areas and playgrounds, there's even a little boating lake. In summer the park is used for all kinds of open-air festivals and concerts, but at this time of year the only people who regularly visit the park in the evenings are dog walkers and winos and groups of kids up to no good.

I paused for a moment, watching the yellow dot on the screen, wondering whether Gloria was actually going into the park or the castle grounds or was just passing by. The dot turned left into Castle Wynd, an ancient pathway that runs alongside the castle grounds. I carried on watching the screen, making sure Gloria didn't double back, then I pulled up my hood against the rain and got moving again.

I took a short cut to the castle, turning down a cobbled street into a maze of narrow lanes that eventually brought me out into the upper end of the park at the bottom of Castle Wynd. The tracker had shown me that Gloria had turned right off Castle Wynd about halfway down and headed into the castle grounds. For the last minute or so, the yellow dot hadn't moved. It had stopped right next to the castle wall.

I couldn't make sense of it. What was Gloria doing there? Or maybe she *wasn't* there, I suddenly thought. Maybe she'd found the tracker and ditched it. I brought up the options menu on my mobile, zoomed in on the map and switched to the satellite view, and suddenly it all made sense. The yellow dot was hovering over a slightly blurred view of a wooden bench in the shadows of the castle wall. *Now* I knew what Gloria was doing. She was sitting on one of the benches that line the base of the wall at the back of the castle.

But why?

Was she waiting for someone? Had she already met them? Who were they? And why would she want to meet them at the back of Barton Castle on a cold rainy night?

I stared at the yellow dot on my mobile screen, but no matter how useful the tracker was, there was only so much it could tell me. If I wanted to find out what Gloria was doing, and who – if anyone – she was meeting, I'd have to do it myself.

I started walking up Castle Wynd. The castle grounds were on my left behind a two-metre-high wire-mesh fence. The fence was covered with a thick growth of ornamental ivy, blocking my view of the grounds, but here and there the dark-green foliage was sparse enough to see through. I waited until I was reasonably close to the castle, but not *too* close, and then I stopped by a thinning patch of ivy and cautiously peered through.

The castle is illuminated at night by powerful

floodlights, and although they're mainly directed at the front and sides of the old stone ruins, there was enough peripheral light at the back for me to make out Gloria sitting on one of the benches. She was on her own. Just sitting there, her handbag clasped in her lap, staring straight ahead.

I heard footsteps and voices then, the sound of people coming up the Wynd behind me, and I suddenly realised how suspicious I must look – a kid on his own, standing by the fence, peeping in through a hole in the ivy . . .

I casually moved away from the fence, put my phone to my ear and started talking – 'Yeah . . . right . . . OK, yeah, that's fine . . .'

The people I'd heard passed by me – a young couple who'd probably just been for a walk in the park. They gave me a quick sideways glance, but they were too interested in each other to care what I was doing. I waited for them to move on past, checked there was no one else coming up the Wynd, and looked through the gap in the ivy again.

Gloria was no longer alone. A man had sat down next to her. He had his coat collar turned up, so I couldn't really see his face, but there was something vaguely familiar about him. They didn't seem to be talking to each other, they were just sitting there side by side, like two strangers sharing a bench. Except, obviously, they weren't strangers. I saw Gloria reach into her handbag and take out a document file. As she passed it to the man, I leaned in closer to the fence, trying to get a better view of the file. It was impossible to tell at this distance, but it *looked* like the file she'd been carrying when I'd surprised her coming out of Grandad's office. The man took the file from her and put it in his coat pocket. He said something to Gloria, she nodded, then he got up and started walking away. He was heading towards me, his face in plain view, and now I knew why he'd seemed so familiar.

It was Winston, the steely-eyed man in charge of Omega.

What the hell was Gloria doing with *him*? I asked myself. And what had she just given him?

I didn't have time to think about it now. Winston was almost at the gate that led out into Castle Wynd, and I had to act fast. He knew who I was, so I couldn't let him see me, but I didn't want to lose sight of him either. I wanted, if possible, to see where he went. It didn't seem likely that he'd come down the Wynd – unless, for some reason, he was going into the park – so my guess was that he'd turn left out of the gate and head up towards the High Street.

I started walking slowly down the Wynd.

After five seconds or so I heard Winston come out of the gate, and I could tell from the sound of his footsteps that I'd guessed right and he was heading up the Wynd. Putting my phone to my ear to half cover my face, I glanced quickly over my shoulder. Winston was walking briskly, his head bowed down, his arms swinging vigorously. As desperate as I was to follow him and find out where he went, I realised now that it was simply too risky. All he had to do was look behind him and he'd see me. And there was Gloria to consider too. I looked at my mobile. The tracker was showing that she was still on the bench, but she could get up and leave any second. If I went after Winston there was a good chance she'd see me, even if he didn't.

There was only one thing for it – I had to let him go.

As I retraced my steps through the maze of narrow lanes, heading back to the High Street, I racked my brains, trying to come up with an innocent explanation of what I'd just seen. But I knew in my heart I was wasting my time. The scene I'd just witnessed could only mean one thing: Gloria was working for Omega. She was passing on information to them, most probably keeping them informed of our investigation into them. She *was* a traitor after all. She'd betrayed us, betrayed Grandad's trust in her.

It was sickening.

I thought about calling Grandad right away, but then I remembered he'd be at the hospital, so he'd probably have his mobile turned off. It didn't really matter though. I was almost at the High Street now, and there was a taxi rank just up the road. I'd get a taxi and be at the hospital in ten minutes.

My mobile rang then.

It was Jaydie.

'Hi, Travis,' she said.

Her voice didn't sound as bright and breezy as usual.

'Are you OK?' I asked her.

'I need to see you about something.'

'What is it?'

'It's best if I don't tell you on the phone. Can I meet you somewhere?'

'What, now?'

'Yeah.'

'I'm kind of busy at the moment. Couldn't it wait till tomorrow?'

'It's *really* important, Trav. It's sort of about Courtney.'

'Courtney?'

'I heard what happened to her. Is she OK?'

'Not really,' I said. 'She's in hospital. I was just on my way to see her. Do you know something about what happened to her?'

'Well, kind of . . . it's a bit complicated. That's why I need to talk to you in person.'

'Where are you now?' I asked.

'On the bus, just coming into town. I can get another bus out to your place and be there in about half an hour.'

'I'm in town now,' I told her, glancing at my watch. 'How about if I meet you in McDonald's?'

'Yeah, that'd be brilliant. I'll be about ten minutes.'

'All right, see you then.'

Just after I'd ended the call my phone honked, warning me that the battery was almost dead. I was a bit surprised as I'd only recently charged it, but when I checked the battery-usage menu I found out that the tracking software had used up 65% of the power. Before turning off the phone to save the remaining battery, I checked Gloria's location on the tracking screen. The yellow dot had left the castle grounds now and was heading back up the High Street at a steady pace. She was on her way home, I guessed. Her dirty work was done for the night.

31

I was leaning against a pillar by the stairs when Jaydie came into McDonald's. She saw me straight away and came over. She was wearing a cool little zip-up jacket, a short skirt over leggings, and a black peaked cap. She looked really nice.

'Do you want anything to eat?' I asked her.

I'd already had a cheeseburger and I still had most of a vanilla shake left.

'No, thanks,' Jaydie said, looking around. 'Can we go upstairs? It's a bit crowded down here.'

The upstairs section was larger than downstairs, so although it was fairly busy up there – groups of kids, families, couples – it was easier to find somewhere with a bit more privacy. Just as we reached the top of the stairs we saw two women preparing to leave a small corner table right at the back, and as they got up, we hurried over and nabbed the table before anyone else could get to it.

As we sat down, and I cleared away the remains of the women's meals, I noticed Jaydie looking around again. She seemed really anxious, worried that someone might see her.

'Are you looking for someone in particular?' I asked her.

'Anyone from the Slade,' she said, keeping her voice

low. 'If I'm seen talking to you, it's bound to get back to Dee Dee.'

'Maybe we should go somewhere else,' I suggested. 'Somewhere less public.'

She shook her head. 'It's all right, I'm probably just being paranoid.' She smiled at me then, a genuinely pleased-to-see-you smile, and she picked up my shake and took a sip from it. 'I mean, we're friends, aren't we? There's no reason we shouldn't be seen together. For all anyone knows, we could be on a date.'

'Well, yeah . . .' I said hesitantly.

'Don't look so worried, Travis. I'm not going to start snogging you or anything.'

I blushed, which Jaydie obviously found amusing.

'You're too sensitive,' she said.

'It's just for show,' I told her. 'I'm a tough guy really. I just pretend I'm the sensitive type to impress the girls.'

'You think we like sensitive types?'

'Don't you?'

'We pretend we do, but actually we prefer tough guys.'

'I *knew* it,' I said, grinning.

She laughed, then took another sip from my shake.

'Are you sure you don't want anything?' I asked her.

'Maybe later.' She looked at me, her face suddenly serious. 'Is Courtney going to be OK?'

'I think they're just keeping her in overnight as a precaution. You know, just in case she's got a concussion or something.'

'They really did a job on her then?'

'It would have been even worse if they hadn't been stopped.'

Jaydie looked hesitant, as if she wanted to say something but didn't know how to say it.

'It was Mason and Lenny, wasn't it?' I said to her. 'They were the ones who saved her.'

She nodded. 'Mase hasn't actually admitted it, but I've been told on good authority that it was him and Lenny and two others.'

'How did they know she was being attacked?'

'Mason's got a network of kids who keep him informed of everything that's going on around the Slade. He'd heard that some of Dee Dee's crew had scared off Raisa, and he had some of his people keeping an eye on her flat. So when Courtney showed up, they called him straight away. He would have got there sooner but he was right over the other side of the estate at the time.'

'Why won't he admit to you that it was him?'

'He won't talk to me about anything any more. Dee Dee, the salon, Mum, Courtney . . . I think he's just totally mixed up about everything. He doesn't know what he should do. He hates Dee Dee for what he's doing to Mum and for what he did to Raisa and Courtney, but he can't quite bring himself to openly go against him because he knows that pretty soon Dee Dee's going to have complete control of the estate. If Mason's his enemy when that happens, his life's going to be hell.'

'Does Dee Dee know it was him who saved Courtney?'

'Not yet. They were all wearing hoods and masks. But Dee Dee's going to do everything he can to find out who they were.'

'Do you think he will?'

'Mason's crew are pretty loyal. I don't think any of them will grass him up. But Dee Dee's got a lot of resources, and he can be incredibly persuasive when it comes to making people talk.' She sighed. 'God knows what'll happen if he does find out.'

'Do you know what happened to Raisa?'

'No one knows. She hasn't been seen anywhere.' Jaydie shrugged. 'Hopefully she's just left the estate and moved somewhere else.'

'You know she's dropped the case against Tanga Tans, don't you?'

'Yeah, I heard.' Jaydie looked at me. 'I also heard that Dee Dee and a couple of his boys came round to your office.'

I quickly told her all about Dee Dee's visit – what he wanted us to do, what he said he'd do to us if we didn't.

'Do you know a girl called Bianca, by the way?' I asked her.

'Bianca Spencer?'

'Yeah, she's Royce's girlfriend—'

'She's not his *girlfriend*,' Jaydie scoffed. 'She just likes to think she is. I don't actually know her personally, but I know her type. She's one of those good girls who like to hang around with bad boys. She's not from the Slade, she lives up by the golf course somewhere. You know – nice house, good school, well-off parents. She's the kind of idiot who thinks it's exciting to hang out with gangsters.'

'She works for Jakes and Mortimer,' I said. 'I'm pretty sure that's how Dee Dee found out about Raisa's compensation case.'

'Ah, well, that explains it,' Jaydie said knowingly. 'Royce probably knew all along who she worked for. I expect he followed her around for a bit, then chatted her up at a pub or a club or something. He would have charmed the pants off of her, let her think he was in love with her, then got her to tell him everything she knew about the case. Unless he needs anything else from her, he's probably already dumped her by now.'

'Sounds like a nice guy,' I said.

'It's what they do, Trav. They use people.'

'They hurt them too.'

She looked at me. 'What are you and your grandad going to do? I mean, are you going to do what Dee Dee wants?'

'Not if we can help it. Courtney's like family to us. If we let Dee Dee get away with what he did to her . . . well, you just can't, can you? You've *got* to do something about it. The trouble is . . .'

'He's Dee Dee,' Jaydie said.

'Yeah,' I sighed bitterly. 'The all-powerful Dee Dee . . . Dee Dee the Invincible.'

'What if he's *not* so all-powerful?' Jaydie said tentatively.

I just looked at her.

'What if he's got a secret weakness?' she went on. 'Something that, if it came out, could bring him down? If someone knew what that secret was, *and* they had proof of it, they'd have Dee Dee in the palm of their hand. It'd be a hell of a dangerous thing to do, and if it went wrong . . . well, I don't even want to think about what Dee Dee would do.' Jaydie leaned across the table and took hold of my hand. 'Would you be willing to take that risk?'

'I'm a tough guy, remember?' I said, smiling at her. 'I was born to take risks.'

'This isn't a joke, Trav,' she said seriously. 'If you go up against Dee Dee with what I've got on him, and for some reason it all backfires, you could end up getting very badly hurt. He might even want to shut you up permanently.'

'All right,' I said, looking her in the eye. 'Why don't you just tell me what you've got on him first, and then we can take it from there.'

She looked around the restaurant again, checking that no one could overhear us, then she leaned in closer and started telling me about Dee Dee's secret.

32

It was just over a year ago when Jaydie and Mason had found out that Dee Dee was a police informant. It had happened purely by chance. They very rarely went out anywhere together as a family, but on this particular day they'd been with their mum to see a specialist at the hospital. She'd recently discovered a small lump in her throat, and because she was so worried about it, Jaydie and Mason had gone with her to get the results of her tests. Their mum didn't have a car, but she'd borrowed one from a friend for the day, and they'd left it in a multi-storey car park a few streets away from the hospital.

'It turned out that Mum's lump was nothing to worry about,' Jaydie explained. 'It was just a cyst, nothing cancerous or anything, so when we left the hospital we were all in a pretty good mood. It was kind of nice all being out together, and Mum was really relieved that she wasn't going to die after all, so we were all kind of messing about and having a bit of fun. We'd stopped off at the Pound Shop on the way back to the car park, and me and Mase had bought these stupid little Disney masks, you know, like Donald Duck or Mickey Mouse or something. I can't remember what they were. We were just acting like kids, you know? We still had the masks on when we got to the car park. The car was on the top level, and while we were waiting for the lift, Mason suddenly decided to have a bet with Mum that we could run up the stairs and get to the top quicker than the lift. She bet him 50p that we couldn't, and we started racing up the stairs. It was when we got to the third floor that we saw Dee Dee. He was with an older guy in a suit, the two of them kind of half hidden away at the end of a little corridor off the stairwell. When Mason stopped suddenly and looked at them, Dee Dee glared at him and told him to eff off. Luckily for us we had our masks on, so Dee Dee didn't recognise us. He probably thought we were just a couple of dumb kids. So anyway, we carried on running up the stairs, and when we got to the top, Mason told me that the guy talking to Dee Dee was a cop. He said his name was Bull, Detective Inspector Ronnie Bull—'

'Ronnie *Bull*?' I blurted out.

'*Shh!*' Jaydie hissed, glancing around. 'Keep your voice down.'

'Sorry,' I said quietly, leaning in closer to her. 'Was Mason sure it was Bull?'

She nodded. 'He was absolutely positive. He said that everyone on the estate knew Ronnie Bull, and they all knew he was the dirtiest cop in Barton.' She gave me a quizzical look. 'How do *you* know him?'

'I don't. My grandad told me about him. Bull was involved in the investigation into my mum and dad's car crash.'

'Really?'

'Grandad said there were rumours that Bull will do almost anything for the right price.'

'They're not just rumours,' Jaydie said. 'There's nothing Ronnie Bull won't do. He takes bribes, he gets paid by criminals to tip them off if they're being investigated. He raids drug dealers, steals their gear, then sells it on to other dealers. He plants evidence, fits people up . . . he's just as much a crook as the bad guys he's supposed to be catching.'

'What do you think he was doing with Dee Dee?'

'The only possible explanation that me and Mase could come up with was that Dee Dee and Bull have got some kind of deal going. Dee Dee passes on information to Bull about certain guys he wants taken out, and in return Bull makes sure that Dee Dee and his crew are left alone. Bull probably gets regular payments from Dee Dee too.'

'Can you prove any of this?'

'Well, Mason always keeps a close eye on what's going on around the estate, and after that day he started watching and listening even more carefully. Now that he knew about Dee Dee and Bull, a lot of stuff began to make sense, and the more Mase thought about it, the more he began piecing it all together – like how it was that Dee Dee's business deals rarely get busted, but the cops always seem to know in advance when his rivals are planning big operations. None of it's done *too* obviously. The cops don't *always* bust his rivals' deals, and sometimes members of Dee Dee's crew get caught and taken down, but they're mostly pretty low-ranking guys. Even if anyone did suspect there was a grass on the estate, no one would ever think it was Dee Dee. Everyone hates the cops, but it's a well-known fact that Dee Dee absolutely *despises* them. He'd *never* do a deal with a cop, not in a million years.'

'Right,' I said, 'but Mason's 100% sure that Dee Dee's a grass.'

'We both are.'

'But, like I said, you don't have any proof.'

She shook her head. 'We talked about whether or not we should do anything about it, but in the end Mason decided it wasn't worth the risk. Even if we could get proof – which neither of us could work out how to do anyway – what were we going to do with it?'

'Give it to his rivals,' I said. 'They'd take him out.'

'And where would that leave us? Even if Dee Dee himself was gone, most of his crew would still be around, and eventually they'd find out it was me and Mase who'd shopped Dee Dee.'

'Yeah, but surely they'd be grateful to you for revealing him as a grass.'

Jaydie shook her head. 'Grassing someone up, even someone who's a grass himself, is *the* worst thing you can do on the Slade. If it ever got out that me and Mase had stitched up Dee Dee, our lives – and Mum's – wouldn't be worth living.'

'But if Dee Dee was gone, your mum wouldn't have to keep working at the tanning salon, would she?'

'No, she wouldn't,' Jaydie agreed. 'But if you had the choice between doing a crap job to pay off your debts or having your entire family branded as outcasts and living in fear for the rest of their lives, which one would you choose?'

'Right . . .' I said, nodding slowly, beginning to get it now. 'So you and Mason decided to just leave things as they were?'

'I know it sounds like the wrong thing to do, but all Mason ever cares about is what's best for me and Mum.'

'There's nothing wrong with that.'

Jaydie lowered her eyes, suddenly looking ashamed of herself. 'He made me swear on my life that I'd never tell *any*one what we know about Dee Dee.'

'Hey,' I said gently, 'it's all right. You don't have to feel bad about it. It's not always possible to keep your promises. Stuff happens, things change . . . you wouldn't have told me unless you had a good reason.'

She slowly looked up. 'But that's the thing, Trav. I'm not even sure why I *am* telling you. I mean, it was just . . . I don't know. I just keep thinking about Mum and Courtney and the state Mason's got himself into, and it's all because of Drew bloody Devon. I'm just so sick of it all. Sick of *him*. I don't know why, but I just *had* to tell you . . .' She sighed. 'I suppose I was kind of hoping that once you knew the truth about Dee Dee,

maybe you and me could work something out together.'
She looked at me. 'What do you reckon, Trav? Are you
willing to give it a go?'

I didn't even have to think about it.

'The first thing I need to know,' I said, 'is how Dee
Dee and Bull get in touch with each other.'

33

'Dee Dee's incredibly careful about using phones,' Jaydie told me. 'He doesn't own a mobile, and he'll only use someone else's if it's absolutely necessary.'

'So how does he communicate with anyone?' I asked.

'He uses his people. They make all his calls for him, and if anyone wants to get in touch with him, they have to go through them.'

'But he can't use his people to get in touch with Bull, can he?'

'There's a phone box on the Slade, not far from where he lives. It's the only one on the whole estate that actually works, and basically it belongs to Dee Dee. Everyone knows it's his, and if anyone else uses it or vandalises it or anything, they're soon made aware of their mistake. Dee Dee has a network of kids whose only job is to keep an eye on the phone box all the time. If anyone goes near it, they let him know.'

'And you think that's how he contacts Bull?'

'Well, most people assume he uses the phone box for arranging business deals, which he probably does, but me and Mase were thinking about it and we suddenly realised that it was kind of weird how he feels safe using the phone box when he's so paranoid about using any other phones. Mason reckoned the only answer was that he uses the phone box to contact Bull.'

'Because Bull's got the resources to make absolutely sure that the phone box isn't bugged,' I said.

'Exactly. And Dee Dee knows he can trust Bull to keep the phone box clean because it's just as important for Bull to keep their deal secret as it is for Dee Dee.'

'So if we want to get evidence of Dee Dee's connection with Bull, we need to get access to the phone box . . .' I paused for a moment, thinking about the practicalities. It wasn't hard to work out what needed to be done. The tricky bit was figuring out how to actually do it. 'The best way of doing it,' I told Jaydie, 'would be to put a voice-activated recorder into the phone box, and somehow get a tracker on Dee Dee. So when Dee Dee calls Bull we can record what they're talking about, and if they set up a meeting we'll know when and where it's going to be. Even if they use some kind of code, we can follow Dee Dee with the tracker to the meeting. Then all we've got to do is take photos of them together, or even better video the meeting, with audio if possible, and we've got all the evidence we need.'

Jaydie smiled. 'Simple as that.'

'Yeah . . .'

'What do we do once we've got the evidence?'

'I think we need to concentrate on getting it first. That's going to be hard enough as it is. We can work out what to do with it later.'

'Right,' Jaydie said. 'So what's your plan?'

The problem was, I didn't actually have a plan. The idea itself was simple enough, but I just couldn't think how to put it into action. There was certainly no way that I could get into the phone box to plant the voice-activated recorder without being spotted, and I definitely couldn't go anywhere near Dee Dee myself, so I couldn't plant the tracker on him either. When I asked Jaydie if she thought Mason could do it, she was adamant that he mustn't know anything about what we were doing.

'If he knew what we were planning,' she said, 'he'd have a fit. Honestly, Trav, he'd go ballistic. We can't tell him *anything* about this, OK?'

'All right,' I agreed.

'You promise?'

'I promise.'

'Cross your heart and hope to die?'

'Yes,' I sighed. 'But I can't see how else we're going to do it.'

'It seems pretty obvious to me.'

I frowned at her, not getting what she meant.

'*I* can do it,' she said simply.

'You?'

'Yeah, why not?'

I just looked at her, not sure what to say.

'You think I'm not *capable* of doing it?' she said.

'No, it's not that . . .'

'What is it then? Is it because I'm just a little *girly*? You think I'll get scared and start blubbing or something?'

'Of course not. I just don't want you to get hurt, that's all.'

She grinned. 'So you do care about me after all.'

'Yeah,' I said seriously. 'I care about you.'

'Really?'

'Yeah . . . I mean, you know . . .'

She reached across the table and took hold of my hand. 'I can do it, Trav. Trust me. I'm a Slade girl. I know how to look after myself. And besides, I wouldn't be doing it on my own anyway. Dee Dee and Mason aren't the only ones on the estate with a crew. I've got my own little posse of trusted friends.' She smiled. 'We might not be as big and tough as Dee Dee's mob, but what we lack in numbers and size we make up for in brains and sneakiness.' She squeezed my hand. 'I can do this, Travis. I *want* to do it.'

'All right,' I said. 'Let's do it.'

I don't know how long we sat there, working out how Jaydie and her friends were going to get the job done, but when I suddenly remembered that my phone was still turned off, and I turned it back on and found three missed calls from Grandad, I was surprised to realise that it was gone ten o'clock.

'Where the hell are you?' Grandad said when I called him back. 'And why's your phone been turned off? I've been trying to ring you for ages.'

'Sorry, Grandad. I turned it off to save the battery and forgot to turn it back on again. Are you still at the hospital?'

'Yes, and you need to get yourself down here as soon as possible.'

'Why, what's happened?' I said quickly. 'Is Courtney all right?'

'She's taken a turn for the worse, Trav. It's kind of complicated . . . I'll explain everything when you get here. Just get in a taxi right now, OK?'

'I'll be there in fifteen minutes.'

'What's happened?' Jaydie asked as I hung up.

'I'm not sure,' I said, getting up. 'Grandad just said that Courtney's taken a turn for the worse. I have to get going right now.'

'Yeah, of course.'

'Will you be OK getting home?'

'Yeah, don't worry about me. Just go.'

'I'll call you in the morning.'

'OK.'

I hurried downstairs and rushed out into the street. The taxi rank was just along the road. There was a cab waiting, and no one in the queue. I jumped in and told the driver to take me to the hospital.

'You got enough money, kid?' the driver said.

I took out a ten-pound note and showed it to him. 'All right?'

He nodded, put the taxi into gear and got going.

34

Grandad was waiting for me outside Courtney's room when I got there. He quickly told me that just over an hour ago Courtney had suddenly developed an intensely painful headache. The doctors had immediately rushed her off for X-rays and a cranial CT scan, and at the moment she was resting quietly in her room, no visitors allowed.

'Their main concern was that she might have developed a blood clot in her brain,' Grandad explained. 'It can happen sometimes after a head injury. It's basically internal bleeding between the skull and the brain, and it can be really serious, possibly even fatal.'

My heart sank, and I could feel my legs going weak.

'It's OK, Trav,' Grandad said gently, guiding me over to a chair and sitting me down. 'So far the results are negative. There's no sign of blood-clotting on the X-rays, but they're still waiting for the results from the CT scan, which apparently is a more reliable test. I spoke to Dr Adams about ten minutes ago, and although he won't really tell me anything at the moment, I get the feeling that he's cautiously optimistic.'

I let out a sigh of relief.

'She's not out of the woods yet though,' Grandad went on, sitting down next to me. 'Even if the CT results are negative, they're going to want to keep her in for a while yet.' He leaned back and ran his fingers through his hair. He looked exhausted, and I felt bad for not having been here when he needed me. Not that I could have done much to help, but at least I could have shared some of his worry and concern for Courtney.

'When can we see her?' I asked.

'Not for a while. Maybe a couple of hours or so.' He looked at his watch. 'Nan should be here soon. She went over to Courtney's to pick up some nightclothes and stuff.'

'What about Courtney's mum?' I asked. 'Is she on her own?'

Grandad shook his head. 'Her carer's staying with her tonight. We'll have to arrange for someone else to take over in the morning. I'll make some calls first thing.'

'Why don't you go home and get some rest?' I suggested. 'I can stay here with Nan. We can call you if anything happens.'

'I'm not going anywhere,' he said firmly. 'If I hadn't let Courtney go to Raisa's on her own, she wouldn't be here. I'm not going to leave her now until I know for sure that she's going to be OK.'

'It's not your fault, Grandad,' I told him again. 'The only people to blame for beating her up are the ones who actually did it and Dee Dee for telling them to do it.'

'I know,' Grandad said. 'But that doesn't mean I'm not partly responsible.' He looked at me. 'I'm not wallowing in guilt or anything, Travis, I'm just stating a fact. I made a mistake. I messed up. All I'm doing now is trying to make amends for it.' He smiled wearily at me. 'That's what you do when you get things wrong. You accept it, try to fix it, and make sure you learn from it. So don't worry, I'm not moping around drowning myself in guilt and self-pity, I'm just trying to put things straight. OK?'

'OK.'

Nan turned up about twenty minutes later. She'd not only brought nightclothes and stuff for Courtney, she'd also brought fresh clothing for Grandad and me, which turned out to be a really good idea as the three of us ended up staying the rest of the night at the hospital. When the results of Courtney's CT scan finally came through, there was no sign of a blood clot, and no indication of any other long-term damage. Dr Adams talked a lot about the complexities and uncertainties of head trauma injuries, but it was pretty obvious that he had no real idea what had caused her severe headache. I don't know why he didn't just admit that he simply didn't know. I mean, it wasn't as if anyone was going to blame him for not knowing everything. I felt like telling him what Granny Nora had told me. *There are so many things that none of us will ever understand, things that simply don't have answers, but the trick is to realise that we don't have to know all the answers. We live in a mysterious universe that has no purpose or reason. We don't have to feel frightened of not knowing things.*

I didn't tell Dr Adams that, of course. I didn't think he'd appreciate it.

We were allowed in to see Courtney for a short while, and although she still looked terrible – her face a swollen mess of yellow and purple bruises – she didn't seem too bad in herself, smiling and joking, trying to make light of everything. Underneath it all though, I think the shock of what had happened to her – and what *could* have happened to her if Mason and his friends hadn't intervened – was beginning to really sink in. I could see it in her eyes, a haunted and fearful look. I'd never seen anything like that in Courtney before, and it really got to me. It gripped me deep down inside, filling me with a hatred so powerful that it was actually quite frightening.

I didn't tell Nan or Grandad what I'd found out about Gloria's betrayal or Dee Dee's connection with Ronnie Bull. Grandad was so exhausted that he could barely keep his eyes open – every time he sat down he kept dozing off – and I thought it was best to let him get as much rest as possible. And although it was very tempting to tell Nan about Gloria – and I almost gave in to the temptation once or twice – I decided in the end that it just wasn't the right time or place. Our one and only concern at that moment was Courtney. And I wasn't going to do anything to change that.

35

At eight o'clock the next morning we all set off from the hospital in Grandad's car. Grandad had tried to arrange a replacement carer for Courtney's mum, but he hadn't had any luck, so Nan said she'd look after Mrs Lane for the day. The plan was that Grandad would drop Nan off at Courtney's house, take me to school, then drive back to the hospital to stay with Courtney. She hadn't suffered any further headaches, and when she'd woken up at seven o'clock she was feeling, and looking, a lot better. She'd eaten some breakfast, had a shower, and she was already starting to moan about having to stay in hospital.

'I've got a lot of things to do,' she told Dr Adams. 'I haven't got time to lie around in bed all day. Just give me some painkillers and I'll be fine.'

'I'll decide if you're fine or not, Ms Lane,' he told her. 'You've taken a serious beating. Your body needs time to recover.'

'Yes, but—'

'No buts,' he said firmly. 'I'm keeping you under observation for at least another twenty-four hours. If you're still doing well then, we'll consider discharging you. In the meantime, you need to get as much rest as you can.'

Apart from a resigned shake of her head and a glare

of disapproval, she hadn't put up much of an argument, and I think, deep down, she knew he was right. The haunted look in her eyes that had pained me so much the night before wasn't nearly so obvious now, but she was still a long way from being back to her usual feisty and fearless self. I'm pretty sure that's why Grandad wanted to carry on staying with her. Physically, she was on the mend. But mentally and emotionally she was still in a bad way, and Grandad was determined to give her as much help as he could, even if that just meant being there for her.

After we'd dropped Nan off at Courtney's house and were heading out of town towards school, I wondered if now was the time to bring Grandad up to date on things – Gloria's betrayal, her meeting with Winston, Jaydie's revelation about Dee Dee and the plan we'd worked out to prove that he was hooked up with DI Bull – but as I was considering it, Grandad asked me how the changing-room investigation was going, and by the time I'd finished telling him as much as I could remember about the day before – which, now that I was looking back at it, felt like three days rolled into one – we were already approaching the school gates.

'So when's the Cup Final?' Grandad asked, pulling up at the side of the road.

'Tomorrow afternoon,' I told him. 'One thirty kick-off.

'Well, hopefully you'll have better luck catching your thief then.'

He was doing his best to sound interested, but I could tell his heart wasn't really in it. His mind was still focused on Courtney.

'She'll be OK, Grandad,' I said. 'She's tough. She'll get through it.'

'I hope so.'

'You'd better get going,' I said, unbuckling my seat belt. 'You'll call me if there's any problems or anything, won't you?'

'Of course.'

'I'll come round to the hospital straight after school.'

'OK.' He forced a smile. 'Enjoy your lessons.'

'I won't.'

Lessons didn't start until nine o'clock, and it wasn't even eight thirty yet, so there weren't many kids or teachers around as I made my way over to the bike shed. As I unlocked my bike, I wondered again why I hadn't told Grandad what I was planning to do this morning. I tried telling myself that it was simply because I was skipping school, and no one in their right mind tells their parents – or in my case grandparents – that they're skipping school, but in all honesty I knew there was more to it than that. The real reason I hadn't told him what I was doing was that I knew if I had, he would have done everything in his power to stop me. He would have told me it was far too dangerous, too risky, too stupid, and he probably would have been right.

But as he'd told me himself, the sensible option isn't always the right option. Sometimes you have to follow your heart. And my heart, filled as it was with a burning desire for revenge, was telling me to do everything in *my* power to make Dee Dee pay for what he'd done to Courtney.

It usually takes me between twenty and twenty-five minutes to cycle from Kell Cross to Delaney & Co's office, but speed was of the essence that morning – I wanted to be in and out before Gloria arrived – and by going full-pelt all the way, I managed to get there in just over fifteen minutes. It was 8.43 when I entered the office, which meant that if Gloria was as punctual as she usually was – nine o'clock on the dot, every morning – I had exactly seventeen minutes to get what I needed and get out.

It wasn't absolutely crucial that I avoided Gloria, it just made everything a lot easier if she didn't see me, so although I was hurrying as much as possible, I wasn't in a state of panic or anything.

I went into Grandad's office and headed straight for the cupboard by the window. I opened it up, pulled out the gadget case, and began searching through it for what I needed. It took me a couple of minutes to find the two bits of kit I wanted – a small voice-activated recorder and the second of the two new trackers – and then I had to spend another two or three minutes opening up Grandad's laptop and connecting the new tracker to my mobile. By the time I'd done all that and put the case back in the cupboard it was 8.56.

Four minutes to go before Gloria was due to arrive.

'Plenty of time,' I muttered to myself, hurrying out of the office and locking the door behind me. 'No need to rush . . . just stay cool . . .'

I didn't dare look over my shoulder as I rode off towards town along North Walk, I just kept going until I'd turned the corner at the end of the street. I felt childishly exhilarated, like a little kid who's just got away with nicking a Twix from a sweetshop.

While I stopped to get my breath back, I turned on my phone and quickly texted Jaydie. We'd already arranged the night before to meet at McDonald's at ten this morning, so all I texted was – *all ok, il b there n 5. c u wen u gt there. trav x*

While I was waiting for Jaydie upstairs in McDonald's, I called the receptionist at school and told her that I wouldn't be in today because a close friend of mine had been taken to hospital after a serious assault. I pretended to be all shaken up and emotional about it, and the receptionist was really kind and understanding, which made me feel a bit ashamed of myself, but it did the trick. She said she'd let my teachers know, and asked me to pass on her best wishes to my friend.

*

Jaydie arrived at about 9.45. I bought us each a Big Breakfast, and while we ate, I went through the plan with her again.

'This is the voice-activated recorder,' I said, passing her the bug, 'and this is the receiver.' She took both devices and had a good look at them. The recorder was similar in size and shape to the tracker, and like the tracker it was magnetic. 'It should be easy enough to find somewhere in the phone box to fix it to,' I told Jaydie. 'Just make sure it's not visible.'

'Duh,' she said, grinning at me.

'The receiver's got a range of a thousand metres, so you shouldn't have any problem getting a signal in your flat. How far do you reckon the phone box is from your place?'

'A lot less than a thousand metres,' she said, examining the receiver. 'How do I turn it on?'

'See that switch that says on and off?'

She smiled sheepishly at me.

'Duh,' I said.

She laughed.

'Just keep it turned on all the time,' I explained. 'Once the recorder picks up the sound of a voice, it'll start recording and you'll hear a series of beeps from the receiver. The receiver will automatically record everything, but if you want to listen to it in real time, you press this button here.' I pointed out a little switch labelled *LIVE AUDIO*. 'All right?'

'No problem.'

'Call me as soon as you hear *anything*, OK?'

She nodded.

'This is the tracker,' I said, passing her the device. 'Somehow you've got to get it planted on Dee Dee. Does he usually carry any kind of bag with him?'

'Yeah, he's got this really nice little Louis Vuitton handbag.' She smiled at me. 'He never goes anywhere without it.'

'You know what I mean,' I said, momentarily grinning back at her. 'Does he carry a rucksack or a sports bag or anything?'

She shook her head, suddenly serious again. 'I've never seen him with one.'

'All right, so we'll probably have to put the tracker in his clothing. That suit he wears . . . does he wear it all the time?'

'Not always, but a lot of the time, yeah. He thinks it makes him look like a businessman.'

'Try to get the tracker in the top pocket of his jacket. We'll just have to hope he's wearing it when he calls Bull.' I looked at her. 'Are you sure this plan of yours is going to work?'

When we'd talked about it the night before, Jaydie had come up with a way of getting the tracker into the phone box without being seen, and she'd worked out a possible way of getting close enough to Dee Dee to plant the tracker on him. Both plans were full of risks, and I still wasn't sure about them at all.

'Don't worry about it, Trav,' Jaydie said. 'I talked it through with my girls last night and we've got it all worked out. Just leave it to us, OK?'

'Well, all right,' I said hesitantly. 'But if there's any hint of trouble, even the slightest possibility that something might be going wrong, just call it all off immediately. Have you got that?'

'Yes, sir,' she said, giving me a mock salute. 'Message received and understood.'

'I'm serious, Jaydie. I don't want you or anyone else getting hurt.'

'We know what we're doing, Trav. Trust me.' She stared into my eyes. 'We don't need anyone to hold our hands. We know *exactly* what we're doing.'

I'd always known how tough and smart Jaydie was – she had to be to survive on the Slade – but what I hadn't realised until now, as I sat there looking back into her eyes, was just *how* determined and capable she was. It was such a powerful sense that I could feel it drilling into me, filling me with a feeling I didn't quite understand. Whether she'd always been so strong, and I just hadn't realised it before, or whether this was another part of that indefinable change in her that I'd noticed the other day in her flat, I didn't really know. All I knew for sure was that, at that precise moment, it was impossible *not* to believe in her.

'Why are you looking at me like that?' she asked, frowning at me.

'Like what?'

'Like you've just had an epiphany or something.'

'Epiphany?'

'It means a sudden revelation.'

I grinned, shaking my head. 'I was just thinking about something, that's all.'

'That's the problem with you.'

'What?'

'You think too much.'

'You think so?'

She smiled. 'I know so.'

36

I didn't intend to sleep for the rest of the day, all I really meant to do was go home for a few hours and get some rest – take a shower, spend some time on my own, just hang around doing nothing for a while. But I suppose I must have been a lot more tired than I thought, because as soon as I went up to my room and lay down on my bed, I was out like a light.

While I was sleeping like a baby, Jaydie – as she told me later – was busy doing her stuff.

Like most of the so-called gangs and crews on the various estates in and around Barton, Jaydie's 'posse' wasn't really an organised gang at all, just a group of friends who hung around together and looked out for each other. There were a few 'proper' criminal gangs – like Dee Dee's crew and Joss Malik's boys – and these gangs *were* organised, at least to a certain extent, but a lot of what passed for 'gang activity' on the estates wasn't structured or coordinated at all. It was just groups of kids who stuck together and sometimes had fights with other groups of kids. They might give themselves names that gave the impression they were genuine organised gangs – *Young Beacon Boys* or *Barton Bloodset* or whatever – but according to Mason, it was the crews without names that you really had to worry about, the ones that didn't have to try to impress anyone.

Jaydie's 'posse' was exactly what she'd told me it was – just a little group of trusted friends. There were only about fifteen of them. Some of them were the same age as her, but most of them were older. They didn't call themselves anything, they didn't go looking for trouble, and although the older girls were generally more respected – and listened to – than the younger ones, there weren't any leaders as such. They were simply a group of friends who'd grown up together and were always there for each other.

When Jaydie had first explained her plan to me, she'd told me that although she was only going to need help from two or three of the girls, she'd still have to tell the rest of them what she was up to. The problem with that – from my point of view – was that there was no way of explaining things without revealing Dee Dee's relationship with Bull. To me, that sounded far too risky.

'What if one of the girls tells someone else?' I'd said to Jaydie. 'If it got out *now* that Dee Dee's in with Bull, and he found out about it, it could ruin everything.'

'It won't get out,' Jaydie assured me. 'I can absolutely guarantee it. Whenever we talk together, if one of us reveals something that we don't want anyone outside the group to know – whatever it is, and for whatever reason we want it kept secret – it never goes any further. And when I say never, I mean never.'

I still didn't like the idea of putting my trust in people I'd never even met, but Jaydie was adamant that that was how it had to be, so I'd told her to go ahead, and that's what she'd done. She'd told the whole group about Dee Dee, and they'd all agreed to keep it secret, and then she'd taken aside the two girls she'd chosen to carry out her plan, and they'd sat down together and worked out precisely how they were going to go about it.

The first part of the plan – getting the recorder into the phone box – was relatively simple. It was all a matter of timing. As Jaydie had explained to me, Dee Dee had a network of kids whose one and only job was to keep an eye on the phone box and make sure no one went near it. So in order to plant the recorder without being spotted, Jaydie had to somehow distract the kid who was watching it. The problem was, it was impossible to tell which kid was on duty – and where they were – at any given time. Jaydie's solution to this problem was brilliantly simple. She planned to create a distraction that was so spectacular that no one on the entire estate could ignore it, so it didn't matter who was watching the phone box or where they were watching it from. Whoever and wherever they were, they'd be distracted.

The girl Jaydie chose to help her with this was a somewhat troubled sixteen-year-old called Della Hoyt. Even by Slade standards, Della had had a really tough life, and while she'd never actually been convicted of anything, she had a long record of arrests and cautions for relatively minor offences – shoplifting, possession of drugs, threatening behaviour. According to Jaydie, she wasn't really a 'bad' girl, she just had a lot of emotional problems that sometimes got too much for her. Della had learned all about explosives from her older brother Eric who'd been a militant animal-rights activist. Eric had died when Della was fourteen, accidentally blowing himself up during a raid on a cosmetics company that tested their products on animals.

When Jaydie asked Della if she could produce an explosion that was big enough and loud enough to be heard all over the estate, but that wouldn't hurt anyone or cause any damage, Della said simply, 'No problem. When do you want it and where?'

The 'when' was today, Tuesday, at precisely midday; the 'where' was a patch of wasteground at the back of the block of flats where Dee Dee lived.

So, at exactly one minute to twelve, Jaydie was sitting on a brick wall about fifty metres away from the phone box. She had her mobile in her hand and was going through the motions of writing a text. In reality, she was just staring at the clock on her phone, counting down the seconds. At 11.59 and thirty seconds, she got to her feet and started ambling towards the phone box. She'd already done a trial run, timing how long it took to get from the brick wall to the phone box, so as long as Della's timing was spot on, everything should be OK. Jaydie's heart was beating hard now, and she was finding it really hard to keep looking inconspicuous. *You're just strolling along*, she kept telling herself. *You're not going anywhere in particular, you're not up to anything, you're just wandering across the square . . .*

She was about two metres away from the phone box when the explosion went off, an almighty *KA-BOOM!* that shook the ground and sent a thick cloud of black smoke billowing into the air. Even though she was expecting it, the sudden explosion still gave Jaydie a shock, but she recovered almost immediately and rapidly went to work – nipping quickly into the phone box, taking the recorder from her pocket, crouching down and fixing it to the underside of a metal ledge, right at the back so it was completely out of sight.

She was in and out in less than five seconds.

Job done.

To avoid looking suspicious, she headed off towards the patch of wasteground, joining the throng of residents who were already pouring out of their flats to find out what the hell was going on.

At the exact moment the explosion went off, the second part of Jaydie's plan was reaching its conclusion. The friend she'd picked to carry out this part of the operation was the oldest one of the group, a nineteen-year-old girl called Jazz Lipka. Jazz was chosen for a number of reasons – she was fearless, well-connected, brimming with self-confidence – but above all she was astonishingly beautiful.

'I mean, compared to Jazz,' Jaydie told me, 'Angelina Jolie looks like a bag lady.'

Jazz had used her connections to get a message to Dee Dee that she had something really important to tell him, something that she could only tell him in person. If it had been anyone else, there was a good chance that Dee Dee would have either ignored the message or simply refused to see her. But another reason that Jazz had been chosen for this part of the plan was the fact that she was in a long-term relationship with another girl, and that everyone on the estate, including Dee Dee, knew about it. As Jazz herself said, 'Dee Dee's the kind of idiotically arrogant Neanderthal who just can't accept that a woman would rather be with another woman than with a hunk of man like him. Morons like Dee Dee think of girls like me as a challenge. He won't pass up the chance to sway me with his manly charms.'

So a meeting was arranged – and even for Jazz it took a lot of string-pulling to make sure the meeting took place at midday on Tuesday – and at 11.55 she showed up at Dee Dee's flat. She knew she'd be checked for weapons and wires, so she had the tracker hidden under a clip in her hair, which was further covered up by a baseball cap. As she'd guessed, Dee Dee's bodyguards were hired for their muscle not their minds, and although they checked her cap, it never occurred to them to look any further.

At 11.58 she was finally shown into Dee Dee's flat.

'And there he was,' she told Jaydie later, 'sitting in a red velvet chair, smoking a cigarette and drinking brandy, surrounded by a bunch of wannabe girlfriends and fawning hangers-on, like he was some kind of big-shot gangster rapper or something.'

In case things went wrong – say the explosion didn't go off, or Dee Dee wasn't wearing his usual suit – Jazz had a back-up plan. She was going to tell him that she'd heard from a friend, who'd heard from another friend, that Joss Malik was planning a raid on his flat. And if Dee Dee asked her for more details, she was going to plead ignorance and tell him that that was all she knew, but that she'd do her best to find out more.

In the end though, she didn't need Plan B, because just as Dee Dee asked her what she wanted to see him about, the explosion went off. By now Jazz had taken the tracker from her hair clip and was holding it out of sight in her hand, and she was standing less than a metre away from Dee Dee. At the sound of the explosion – *KA-BOOM!* – Jazz let out a frightened scream and stumbled forward, falling into Dee Dee's lap. She just had time to slip the tracker into his top pocket before he cursed at her and pushed her off, and then all hell broke loose. Dee Dee jumped out of his chair and was immediately surrounded by his bodyguards, some of his wannabe girlfriends started to panic, screaming and running around the flat like headless chickens, and while all this was going on, Jazz was completely forgotten. She got to her feet, smiling quietly to herself, and casually walked out of the flat.

Job done.

37

I woke up to the sound of my mobile ringing. For a moment or two I had no idea where I was, or what time it was, or even what day it was. It was a bit of a scary feeling, but it was one that I'd kind of got used to over the last few months. Even though I felt completely at home at Nan and Grandad's, I still sometimes woke up thinking I was back at my old house in Kell Cross, back in my old bedroom, with Mum and Dad downstairs . . .

This wasn't quite the same kind of feeling, but it was similar enough for me to know how to deal with it. All I had to do was stay calm and wait, and eventually my brain would clear and I'd realise where I was. And after about five seconds, that's exactly what happened. I knew *where* I was now – in my room at Nan and Grandad's – but I still didn't know what time it was. I fumbled for my still-ringing phone and glanced at the clock. It was 16.08.

'Hello,' I said, answering the phone.

'Travis?' a familiar voice said. 'It's Kendal. Are you all right?'

'Yeah,' I muttered, rubbing sleep from my eyes. 'Yeah, I'm fine.'

'I heard about your friend,' he said. 'The one who got beaten up or something? How's she doing?'

'Not too bad. She's still in hospital, but hopefully she'll be out soon.'

'Right . . .'

I could sense his hesitation, and I guessed he was wondering if he had to offer any more sympathies, or if he could just get on with what he really wanted to say.

'Don't worry,' I told him, putting him out of his misery, 'I'll be back at school tomorrow.'

'Great,' he said. 'I mean, I didn't want to pressure you or anything, I was just, you know . . .'

'Yeah, it's all right. I understand.'

'So I'll see you tomorrow then. Cup Final day.'

'Yep.'

'OK. Well, I hope your friend gets better soon.'

'Yeah.'

Like you care, I thought, ending the call.

There was an unopened text on my phone. I clicked on it and saw that it was from Jaydie: *all done*, it read, *no probs. call u wen I hear anyfin. jx*

I texted back – *brilliant! travx*

It was now 16.14.

Time to go to the hospital.

On the way into town, I decided that it was finally time to tell Grandad what I'd found out about Gloria. I still wasn't sure about letting him know what Jaydie and I were up to, mainly because I knew how he'd react if I did. He'd say it was too risky, too dangerous, and he'd do everything in his power to make sure we didn't go ahead with it. But, the way I saw it, we *had* to go ahead with it. It was the only way to bring down Dee Dee and make him pay for what he'd done to Courtney. The trouble with that though, the thing that made me a bit scared of *not* telling Grandad what we were doing – and also, if I'm completely honest, a bit scared of actually doing it – was that Grandad was already so messed up with guilt about Courtney, blaming himself for not looking after her, that if anything happened to me or Jaydie, or anyone else for that matter, it was just going to make things even worse for him. More misplaced guilt, more weight on his shoulders, more burdens to bear. I couldn't do that to him, could I? But at the same time I couldn't just sit around doing nothing either. I couldn't wrap myself up in cotton wool for the rest of my life just so that Grandad wouldn't have to feel guilty if anything happened to me, could I?

Or maybe I could . . . ?

I just didn't know.

And maybe that was why I'd decided to tell Grandad about Gloria. Because it made me feel that at least I was telling him *some*thing, I wasn't hiding everything from him. He wouldn't *like* finding out about Gloria, but at least it wouldn't be something he'd have to feel guilty about.

*

Nan wasn't there when I arrived at the hospital, she was still at Courtney's house looking after her mum until the night carer arrived, but Grandad wasn't on his own. When I walked into Courtney's room, he was sitting on one side of the bed, Courtney was sitting up in bed with a tray of food in her lap, and on the other side of the bed, to my utter surprise and dismay, was Gloria.

'Hi, Travis,' Courtney said, smiling through a mouthful of food. 'Have you had a good day?'

'Uh, yeah, thanks,' I muttered, trying to hide my disappointment. 'How are you doing? You look a lot brighter than you did this morning.'

'I'm as bright as a button,' she said breezily. 'And raring to go. I'm seeing the doc in half an hour, and hopefully he's going to let me go home.'

'That's wonderful news.'

'He didn't say you could go home,' Grandad corrected her. 'He just said that he'll see how it goes and *maybe* you can leave tomorrow.'

Courtney grinned. 'Doctors never mean what they say. Just you wait and see, I'll be out of here by tonight.'

I glanced at Gloria. 'I didn't expect to see you here.'

'Why not?'

I shrugged. 'I don't know . . . I suppose I just thought you'd be keeping things going at the office.'

'I've been "keeping things going at the office" all day, thank you very much,' she said. 'The office can do without me for an hour or two.'

'She brought me some grapes,' Courtney said.

How original, I thought.

'That's nice,' I said.

'You want one?' Courtney said. 'They're on the cupboard. Help yourself.'

It was such a relief to see that Courtney was looking so much better, and that – on the surface at least – she seemed to be getting back to her normal self. I should have been really pleased. And I *was*, for her. But Gloria's presence had put a dampener on everything for me. I didn't want her to be here. She didn't belong here. It was like she was *with* us, and everyone was treating her as part of the family, but I knew what she *really* was. I knew she was a traitor, and I wanted to scream it out loud and let everyone know – *SHE'S A LIAR! A FAKE! A SHAM! SHE'S A DIRTY DOUBLE-CROSSING RAT!*

But I knew I couldn't say anything. Not now. Not here.

When Nan arrived at just gone five, I hoped – and expected – that Gloria would leave. But she didn't. She just sat there, smiling pleasantly at Nan and making polite conversation. I could tell that Nan felt really uncomfortable. She didn't show it, and she was perfectly civil to Gloria, but she couldn't fool me. I knew what she was thinking. *What the hell is she doing here? Who does she think she is?*

Nan stayed for about twenty minutes, but when it became clear that Gloria wasn't going anywhere, she made her apologies to Courtney, explaining that she was really tired, and started getting ready to go.

'I'll come with you, Nan,' I said.

We said our goodbyes to Grandad and Gloria, and we both gave Courtney a gentle hug, and then we just left them to it. We found a taxi on the rank outside that was big enough to take my bike, and we set off home.

On any other Tuesday night I would have gone to my boxing club, but although it probably would have done me a power of good to spend a couple of hours in the gym – pummelling away on the heavy punchbags, working the speedball, maybe a few rounds of sparring in the ring – there was something more important I had to do that night. I *had* to tell Nan what I'd found out about Gloria. It was really wearing me down having to keep it to myself, and as I seemed to have a problem telling Grandad – forever finding excuses not to – I'd decided that Nan was my best bet. Besides, if anyone deserved to know the truth, it was Nan. She was the one who'd suspected Gloria from the start, so maybe it was only fitting that she found out the truth about her first.

All I had to do now was wait for the right moment to tell her.

I thought that moment had come when Grandad rang around seven to let Nan know that Dr Adams had decided to keep Courtney in for one more night, just to be on the safe side, and that he was staying the night with her again.

'Is Gloria still there?' Nan asked him.

She listened to his reply, then said, 'You *know* why.'

They talked for a few more minutes, and when Nan eventually put down the phone she didn't look very happy at all.

'*Is* she still there?' I asked her.

'Not according to your grandad,' Nan muttered. 'He *said* she left half an hour ago.'

'He wouldn't lie to you, Nan,' I said gently. 'You know that.'

She glared at me, and just for a moment I thought she was going to snap at me and tell me that it was none of my business, but almost immediately the anger faded from her eyes and she came over, put her arms round me, and gave me a big hug.

'I'm sorry, love,' she said tearfully. 'I'm just being silly. I know your grandad wouldn't lie to me. It's just . . . it's just . . .'

She gave a little gulp then and started sobbing, and for the next minute or two we just stood there hugging each other tightly. Despite all the sadness and tears, it actually felt kind of nice – just me and Nan, on our own, not talking about anything, just *being* together – and I began to think it would be a shame to spoil things by bringing up the subject of Gloria. I knew I had to though. I couldn't put it off any longer.

'Listen, Nan,' I started to say. 'About Gloria—'

'Not now, eh?' she said softly, letting go of me and wiping her eyes. 'I'm sick to death of thinking about Gloria Nightingale.' She smiled sadly at me. 'Let's just try and have a nice normal evening together, shall we?'

'Yeah, but I need to tell you—'

'*Please*, Travis,' she pleaded, 'I really can't deal with it at the moment.' She sighed. 'Look, love, I know I should have talked to you about all this business with Gloria and Grandad and me, and I'm really sorry you had to find out about it from Granny Nora instead of me.'

'How do you know I talked to her? Did she tell you?'

Nan shook her head. 'I just put two and two together.'

'She was only trying to help,' I said defensively.

'It's all right, Trav. I don't *mind* you talking to her about it, I'm just sorry you felt you had to. If I hadn't been so wound up with my own stupid feelings . . .' She paused, letting out a long and weary sigh, and I could see that she was really struggling – her shoulders were slumped, her eyes were heavy, she was so frail and exhausted she could barely stand up straight.

'It's all right, Nan,' I said, putting my arm round her shoulders. 'We don't have to talk about anything now.'

'I've just been so worried about everything,' she muttered. 'Courtney, her poor mother, Grandad, you . . . Gloria. I'm sorry, Travis, but the last thing I need right now is a conversation about that woman.'

'You go and sit down,' I told her. 'I'll put the telly

on and make us something to eat.'

She smiled at me, not so sadly this time. 'We'll talk tomorrow, I promise. Grandad will be home by the time you get back from school. We can all sit down together and discuss things properly. Is that OK?'

'Of course it is,' I said, ushering her into the front room. 'Now, what do you want to eat?'

'Thanks, Travis, but I'm not really hungry.'

I gave her a serious look. 'If I'm looking after you, you're going to eat something reasonably healthy at least once a day. Understood?'

'Yes, sir,' she said, grinning at me.

I smiled. 'How does beans on toast sound?'

She laughed.

It felt OK.

For the next few hours we did what Nan had suggested – we had a nice normal evening together. We ate our beans on toast, I made us some tea, we watched some rubbish on TV together. And the only things we talked about were things that didn't really mean anything – my investigation into the changing-room thefts, TV celebrities, schoolwork, exams . . .

It was fine.

Perfectly nice and normal.

At around ten o'clock, Nan thanked me for looking after her, said goodnight, and went upstairs to bed. I wasn't tired at all – I'd been asleep most of the day – so I just went up to my room and sat around, not doing anything in particular, until about one o'clock in the morning. I played a few games of computer chess, read a book for a while, watched some old *CSI* repeats on my little TV . . . but mostly I just sat around thinking.

I had a lot to think about.

38

At one thirty on Wednesday afternoon I was sitting on the bench with the rest of the substitutes waiting for the Under-15 Twin Town Cup Final to kick off. Kell Cross Secondary v Slade Lane Comprehensive. Although we were the home team, Slade Lane were the odds-on favourites to win. As far as I could remember, we'd never beaten Slade, our best result being a 0–0 draw two years ago, and that was only because most of Slade's regular first team had been taken ill with a stomach bug.

The weather was surprisingly OK. It was cold, but it wasn't raining, and the sky was bright and clear. 'Cup Final weather', as Mosh Akram had noted while we were getting changed. A massive crowd had turned up for the game: hundreds of Kell Cross kids, and almost as many Slade Lane supporters; teachers and parents from both schools (although there weren't that many Slade Lane parents); teachers and kids from the German and French schools; dozens of reporters, photographers, and sponsors, and quite a few scouts and representatives from both Premier League and lower league clubs. As well as all the kids and teachers I knew, there were a few other familiar faces in the crowd too. Evie Johnson was there with her boyfriend Daniel. Royce Devon was there too, this time without Bianca. I guessed Jaydie was right – he'd got what he wanted from her, and now he'd dumped her. There were a few other faces from the Slade I recognised too, including the kid I'd knocked out in the square when he'd tried to take my phone. His jaw was still bruised and swollen, and I was pretty sure that if he spotted me – which he didn't seem to have done yet – he was bound to recognise me, and he might even be tempted to try getting his own back. I doubted it though. I'd already bettered him once, and this time I was on *my* home ground, and I wasn't outnumbered either. Revenge is a powerful emotion though, and it doesn't always listen to reason – as I knew from my own experience – and in view of that I made a mental note to keep half an eye on the kid with the busted-up jaw, just in case he was stupid enough to try something.

The teams were getting ready to kick off now, and there was a real sense of excitement in the air. I was feeling kind of excited myself, to be honest. But, of course, I had other things on my mind as well as the actual match.

I'd come in early to check on the motion sensors in the changing rooms, and they both seemed to be working OK. The car park was so full that I couldn't see the changing-room doors from the subs bench, but I knew that Mr Wells was guarding the home dressing room again and Mr Ayres was outside the away dressing room. This time, both rooms had been thoroughly checked to make sure that no one was hiding inside before the doors were locked.

I'd called Jaydie earlier to check if she'd heard anything from the voice-activated recorder yet, but she hadn't. And, as she told me, she would have let me know if she had.

I'd also been keeping an eye on Dee Dee's whereabouts, following the tracker Jazz had planted on him on my mobile. I'd set up the tracker to show as a green dot on the screen. So far the green dot had been moving around the estate quite a lot, but it hadn't gone anywhere near the phone box.

I'd heard from Grandad that Courtney had finally been discharged, but only on the condition that she spent the rest of the day at home. So she'd gone back to her house, Grandad had gone into the office, and here I was, sitting on the subs bench, wondering what the day was going to bring.

The ref blew his whistle and Slade Lane kicked off. They immediately gave the ball to Quade Wilson, Evie Johnson's half-brother, and he set off on a mazy run towards our goal, skipping past four Kell Cross players as if they weren't there. Although I'd heard how good he was, this was the first time I'd actually seen him play, and as I watched him glide past our defensive midfielder, leaving him rooted to the spot, I shook my head in amazement. He was *unbelievably* good. The way he looked, and moved with the ball, reminded me a lot of Lionel Messi. He was quite short and slight, but deceptively powerful, and however much he jinked and turned, he never lost control of the ball. It was an awesome thing to see.

He was approaching our back four now, and although he had teammates either side of him, it looked as if he was going all the way on his own. On the touchline, Mr Jago was yelling at the top of his voice – 'CLOSE HIM DOWN! GET TIGHT! CLOSE HIM *DOWN*!' Quade was about two metres outside our penalty area now, and both our centre backs – Kendal and another big lunk of a kid called Des Bowker – were closing in on him. I saw Kendal say something to Bowker, and as Bowker slowed down and backed off to the right, Kendal launched himself at Quade. He clattered into him like a bulldozer, knocking him clean off his feet, and everyone could see that he'd made no attempt to play the ball. As the ref blew his whistle, and Quade just lay there on his back, gasping for breath, the Slade supporters went crazy – booing and jeering – and every one of Quade's teammates, including the goalkeeper, rushed over towards Kendal. He backed away, holding up his hands in apology, trying to make out that he hadn't meant to hurt Quade, he'd simply mistimed his tackle. It didn't fool the Slade players for a second, and they all piled in after Kendal, which in turn provoked all of our players, and both teams ended up in a mass scuffle on the edge of the penalty area. The referee and his assistants did their best to calm everything down, and after about a minute or two they finally succeeded. There was no doubt that Kendal's tackle – or so-called tackle – deserved a straight red card, but somehow he managed to get away with just a yellow. To add insult to injury, Slade's left back was also shown a yellow card for swearing at one of the ref's assistants in the heat of the scuffle.

As everything settled down, and players from both sides began getting ready for the free kick, I saw Kendal glance over at Mr Jago and flash him a quick smile. Jago gave him a discreet nod in return.

My mind flashed back to Jago's last-minute team talk in the dressing room before the game. He'd gathered us all round, told us to shut up and listen, and then reminded us one more time of the game plan.

'Right,' he'd said, 'we all know this Wilson kid can play, and if we try and outplay him, he's just going to make us look stupid. But remember what I told you: he might be a genius, but he's got no bottle. He cracks under pressure. So what do we do?'

'Put him under pressure,' Kendal had said.

'Right. And how do we do that?'

'We get stuck into him.'

Jago nodded. 'Every time he gets the ball, we make sure he gets hurt. Hit him hard, and keep hitting him hard. But spread it around, OK? Take it in turns. And once you've got a yellow, lay off the dirty stuff. We can't afford to go down to ten men. Is that clear?'

I wasn't the only one who hated Jago's 'tactics' – there were at least another five or six in the squad who'd rather lose the game than play it Jago's way – but none of us voiced our opinions. I suppose we all realised that even if we did speak up, it wouldn't make any difference. Jago wouldn't change his mind, all he'd do was kick us off the squad. So we all just kept our mouths shut.

The free kick was about to be taken now. It was right on the edge of the penalty area, and Quade Wilson had recovered enough to take it himself. He placed the ball carefully, took three steps back, and then stood there, with his hands on his hips and his eyes on the goal, waiting for the whistle. The ref blew, and Quade just stepped up to the ball and almost lazily swung his foot at it. He didn't seem to hit it with any power, but it left his boot like a rocket. Instead of trying to curl it round the wall, he went for a straight up and over dipping shot. It very nearly worked. It easily cleared the wall, then dipped wickedly towards the goal. It moved so fast that our goalie never even moved, he just stood there and watched as it arrowed down towards the top right-hand corner, hit the top of the bar, and flew off behind the goal.

The crossbar rattled, the crowd went 'Ooohh!', and everyone on the bench started breathing again.

'It's going to be a long eighty minutes,' Mosh said.

'Seventy-four minutes,' I corrected him.

'Oh, right,' he said, grinning at me. 'Well, that's not so bad then, is it?'

The rest of the first half carried on as it had begun. Quade Wilson got hacked down almost every time he got the ball, and Slade Lane quickly resorted to the same kind of tactics. Their players knew every dirty trick in the book, and as well as the more obvious stuff – shirt-pulling, sly elbows to the face, over-the-top tackles – they were also well-versed in the darker arts of the game. Faking injuries, winding up their opponents, spitting . . . they didn't stop at anything. Despite all that, there was no denying that they played some excellent football too, and as the game went on, we kept getting pushed back into our own half, until eventually we were virtually camped on our own eighteen-yard line with ten players behind the ball. So even when our solitary striker did get the ball, he was completely on his own, massively outnumbered, with no support and nowhere to go.

Because both sides were really getting stuck into each other, there were lots of stoppages for injuries, some of which were quite serious. With half-time approaching, Kell Cross had already lost two players to injuries. Slade had also used two of their substitutes, and one of their midfielders had been hobbling for the last ten minutes, and it didn't look as if he'd last much longer.

It was, to put it mildly, a game of attrition.

It wasn't much fun to watch. No goals, very little goal-mouth action, just twenty-two kids kicking lumps out of each other. The only good thing about it was that, miraculously, we weren't losing.

As the whistle blew for half-time, and a chorus of boos went up, I turned off the motion sensors, got up off the bench, and started heading back to the changing rooms. I was about halfway there when my mobile rang.

It was Jaydie.

'Hey, Jaydie,' I said. 'How's it going?'

'Dee Dee just called Ronnie Bull,' she said excitedly. 'They're meeting later on this afternoon.'

'What time?'

'Five o'clock.'

'Where?'

'Dee Dee just said five o'clock at the usual place. He must have meant the multi-storey car park.'

'Not necessarily.'

'Probably though.'

'Yeah,' I agreed, doing some quick calculations in my head. The match should finish around three fifteen, ten minutes to get changed, half an hour to get into town . . . as long as they *were* meeting at the car park, I should have plenty of time.

'Did they talk about anything else?' I asked Jaydie.

'Nope, nothing at all. Just "five o'clock at the usual place", and that was it. Where do you want to meet?'

'What?'

'Where do you want us to meet?'

'We can't do this together, Jaydie.'

'Why the hell not?' she said angrily. 'It was *my* plan. I set it all up. You can't just shut me out of it now.'

'I'm not shutting you out—'

'No? It sounds like it to me.'

'Look, I've got to follow him using the tracker, OK? If he's not meeting Bull at the car park, I don't know where I'm going to have to go, and I won't know until the last minute. I'm not going to have time to keep calling you and trying to work out where to meet—'

'Why can't we just meet up now? Then you won't have to keep calling me, will you?'

'I'm at the Cup Final now,' I explained. 'I've got this thing I'm working on.'

'What thing?'

'I told you, the thefts from the changing rooms—'

'Who cares about *that*? Just leave it.'

'I can't just leave it.'

'Why not?'

'Because I gave my word that I'd do it.'

'Right,' she said sourly. 'And that's more important than taking down Dee Dee, is it?'

'It's not that simple, Jaydie. It's not just a matter of . . . hello? Jaydie? Are you still there?'

She wasn't there.

The line had gone dead.

She'd hung up.

I tried calling her back, but all I got was her voicemail.

'Damn it,' I muttered.

I wondered then if staying here until the end of the match was the right thing to do after all. Maybe I *should* just leave it, as Jaydie had said. Taking down Dee Dee *was* far more important than catching a petty thief, and it wasn't as if I owed anything to Jago or Kendal, or even to the school.

I checked Dee Dee's tracker on my mobile. He was still on the estate.

I called Jaydie again. *Hi, this is Jaydie, leave a message.*

'You ready?' I heard Mr Jago say.

I looked up and saw him striding towards me, heading back to the pitch. Half-time was already over, I realised. The teams were back out and the changing rooms were locked again.

'Come on, Travis,' Jago said, guiding me back to the subs bench. 'The second half's just about to start. Are the sensors back on again?'

'Uh, yeah,' I mumbled, ending the call to Jaydie and switching screens on my mobile. 'I'm just doing it now.'

'Chop-chop,' he said, patting me on the shoulder. And with that he marched off to his position and started clapping his hands and shouting out encouragement. 'LET'S GO, KELL CROSS! COME ON, WE CAN WIN THIS THING!'

I sighed heavily and sat down.

It looked like I was stuck here whether I liked it or not.

'Sorry, Jaydie,' I muttered under my breath.

'What?' Mosh said.

'Nothing.'

Mosh frowned at me.

I shrugged.

The whistle blew and the game kicked off. The ball went out to our winger, he tried to go past a Slade midfielder, the midfielder hacked him down.

Here we go again, I thought.

39

The second half had only been going for about five minutes when, to the shock and surprise of everyone, and completely against the run of play, Kell Cross took the lead. Even the goal scorer – a kid called Nicky Beale – admitted later that it was pretty fluky. It came from a long punt upfield by our goalie. Nicky was on his own, as usual, the only Kell Cross player in Slade's half, and as the high ball came towards him, instead of trying to win the header he took a chance and slipped round the goal-side of the Slade centre back, hoping that he might misdirect his header or something. As the centre back glanced round at Nicky to see what he was doing, his feet got tangled up and he stumbled over, missing the ball altogether. The other centre back was covering him, but as the ball bounced towards Nicky, he made the decision to back off rather than closing Nicky down. It wasn't a bad decision. Nicky was on his own, still about thirty metres out, and there were two more defenders between him and the goal. So there shouldn't really have been any danger.

Nicky said afterwards that the only reason he went for the shot was that he was too tired to do anything else.

'I'd been running around on my own for the whole of the first half,' he said. 'I was absolutely knackered.'

So he just waited for the bouncing ball to come down

and swung his boot at it. It was the kind of effort that ninety-nine times out of a hundred goes flying up into the air and misses the target by miles, but this time Nicky caught the ball perfectly with a powerful looping volley that sailed up and over the astonished Slade goalkeeper and smashed into the top right-hand corner of the goal. There was a stunned silence for a second, no one quite sure they could believe what had just happened, and then all at once the home crowd erupted and the Kell Cross players went crazy, whooping and yelling, chasing after Nicky and throwing themselves all over him.

It was unbelievable. We'd actually *scored*. 1–0 to Kell Cross.

We were beating Slade Lane in the Twin Town Cup Final!

I couldn't help getting caught up in all the excitement – jumping up off the bench with everyone else, shouting and cheering – and for the next ten minutes, as the match suddenly burst into life, I got so drawn into it that I almost forgot about everything else – the changing-room thefts, Dee Dee and Ronnie Bull, Jaydie, Gloria . . . all I could think about was the game, and the possibility that we might actually win it.

Slade Lane were going all out for an equaliser now, throwing everyone forward, and we were having to defend with our backs to the wall. It was still a very physical game, but a lot of the dirty stuff had been forgotten now, with both teams concentrating on the actual football.

But ten minutes after we'd scored, the violence suddenly flared up again. It happened at a Slade corner kick, and the penalty box was so crowded, with everyone doing the usual pushing and shoving, that it was hard to tell what really happened. Kendal claimed later that as the corner was taken and the ball came in, one of the Slade centre backs – who'd come up for the corner – deliberately elbowed him in the face. It was a vicious blow, breaking Kendal's nose and loosening one of his teeth, and as the blood streamed down his face, he doubled over in agony with his head in his hands. Apparently the referee didn't see what happened, but as the corner kick was cleared by one of our defenders, and the rest of the players started to clear the box, Kendal went over to the guy who'd elbowed him and punched him in the head. The guy went down as if he'd been shot, moaning and clutching at his face, and the referee blew his whistle and immediately pointed to the penalty spot. Kendal started shouting at the ref, complaining that he'd been elbowed first, but the ref just reached into his pocket and pulled out a red card. Then bedlam broke out. Kendal refused to go off, pointing out his broken nose to the ref, the crowd started booing and jeering, and both managers rushed onto the pitch with their first-aid kits to tend to their injured players. While Mr Jago worked on Kendal's broken nose, he also started arguing with the ref, and then Slade's manager joined in, shouting and cursing at Mr Jago *and* the ref . . .

And that's when the alarm on my mobile went off.

40

Although I partly rationalised my decision to deal with the alarm on my own by telling myself that Mr Jago had enough to deal with at the moment as it was – arguing with the ref and Slade's manager, dealing with Kendal's injury – the truth was that I didn't *want* him to know that the alarm had gone off. The thefts from the changing rooms was one of the things I'd spent so much time thinking about the night before, and after taking everything into consideration, I was pretty sure I knew who the culprit was. And if I was right, the situation was going to require delicate handling, which meant keeping Mr Jago as far away from it as possible. He couldn't be delicate if his life depended on it.

As I got up and started heading for the changing rooms, Mosh called out after me, 'Where you going, Trav?'

'Changing rooms,' I told him. 'I forgot something.'

'Jago'll kill you if he comes back and finds you gone.'

I glanced over at the penalty area where the mass argument was still going on.

'It looks like he's going to be a while yet,' I told Mosh. 'I'll be back before him.'

There was actually a good chance that I *wouldn't* be back before Jago, and as I carried on towards the changing rooms, I realised that he was going to want to know why I hadn't told him the alarm had gone off, and I'd better start thinking of a reason.

I was hoping that my theory about the thief was wrong, but when I got to the changing rooms and saw that the home dressing-room door was locked and there was no sign of Mr Wells anywhere, I pretty much knew I was right. I looked back at the football pitch. The ruckus was still going on. I reached up to the door lock and keyed in that day's four-digit entry code (Jago had given it to me earlier on), then I opened the door and went inside.

I *was* right.

When I entered the dressing room, Mr Wells was standing by the row of coat hooks going through the pockets of someone's jacket. His head snapped round as he heard me coming in, and for a fraction of a second he froze – his hand still in the jacket pocket, his eyes wide open in shock, his face visibly paling. I didn't say anything, I just stood there staring at him. His eyes blinked rapidly as he took his hand out of the jacket and stepped away from the coat hooks, and he gave me a nervous smile.

'Goodness *me*, Travis,' he spluttered, 'you gave me a real shock there for a second . . .' He glanced anxiously at the jacket, then turned back to me. 'I hope you don't think I was . . . well, you know . . . you see, the thing is, I was just . . .'

It was painful to see him struggling to come up with

an excuse, and when he looked down at the floor and let out a sigh of resignation, realising that it was hopeless, I was relieved that the charade was over.

'I'm sorry, Travis,' he said sadly, looking up at me. 'I know you're not a fool, and it's unforgivable of me to treat you like one.' He glanced over at the dressing-room door, then turned back to me. 'I assume Mr Jago gave you the entry code?'

I nodded.

He said, 'So I take it you've been working with him to catch the thief.'

I nodded again, then briefly told him about the motion sensors.

'Ah, I see,' he said. 'I had a feeling Mr Jago was up to something. I just wasn't sure what it was.' He looked at me. 'I think it's probably best if I hand myself in to him after the match. Is that acceptable to you? Of course, it's entirely up to you how you want to go about it, and I'll happily go along with whatever you say. I just thought it might make it easier for you if I were to give myself up.'

'You're not a thief, are you?' I said to him.

'I'm sorry?' he said, looking puzzled.

'I mean, I know you've been stealing stuff from the changing rooms over the last few months . . .'

'You know?'

'I worked it out last night. I should have realised before, really. I mean, the thief wasn't breaking in, so it *had* to be someone who knew the entry code, which narrowed it down to you, Mr Ayres, Mr Jago, or Kendal Price. Mr Jago and Kendal wouldn't have hired me to look into the thefts if it was one of them, which left either you or Mr Ayres. And when we caught you in here the other day, and you told Mr Jago that you'd only come in because you thought you'd heard someone in here . . . well, it just wasn't very convincing.'

He smiled. 'I'm not a very good liar, am I?'

'I just don't get it,' I said, shaking my head. 'I mean, you're *not* a thief, are you? You're a decent man. What on earth possessed you to start stealing things?'

'That's a good question, Travis. And I wish I knew the answer.' He sat down wearily on a bench. 'I suppose a psychoanalyst might say that I'm somehow trying to compensate for the guilt I feel about my son's death, or that I'm subconsciously punishing myself by acting out his wrongdoing, *his* thieving, that indirectly led to his death.'

'Do *you* think that's why you're doing it?' I asked.

'I have absolutely no idea,' he said emptily. 'It was just something that took hold of me . . . something I felt I *had* to do. I took no pleasure from it. It gave me no comfort. All it did was make me despise myself even more.' He shrugged. 'Perhaps *that* was why I did it . . .'

'You told me once that grief is something that gets inside you,' I reminded him. 'Something that's you, but *not* you. And whatever it wants you to do, there's nothing you can do to stop it.'

He looked at me. 'Did I say that?'

I nodded.

'Well,' he said, without a trace of bitterness in his voice, 'there might not have been anything *I* could do to stop myself stealing, but you've certainly put a stop to it.'

A distant roar went up from outside then, the sound of the crowd cheering and whooping. Mr Wells glanced at me and raised his eyebrows.

'Slade had a penalty,' I explained. 'That was either the home crowd cheering because they didn't score, or the Slade supporters celebrating because they did.'

Mr Wells just nodded. He wasn't particularly interested in football, and I don't think he really cared who won the game.

'So,' he said, 'do we agree it's best if I confess to Mr Jago myself?'

'He doesn't *have* to know,' I said.

Mr Wells furrowed his brow. 'I'm sorry, I don't understand.'

'You're a good teacher,' I told him. 'You actually care about the kids you teach. If you own up to the thieving, that's the end of your career, isn't it?'

'And so it should be.'

'Yeah, but what's the point? No one gains from you being sacked. You lose your job, and you'll never get another teaching job, and the school loses a good teacher.'

'I stole from my students,' he said firmly. 'That's unpardonable.'

'You didn't hurt anyone, did you?'

'Well, no, but—'

'Give yourself another chance,' I told him. 'I can forget it if you can. If it ever happens again, I'll obviously have to turn you in. But if you promise to stop, that's good enough for me.'

'What about Mr Jago?'

A voice suddenly boomed from the doorway. 'What *about* Mr Jago?'

We both turned and saw Jago standing there, hands on hips, glowering at us.

'The sensor went off by mistake,' I told him, thinking rapidly, wondering how much he'd overheard. 'I came straight over when the alarm went off and told Mr Wells I needed something from the dressing room. He didn't want to let me in, not after the last false alarm, but I told him it was really important. He was just worried what you'd think about him letting me in.' I glanced at Mr Wells. 'Isn't that right, Mr Wells?'

'Uh, yes . . .' he said, looking at Jago. 'I wasn't sure if I was doing the right thing or not.'

Jago glared at me. 'He knows about the sensors?'

Damn, I thought. I'd forgotten that Mr Wells wasn't supposed to know about them. 'The one in here started making a crackling noise,' I told Jago. 'There's something wrong with it. That's why it went off in error. Mr Wells thought there was something wrong with the air-freshener and he was going to take a look at it. He was bound to find the sensor, so I thought I might as well tell him about it.'

'You could have let me in on it, John,' Mr Wells said to Jago, playing along with the lie. 'You could have trusted me, you know.'

Jago sniffed. 'It wasn't a matter of trust, Ralph. We just thought that the fewer people who knew about it the better, that's all.'

I sighed quietly to myself, pretty sure now that Jago hadn't heard what we were talking about and that he'd swallowed my story.

'Anyway, look,' he said to me, 'forget about the bloody sensors for now, we need you back on the bench. Nicky Beale's gone off with a hamstring injury and we're running out of players.' He looked at Mr Wells. 'You might as well stay in here for the rest of the match. We'll sort out the sensors afterwards.'

'Right,' Mr Wells said. He turned to me then and looked me straight in the eye. 'Thank you, Travis.'

'No problem,' I told him.

'Come on, then,' Jago said to me. 'Let's get a move on.'

As I followed Mr Jago out of the dressing room and we started heading across the playing fields, I wondered briefly what was going to happen when he and Kendal realised that the thefts from the changing rooms had stopped. That was if Mr Wells *did* stop, of course, but I was pretty sure he would. So I'd know why the thieving had stopped, and so would Mr Wells, but all Jago and Kendal would know was that it wasn't happening any more. The question was, would they simply be relieved that we didn't have a thief any longer – no more potential embarrassment for the school – and would they be happy to leave it at that, or would they still carry on looking for answers? Who *was* the thief? Why had they stopped? Had we scared them off for good? Or were they just biding their time until things cooled down again?

I also found myself wondering what Jago and Kendal would think of me when they realised the thieving had ceased. Would they think I'd done a good job in frightening off the thief, or would they think I'd failed because I hadn't actually caught them?

I glanced at Mr Jago – striding along ahead of me like a crazed sergeant major, his eyes fixed manically on the match up ahead – and I thought to myself, *Look at him, he's half out of his mind. What do you care what he thinks or does about anything?*

'Did Slade score from the penalty?' I asked casually, trotting up behind him.

He grinned. 'Wilson got too clever. He tried to send our goalie the wrong way and then dink it down the middle, but he slipped on his run up and completely fluffed his shot. The ball barely reached the goal line.'

'So we're still winning?'

'Yep.' Jago glanced at his watch. 'Ten minutes to go. Plus added time.'

Just as he finished speaking, I looked up and saw Quade Wilson with the ball at his feet on the edge of our penalty area. Four Kell Cross defenders were in front of him, and the nearest Slade players – one to his left, another to his right – were both closely marked. Quade didn't seem to have any options. But then he took a step back, rolled the ball under his right foot, flipped it up into the air, and with virtually no back lift at all, volleyed it with the outside of his left foot. The ball swerved up and over the four defenders and curled into the net like a guided missile, and the Slade supporters went berserk.

Mr Jago let out a string of four-letter words, and when I looked at him – a bit taken aback by his language, to be honest – his face wasn't just red with anger, it was almost purple.

Yep, I thought, *he's definitely at* least *half out of his mind.*

I was going to ask him if he still thought Quade Wilson was 'too clever', but I thought if I did he'd probably explode, so I decided to keep my mouth shut.

Kell Cross 1, Slade 1.

Nine minutes and fifty seconds to go. Plus added time.

41

With Kendal having been sent off, we were down to ten men now, and we were basically playing four at the back and five in midfield, with all the midfielders taking up defensive positions. As well as Nicky Beale going off with a hamstring injury, we'd also lost our best attacking midfielder (ankle strain) and our right back (suspected concussion). Mosh Akram had gone on in place of the midfielder, and our substitute left back was playing at right back. Although the substitution rules for the Twin Town Cup tournament allowed for more subs than normal games (up to six from a squad of twenty-three), Mr Jago had decided in his wisdom that we didn't need a squad of twenty-three, and that five substitutes on the bench was more than enough. So now there were only two of us left: me and a kid called Paul Ryman. Ryman was an out-and-out goal poacher. A short, slightly chubby kid, he wasn't much good at anything except scoring goals. He couldn't pass the ball, couldn't dribble, couldn't tackle, and he was absolutely useless in the air. But put him in the six-yard box and he was almost guaranteed to get you a goal. Unfortunately for him, a goal poacher was the last thing we needed right now. All we were doing was trying desperately to hold on to the draw.

Because it got dark around four o'clock, and the

school didn't have any floodlights, there was no extra time scheduled for the Twin Town Cup Final. The rules were that if the score was level at full-time, the match would go straight to a penalty shoot-out. And that was our only hope. If Slade scored again now, the chances of us getting an equaliser were virtually non-existent. But if we could just hold on for another five minutes . . . well, anything can happen in a penalty shoot-out.

'CONCENTRATE, KELL CROSS!' Jago was shouting. 'KEEP YOUR DISCIPLINE, DON'T LOSE YOUR CONCENTRATION NOW!'

'It'd be a lot easier to concentrate if he didn't keep shouting at them all the time,' Paul Ryman said to me.

'Maybe you should go over and point that out to him,' I suggested.

Paul grinned.

I held my breath as another Slade corner kick came looping into our box. Their big centre back leapt into the air and met it with a thudding header that looked for a moment as if it was going into the top corner of the goal, but at the last second our goalie – Richie King – flew across the goal and tipped it over the bar for another corner.

I glanced at my mobile. It was almost three thirteen. There were two minutes of normal time to go, but the sending off and the resultant scuffle must have taken up at least ten minutes, if not longer, so if the ref was keeping time properly, there should be at least ten minutes' added time.

As Slade got ready to take the corner, I quickly switched to the tracker screen on my mobile. The green dot was moving quickly now, speeding away from Slade Lane. It looked like Dee Dee had left the estate and was driving (or being driven) into town. It was far too early for him to be going straight to his five o'clock meeting with Ronnie Bull, and I just hoped he was leaving now because he was going somewhere else before his meeting. If he wasn't, if he was leaving now because he was meeting Bull somewhere else, somewhere that was going to take him an hour and forty-five minutes to get to, there was no way I was going to be able to follow him.

'What's that?' Paul Ryman said, leaning over to look at my mobile. 'Is it some kind of game?'

'Uh, yeah, kind of,' I told him, quickly closing the screen.

'I'd put it away if I were you,' he said. 'If Jago catches you messing around on your mobile now, he'll flip his lid.'

I put my phone in my tracksuit pocket and turned my attention back to the game. The corner kick had just been taken, and as it swung into the six-yard box, Richie King shoved his way through the crowd of jostling players, leapt into the air, and caught it with both hands.

'WELL DONE, RICHIE!' Jago called out. 'NOW HOLD IT! *HOLD* IT! PLAY IT SHORT!'

Clutching the ball to his chest, Richie looked round, trying to find someone who was free. With the advantage of an extra man though, Slade had everyone marked. Richie began to panic, realising that if he didn't get rid of the ball soon, he might give away a free kick or get booked for wasting time. So instead of playing it short, he just booted it as far as he could upfield. It bounced once, just over the halfway line, and went straight to Slade's centre back.

'WHAT ARE YOU *DOING*?' Jago yelled. 'I SAID *HOLD* IT!'

Slade launched another attack, which ended with Mosh Akram tackling Slade's right-winger and putting the ball out for a throw-in. A Slade player hurried over to get the ball, and Mosh casually kicked it away. The ref booked him.

Slade launched another attack.

Then another, and another, and another . . .

We defended like demons – keeping ten men behind the ball, tackling hard, throwing bodies all over the place, clearing shots off the line. We committed fouls, we wasted time, and on the rare occasions when we did get the ball, we didn't even think about using it, we just took it into the corner and kept it there for as long as possible. Our supporters started whistling for full-time after about two minutes of added time, and after another few minutes Mr Jago began haranguing the referee.

'COME ON, REF! HOW MUCH LONGER? BLOW YOUR WHISTLE!'

The ref just ignored him, but as the period of added

time got closer to ten minutes, he started glancing at his watch and looking across at his assistants. The home crowd were really going crazy now, whistling and jeering, berating the ref, but despite all the pressure, he still didn't blow his whistle.

Out on the pitch, our players were getting increasingly annoyed with the referee too, and that – as it turned out – was their downfall. As we gave away yet another free kick – out on the right touchline, about thirty metres from goal – three or four of our players took their eyes off the ball for a moment as they surrounded the ref, pointing at their wrists, complaining that he was adding on too much time. As he backpedalled away from them, waving them away, the ref raised one finger, indicating that there was one minute to go. Slade took the free kick quickly, passing it down the touchline to Quade Wilson, who immediately spotted the gap in our defence where our arguing players should have been. He went straight for it, cutting inside our left back and making a beeline towards the eighteen-yard box. There was no one between him and the goal now except Richie King, and as Quade raced into the penalty area, Richie came running out. It was a classic one-on-one situation, striker versus goalkeeper, and with less than a minute to go, everyone knew that this was the defining moment of the match. If Quade scored, the game was over; if Richie stopped him, the match was going to a penalty shoot-out.

Quade was moving fast, keeping the ball close to his

feet, and as Richie came out to meet him, I could see the indecision in his eyes. Should he stay on his feet and make himself as big as possible, guarding against Quade taking a shot? Or should he dive at Quade's feet and go for the ball? Quade made the decision for him, suddenly changing direction and jinking to his left, trying to take the ball past Richie. Richie dived full-stretch to his right. It looked for a second as if he was going to get the ball, but at the very last moment Quade flicked it out of his reach, and as he veered to Richie's right, Richie's flailing hands caught his ankles and brought him down. It wasn't intentional, he was genuinely going for the ball, but that didn't make any difference. He hadn't got the ball, he'd taken Quade's legs from under him. It was a penalty, no question about it.

But that wasn't all.

As Quade got to his feet, and Richie looked pleadingly at the ref, the ref took out his red card and showed it to Richie. He'd denied Quade a clear goal-scoring chance, and there were no other defenders between Quade and the goal. It was a straightforward sending-off offence.

Richie and a few other players made a bit of a scene, surrounding the ref and trying to make out that Quade had dived, but their hearts weren't really in it. They knew the ref was right. Even Mr Jago accepted the decision without *too* much shouting and swearing.

I'd got so used to thinking of myself as a spectator that it never even occurred to me that I might be called on to go in goal. As Richie trudged off the pitch, taking off his gloves, and Mr Jago called over Mosh, I just assumed he was going to put Mosh in goal for the penalty, and was calling him over to give him instructions. As far as I knew, Mosh had never played in goal before, so I thought it was a pretty odd decision. But then, as far as I knew, no one else in the team had played in goal before either, so I just took it for granted that Jago knew what he was doing. It wasn't until he turned to me and told me to get stripped off that it finally dawned on me that he wasn't putting Mosh in goal, he was taking him off so that he could bring me on.

'You want *me* to go in goal?' I asked him incredulously.

'You're a goalkeeper, aren't you?' he said.

'Well, yeah, but—'

'We've got a penalty to save. We need a goalkeeper.' He glared at me. 'Come on, what are you waiting for? This is your big chance to be a hero.'

Yeah, right, I thought, as I fumbled my way out of my tracksuit. *It's also my big chance to be a total zero.*

42

Just as I was getting ready to go on, Jago came over to me and gave me some last-minute instructions.

'Right, listen,' he said quietly. 'Wilson's going to take the penalty, OK? He tried dinking it straight down the middle the last time and made a complete mess of it, so he's not going to do that again. He's going to go for the left or right corner of the goal, probably keeping it low. He'll try to send you the wrong way. So watch his eyes, all right? If he looks to your right, dive to your left. If he looks left, go to your right. Got that?'

'Yeah.'

'OK,' Jago said, slapping me on the shoulder. 'Just get out there and do it. If you save this one, they're all going to be so devastated that we'll win the penalty shoot-out with our eyes closed.'

I'd forgotten all about the possibility of going to penalties, and now that Jago had reminded me, I was even more nervous than before.

Thanks a lot, Johnny, I thought to myself as I started jogging out onto the pitch. *Thanks for filling me with confidence.*

The goal I was heading for seemed to be about a thousand miles away, and as I trotted towards it, pulling on my goalkeeping gloves, I'd never felt more alone. I couldn't bear to look around at the crowd or the other players, so I was keeping my eyes fixed firmly on the ground, but I could sense everyone watching me, and I could hear the shouts of encouragement from the Kell Cross supporters – *COME ON, TRAV, YOU CAN DO IT! TRA-VIS! TRA-VIS!* – and the comments from Slade supporters trying to put me off – *YOU GOT NO CHANCE! LOS-ER! LOS-ER!* It seemed to take for ever to get to the goal, and no matter how hard I tried to empty my head and not think of anything, my mind was spinning with all kinds of confusing questions. For a start, I couldn't help wondering how Quade Wilson was feeling right now. This was his big moment, his chance to show everyone that he *could* cope with the pressure. I remembered what his sister Evie had told me about him – *Football's his whole life. Being a pro is all he's ever wanted . . . he gets kind of anxious sometimes. I mean really anxious.* And when I'd asked her if the big clubs who were interested in signing him knew about his lack of self-belief, she'd nodded and said – *That's why they're watching him all the time – they want to see how he copes when he's put under* real *pressure.* And there was no doubt that this *was* a pressure situation for him. He'd already missed one penalty, and now he was getting ready to take another one, one that could win or potentially lose not just the match but the whole tournament. If he messed up *this* one, with all the scouts and representatives from the big clubs watching, it could ruin his chance of becoming a pro.

If I saved his penalty, I realised, it was possible I could be shattering his dream.

But was that really anything to do with me? I asked myself. Should I even be thinking about Quade? My only responsibility was to do my best for the team and the school, wasn't it?

Another thing that occurred to me was that if I saved the penalty, or Quade missed, and we went to a penalty shoot-out, that was going to take up at least another twenty minutes or so, maybe even longer, and I was already pressed for time as it was. Dee Dee was meeting Ronnie Bull at five. It was around three forty now. If the meeting *was* at the car park in town, and the game finished in a few minutes, I'd still have enough time to get there. Five minutes to get off the pitch and into the dressing room, another five minutes to take a quick shower and get changed, say half an hour to cycle into town . . . I reckoned I could get to the car park by about four thirty. But not if the match went to penalties. By the time all the arrangements had been sorted out – which end of the pitch the shoot-out was going to take place, which players on each side were going to take the penalties – it would already be getting on for four o'clock. Then the shoot-out itself could take another twenty minutes. I'd never get to the car park by five.

But again, I thought, surely I couldn't deliberately let the team down.

Could I?

Something else popped into my mind then, a realisation that almost made me laugh out loud. All this thinking about whether or not I should let Quade score, and I'd forgotten one simple fact: I wasn't a very good goalkeeper. Even if I did decide that the right thing to do was make every effort to save the penalty, the chances of actually doing it were pretty slim, to say the least.

I was approaching the penalty area now, and my teammates were coming up to me and wishing me luck – patting me on the shoulder, bumping fists, slapping my hand. *Come on, Trav. You can do it. Get in there, Trav.*

I just nodded at them, looking serious and keeping quiet. Even though I hadn't actually done anything disloyal, I still felt a bit of a fraud. *If they could read my mind*, I thought. *If they knew what I was thinking . . .*

Quade Wilson had already placed the ball on the penalty spot, and as I approached him he was standing next to it with his hands on his hips. Our eyes met as I walked past him towards the goal, and we both nodded at each other.

'You're Travis Delaney, aren't you?' he said.

'Yeah.'

'You know Evie.'

'Yeah.'

'She says you're a good kid.'

'Yeah?'

I was certainly impressing him with my conversational skills.

'So,' he said, grinning at me, 'are you going to let me score?'

'I was hoping you'd let me save it.'

The ref came over then and told us to get a move on. As I walked off towards the goal, I could still see Quade's eyes in my mind. He might have come across as casual and light-hearted, but I'd seen the intense anxiety in his eyes. He knew how much this penalty meant, and it was obvious that it was tearing him apart. It briefly crossed my mind that if he really couldn't cope with this kind of pressure, maybe it'd be best if he didn't make it as a professional footballer. If he couldn't deal with this level of tension, how on earth was he going to deal with the high-pressure lifestyle of a celebrity footballer?

It's not your problem, I reminded myself, turning to face him. *And there's nothing you can do about it anyway, remember? He's a very skilled footballer, you're not even good enough to get a game with the reserve team.*

I got myself into position – slightly to the left of the centre of the goal, legs bent at the knees, arms out at my sides – and only then did I look up at Quade. He was ready to take the kick. He wasn't taking much of a run-up, three or four steps at most, and he was just standing there, staring at the ground, taking a few deep breaths, trying to compose himself. I don't know what it was – his posture, maybe, his reluctance to look at me – but there was something about him that gave off an air of anxiety. He didn't look very confident at all.

I tried to ignore the see-sawing thoughts in my head – *save it, don't save it, do the right thing . . . what* is *the right thing?* – but even as Quade finally looked up, I still had no idea what I was going to do. Quade's eyes met mine for a moment, and I could see the fear of failure in his mind. He was just as uncertain about what he should do as I was. Should he go for the audacious chip down the middle again, the option that failed so miserably last time? Or should he hammer the ball low into the corner? Or maybe high into the corner?

The ref blew his whistle.

Quade hesitated for a moment, blew out his cheeks, then started his run-up. I watched his eyes, as Jago had suggested, and I saw him glance to my right. Which could mean that he was trying to fool me, and that he was in fact planning to put it to my left. Or it could be a double bluff. From the shape of his body it looked like he was going right, and I was still trying to make up my mind what to do and which way to go when, at the very last moment, he half faltered in his run-up, deliberately taking a hesitant step, and I just knew then that he was going for the same trick he'd tried before – hesitate for a fraction of a second, wait for me to dive, then dink the ball into the middle of the open goal. I don't know how I knew it, I just did.

What I don't know, even now, is whether I'd already committed myself to the dive or whether – subconsciously, at least – I'd decided to let him score. I honestly don't know the answer. But I did dive, flinging myself across the goal to my left, and he did put the ball into the space where I'd been. And this time he didn't fluff it. He timed his move to perfection and caught the ball just right, chipping it delicately – but firmly – into the middle of the goal. I vainly tried swinging my boot at it, but I knew it was hopeless. As I sprawled across the ground, the ball dropped sweetly into the back of the net, and that was it.

Game over.

Kell Cross 1, Slade 2.

Quade didn't really celebrate his goal – he looked more relieved than anything else – but his teammates went crazy, jumping all over him, whooping and shouting, and the Slade supporters erupted in a cacophony of cheering and singing. Some of our players slumped to the ground, holding their heads in their hands, while others just stood around, staring into space or looking down miserably at their feet. A couple of them came over and commiserated with me, telling me not to worry, it wasn't my fault, I did my best . . .

I appreciated their sympathy, but in my heart I still wasn't sure whether I *had* done my best or not. Could I have saved the penalty? Had I been sure that Quade was going to put the ball down the middle?

I honestly didn't know.

As I left the celebrating Slade players behind and started making my way back to the subs bench, Quade jogged over and fell in beside me.

'Hey,' he said, looking at me.

'Well done,' I told him. 'It was a good match.'

He smiled. 'A bit rough at times.'

'Yeah, well . . . that's all part of the game, I suppose.'

He nodded, then went quiet for a few moments, just walking along beside me. Eventually, without looking at me, he said, 'Why did you dive?'

'What?'

'You knew where I was going to put it. I could see it in your eyes.'

'I thought you were going for the corner,' I said.

'Really?'

'Yeah, really.' I looked at him. 'If I knew you were going to chip it down the middle, I would have stayed where I was, wouldn't I?'

He looked into my eyes, trying to work out if I was telling the truth or not. I held his gaze. He could look for the truth as long as he wanted. If *I* didn't know what it was, he certainly wasn't going to find it.

'I guess I must have been wrong then,' he said after a while.

'We all make mistakes.'

'Yeah . . .'

'Anyway,' I said, 'I've got to get going, if you don't mind.'

'No problem.' He glanced over his shoulder. 'I'd better get back for the cup presentation.'

'Good luck with everything,' I told him. 'I hope it all

works out for you with one of the big clubs.'

'Yeah, thanks.'

He gave me a final searching look, then shook his head, patted me on the shoulder, and headed off back to his teammates.

I carried on over to the subs bench and put on my tracksuit. I took out my mobile and checked the tracker screen. The green dot wasn't moving any more. It had stopped halfway down Haven Road, a street full of nightclubs down at the docks. Maybe Dee Dee was meeting Ronnie Bull in a club, I thought. Or maybe he was just meeting someone else or having a drink before going on to the car park. Either way, at least he was still in town.

It was almost four o'clock.

I tried Jaydie's mobile again, quickly gave up when I heard her voicemail, then headed off to the changing rooms.

43

I was supposed to stay for the cup presentation ceremony, but I managed to slip away without anyone noticing, and by four thirty I was sitting on a bench by a bus stop at the top of a street near the hospital. The multi-storey car park was only a couple of streets away. I could see the top few levels from where I was – the car-park lights glimmering in the winter darkness, the massive grey concrete walls looming dimly against the coal-black sky. I had my phone out and was watching Dee Dee driving away from the docks and up towards town. It looked like he was heading this way.

I switched screens on my mobile and sent a couple of quick texts, firstly to Jaydie – *sry j, i dint mean to upset u. plz dont b mad at me. cll u ltr. travx* – and then to Gran – *hi nan. futbl stil goin. ill b a bit late back, cu soon. travx*.

I switched back to the tracker screen again. I couldn't be absolutely sure, but from the route Dee Dee was following, it seemed almost certain that he *was* meeting Ronnie Bull at the car park. Depending on the traffic, I reckoned it would take him between five and ten minutes to get here. So if I wanted to get myself into position before he arrived, I had to get going right now.

I jumped on my bike and got going.

*

I remembered Jaydie telling me that when she and Mason had seen Dee Dee with Ronnie Bull, they'd been half hidden away at the end of a little corridor off the stairwell on the third floor. It didn't necessarily follow that the third floor was the 'usual place' that Dee Dee had referred to when he'd arranged the meeting with Bull – the 'usual place' could just mean the car park in general – but I had to pick somewhere to wait for them, and the stairwell on the third floor seemed like a reasonable choice. And besides, I could always move if the tracker told me they were meeting somewhere else.

I left my bike locked to a lamp post outside the car park and made my way up the stairs to the third floor. I could have used the lift, but the display above it was showing that it was on the sixth floor, and it didn't seem to be in a hurry to move, and I didn't have time to wait.

There weren't all that many people around, but the car park was far from deserted. I passed two women chatting idly to each other going up the stairs, and a young couple with two little kids went past me on the way down, the kids running on ahead of their mum and dad, clattering excitedly down the stairs, making as much noise as possible. Despite the presence of other people, and the playful sounds of the little kids, the car park still had a slightly spooky feel to it. The echoing of the sounds around the stairwell, the lifeless gloom of the cold grey concrete, the lingering smell of sick and urine on the stairs. It wasn't the nicest place in the world. But then, I don't suppose it was meant to be. It was a car park, not a theme park. It wasn't meant to make you feel good. It was just somewhere to leave your car.

The corridor Jaydie had told me about led off from the stairwell and was about twenty metres long. There was a sign on the wall saying NO PUBLIC ACCESS – SERVICE PERSONNEL ONLY. A light on the ceiling showed three doors at the end, one on either side, and one in the far wall. There were a number of grey metal units fixed to the walls along the corridor. I guessed they housed controls of some sort – electrics, lighting, maybe security.

I checked Dee Dee's tracker. He was approaching the car park now, just turning right into the street outside. It was almost four forty-five. I wondered where Ronnie Bull was. Was he in the car park already? Was he waiting for Dee Dee in his car somewhere? Or was he meeting him right here in the corridor? For all I knew, he could be on his way here right now, coming down the stairs, or on his way up . . .

I headed off down the corridor, looking for somewhere to hide.

There was nowhere suitable along the corridor itself, so the only option I had was whatever lay behind the doors. The two doors on either side of the corridor were marked CENTRAL A1 and CENTRAL A2, and the other one, the door facing me, was labelled MAIN. CENTRAL. I assumed they were maintenance rooms of some kind. They weren't ideal surveillance locations, because unless they had another exit – which I doubted – I wouldn't have an escape route if something went wrong. But it was either one of the rooms or nothing.

All three doors were locked. I quickly started going through my pockets, looking for something I could use to pick one of the locks.

My dad had taught me the basics of lock-picking when I was around eleven or twelve. Grandad had taught him how to do it when he was a kid, and the first thing Dad had done before showing me how it was done was make me promise what Grandad had made him promise when he was teaching him.

'Lock-picking is an art, Travis, an age-old skill,' he'd told me, 'and apart from genuine emergencies, it's *never* to be misused. There are plenty of old locks in the garage for you to practise on, and Grandad's got boxes full of them in his attic. You can play around with those as much as you like. But once you've learned how to do it, you *don't* go showing off to your friends, and you *don't* open locks that you're not supposed to. Do you understand? I need you to give me your word on that.'

I'd given him my word, and although I'd been tempted to break it on a number of occasions, I hadn't. But I was sure that if Dad had still been alive, he would have agreed that this was a genuine emergency, and that I wasn't misusing my skill.

I took my key ring from the inside pocket of my parka and removed the miniature penknife from it, and from the side pocket of my coat I fished out a mini-screwdriver that I'd been using a couple of days ago to fix a loose screw on the mudguard of my bike. They weren't the ideal tools for picking a lock, but they were all I had, so they'd have to do. I set to work on the door marked *MAIN. CENTRAL*.

The reason I chose that door was that the top half wasn't solid wood, it was thickened glass covered with a fine metal mesh. The mesh was so fine that you couldn't see through it into the room, but I was hoping that if I held my mobile right up against the glass from the inside, I'd get at least some kind of view of Dee Dee and Ronnie Bull. If not, I'd have to make do with an audio-only recording.

But first I had to get into the room.

I was nowhere near as skilled at lock-picking as Dad had been – and he'd never got close to being as good as Grandad – but I wasn't bad at it, and with the right tools I could open a basic lock fairly easily. The lock on this door was an old mortise lock, about as basic as it gets, but I was hampered by the makeshift tools I was using, so it took me a bit longer than it normally would. By the time I finally unlocked it and went into the room, it was four fifty-five. Ideally, I would have liked to have re-locked the door, but there simply wasn't enough time. So I just shut it behind me and made sure it was securely closed.

I checked the tracker screen again. Dee Dee was in the car park now. The green dot was moving, but not in a straight line. It was kind of flickering around in little circles. I guessed that meant that Dee Dee had parked his car and was either coming up or going down in the lift or on the stairs.

I quickly looked around the room. I hadn't turned on the light, for obvious reasons, but there was enough light showing through the meshed glass of the door to see that it was a cramped little place, not much bigger than a large cupboard. The walls were lined with galvanised metal shelving, the shelves piled high with all kinds of bits and pieces: rolls of electric cable, light bulbs, all manner of parking cones, batteries, hard hats, two-way radios, tins of paint. There were no other exits. No doors, no windows.

I turned round and pressed my face up against the door. I could see through the glass and the mesh grid into the corridor outside. It was by no means a perfect view – the combination of thickened glass and fine wire mesh gave everything a slightly blurred and distorted look – but it was good enough to get a reasonably clear picture of the corridor and anyone who happened to be in it.

I could hear heavy footsteps coming down the stairs now. There were no voices, not that I could hear anyway, just the hard slap of footsteps on concrete. It sounded like two people.

Trying to stay calm, I hurriedly opened up the camera function on my mobile and switched it to video. I held the phone against the glass – positioning it in the lower left-hand corner – and quickly looked at the screen. The view was pretty much the same as I'd just seen with my own eyes – a bit blurred and distorted, but not too bad. I tried zooming in to see if it made things any better, but all it did was enlarge the mesh and make everything even more blurry.

The footsteps were getting louder, and I could hear the murmur of voices. There were definitely two people, both of them male, and one of the voices sounded like Dee Dee's. I reset the zoom, putting it back to normal, and just as I was making a final check of the view, two figures appeared at the end of the corridor. One of them was a middle-aged man in a crumpled brown raincoat, the other one was Dee Dee.

44

I pressed the record button on my phone and stepped away from the door, holding the mobile against the glass with my left hand while standing with my back against the wall.

I could hear Dee Dee and the man I assumed was Ronnie Bull coming along the corridor towards me. I was tempted to check that the video recorder had a good view of them, but I resisted it. *As long as they're in the corridor*, I told myself, *they're going to be in view of the video.*

They were getting pretty close to the door now, and I could clearly hear what they were saying.

So do you think Malik's going to try anything? the man in the raincoat said.

I doubt it, Dee Dee replied. *He knows he's outnumbered. He wouldn't stand a chance if he went to war with me.*

I heard there was some kind of explosion near your place the other day. Was that anything to do with Malik?

I don't think so. I'm still looking into it, but I'm pretty sure it was just someone messing around.

They'd stopped now, and from the sound of their voices they were a few metres away from the door. I couldn't help worrying that they'd spot my phone through the meshed glass, but if I wanted to get them on video, there wasn't much I could do about it. I just had to hope they didn't look too closely at the door.

Listen, Ron, Dee Dee said, *I'm getting a bit sick of waiting for you to bust Malik and his boys. Everything's in place with Beacon, the deal's all ready to go ahead. I just need Malik out of the way.*

I'm working on it, Dee. It takes time. I've got to get the go-ahead from my boss, get the warrants sorted out—

I don't care what you've got to do, I just want it done. I'm paying you good money, and you're going to be getting a ton of gear out of it. I want results.

It'll be done in a couple of days, I promise.

It'd better be.

They went quiet for a while then. I knew now that the man in the raincoat was definitely Ronnie Bull, and it sounded like Dee Dee was paying him to arrange police raids on Malik and his boys to take them out of the picture so that he could go ahead with the merger with Beacon Fields. And, with a bit of luck, I had it all on tape. It was damning evidence that Dee Dee was dealing with Bull, and although his crew might be happy with the results, there was no way they'd approve of his close relationship with a cop. The cardinal rule on the Slade – and every other estate like it – is that you *never* talk to the police about anything, no matter what. And you certainly never grass anyone up to them, not even your worst enemy.

Is all that business with Tanga Tans sorted out now? Bull asked Dee Dee.

Yeah, no problem.

What about those private investigators?

Like I said, it's all sorted.

You shouldn't have gone in so hard on the girl who works for them, Dee.

Why the hell not? You've got to let people know you mean business. It's no good just talking tough, you've got to break a few bones now and then.

Yeah, well . . . it might just backfire on you this time.

What do you mean?

The old guy who runs the PI business, Joe Delaney . . . he's a lot tougher than you think.

Dee Dee laughed. *What's he going to do? Come after me with a walking stick?*

Do you remember the guy I brought to you about the riot in North Walk a few months ago?

What about him?

The people he works for have had dealings with Delaney. That's what the riot was all about . . . well, it was about Delaney's son and daughter-in-law actually. They used to run Delaney & Co—

What's your point, Ron?

My point is that these people, the ones who wanted the riot, are incredibly powerful. They're all ex-security services or ex-military intelligence, so they know what they're doing, and they're really well connected too. They've got contacts everywhere – MI5, MI6, Special Branch, CID—

So what?

Bull sighed. *So if the Delaneys can give* these *people problems – which they have – then it stands to reason that they can give anyone problems, including you.*

You reckon?

Don't underestimate them, Dee Dee. That's all I'm saying. They're not going to just lie down and accept what you did to the girl.

I can deal with them.

Well, just watch your step, all right? From what I've heard, you're not the only one who's interested in the Delaneys at the moment. These people I told you about—

Do 'these people' have a name?

Bull didn't answer immediately, but it was obvious who he was talking about. 'These people', as he called them, were Omega. And it was clear now that it was Bull who'd put them in touch with Dee Dee about the riot. So despite the fact that Gloria was double-crossing us, and working for Omega herself, she'd actually been telling the truth when she'd told Grandad that she thought Ronnie Bull might have some kind of connection with them. Which didn't seem to make any sense whatsoever. If she was working for Omega, and she knew that Bull was one of their contacts, why bother mentioning it to Grandad at all? What purpose did it serve? Why not just keep quiet about it?

Bull started talking again then, answering Dee Dee's question as to whether or not 'these people' had a name, so I forgot about Gloria (for now) and refocused my mind on Dee Dee and Bull.

I honestly don't know if they have a name or not, Bull admitted to Dee Dee. *They're as secretive as they are powerful. Anyway, as I was telling you, I've heard they've got unfinished business with the Delaneys, and they're going to be making a move on them soon. So if I were you, Dee, I'd just let them get on with it. There's no point stepping on their toes if you don't have to, and if they take care of the Delaneys, it saves you the bother of having to worry about them, doesn't it?*

Do I look like I'm worried about them?

Well, no, but—

I'll tell you what, Ron, why don't you just concentrate on what you're being paid for, and leave everything else to me? How does that sound?

Bull sighed again. *I need some more cash up front.*

What for?

Expenses, sweeteners, inducements. It's hard to get anyone interested in busting Malik's crew. No one wants to stir up trouble on the Slade. CID, uniform, the CPS . . . everyone thinks it's best to just leave the estate alone. As long as the gangs are only fighting among themselves, no one really gives a toss. So I need something to persuade them to change their minds, to make it worth their while.

You need to grease a few palms.

Exactly.

How much do you want?

Twenty should do it.

Twenty grand! Christ, Ron, you'll make ten times that when you sell all the gear you get from Malik.

I won't get any gear from him if I don't get the go-ahead to bust him. And when I do bust him, think how much you're going to get out of it. A merger with Beacon's got to be worth at least a couple of million to you. What's twenty K to a potential millionaire?

All right, Dee Dee said reluctantly, *it'll be in your account by midday tomorrow. But that's it, Ron, OK? No more. And I want what I'm paying for by next Monday at the very latest. You got that?*

It's a done deal.

Right . . .

From the sound of it – shuffling feet, muffled movements – they were getting ready to go now. I was hoping they were anyway. I'd got all I needed on tape, and my left arm was really aching from holding the phone against the door. I didn't want to take it away yet in case the sudden movement caught their eye. But I wasn't sure how much longer I could keep it there.

It's probably best if we don't meet up for a while, Bull said. *At least until the operation against Malik's over. Just to be on the safe side.*

All right. But if Malik's not behind bars by Monday night—

He will be.

I'll be seeing you if he's not.

Silence.

Then, *I'd better get going.*

Me too.

I heard the sound of them beginning to walk away.

Where are you parked?

Sixth floor.

You go on ahead. I'm on five, but we'd better not be seen together. I'll give you a minute and—

That's when my mobile rang.

45

As I fumbled with my phone, trying to stop it ringing, I could hear Dee Dee and Bull's voices outside.

What the hell's that?

Sounds like a phone.

It's coming from in there!

Christ, there's someone in there.

I finally stopped the call, stuffed the phone in my pocket – mentally kicking myself for not putting it on silent – then I quickly started thinking about what I was going to do.

Maybe it's one of the car-park staff, I heard Bull say.

We'll soon find out.

I rapidly scanned the room, looking for anything I could use as a weapon.

Hey! I heard Dee Dee shout. *Who's in there?*

He was right outside the door.

Come out now, or we're coming in.

I moved away from the wall and stood just to the left of the door, about two metres away from it.

Go on then, open it, Dee Dee told Bull.

You open it.

You're the cop, for God's sake. Just open it.

I was banking on Bull being cautious, hoping that he'd open the door slowly rather than just shoving it open and rushing in.

I waited, bracing myself.

The door handle turned.

The door inched open.

'I'm a police officer,' Bull called out through the gap. 'I'm coming in. Whoever's in there, step away from the door and put your hands on your head.'

I didn't move. I just stood there, staring at the door, waiting for it to open a little wider.

'Don't do anything stupid,' Bull said. 'I'm opening the door now . . .'

It opened another inch, then another . . . and then after a momentary pause, Bull opened it wide enough to put his head through. That's when I made my move. I launched myself at the door, crashing into it with a flying two-footed kick, slamming Bull's head between the door and the frame. As he let out a groan and dropped to his knees, clutching his head, the door swung back open, and I could see Dee Dee in the corridor. He was already backing away – hedging his bets – and as I quickly jumped to my feet, I saw him pull a knife from his pocket. It wasn't much of a thing – just a short-bladed kitchen knife – but it was still perfectly capable of causing serious damage.

Dee Dee smiled coldly when he recognised me, and he immediately stopped backing away. He was about a third of the way along the corridor, maybe four metres away from me.

'Well, well,' he said, 'look who we've got here.'

I glanced at Bull. He was still on his knees, and from the glazed look in his eyes, he was having trouble working out where he was and what had just happened to him. Blood was streaming from a deep gash in the side of his head.

'Ronnie warned me not to underestimate you,' Dee Dee said, moving slowly towards me. 'But I suppose you already know that, don't you? I mean, I'm assuming you didn't just *happen* to be here, so I guess you've not only been listening to me and Ronnie, you've been recording us too.' He moved a little closer. 'Am I right?'

'I've got every word on tape,' I told him. 'Video and audio. I'm sure everyone on the Slade and Beacon Fields will be interested to see it.' I glanced at Bull again. He was shaking his head and blinking his eyes now, trying to clear the fog from his mind. He'd be back on his feet soon. I had to get out before that happened. I turned round and grabbed a tin of paint off one of the shelves. It was an unopened 2.5-litre can with a strong plastic handle. Good and heavy.

'I'll tell you what,' Dee Dee said, edging closer to me. 'You give me the tape, and I'll let you walk out of here.'

'And if I don't?'

He held up his knife. 'You won't walk out of here.'

He was about two metres away from me now. I gently started swinging the can of paint in my hand, getting the feel of it, testing its weight.

Dee Dee laughed. 'What are you going to do with that? Paint me to death?'

Keeping my eyes fixed on him, I began swinging the can more vigorously, building up the momentum. Dee Dee watched me, his eyes narrowed, trying to figure out what I was doing. From the way he was standing, and the way he was holding his knife, I was fairly sure that he thought I was going to rush at him and try to hammer the can into his head. Which was exactly what I was hoping he'd think.

I swung the can up and over in my head in a full circle, then suddenly stepped forward, swinging it again, even faster, and this time – just at the right moment – I let it go, hurling it as hard as I could at Dee Dee's head. He reacted pretty quickly, I'll give him that, realising at the last second what I was doing, and as the paint can went flying towards him, he raised his arm in front of his head and ducked to one side. If my aim had been good, the can probably would have missed him altogether, but luckily for me – and unluckily for him – I'd let go of the paint can just a fraction too early, so instead of flying straight at his head, it went a bit lower, and instead of dodging it, he actually ducked his head into it. His raised arm saved his head from a direct hit, but it didn't deflect the heavy can all that much, and it caught Dee Dee just over his right eye. He staggered sideways against the wall, his legs almost giving way, but somehow he stayed on his feet. I didn't hesitate, I just ran, hurtling along the corridor as fast as I could. Dee Dee made a grab for me as I approached him, but he didn't have his coordination back yet, and all I had to do was feint one way and go the other, and I was past him like a shot.

I knew I wasn't safe yet though, not by a long way, and even before I'd reached the end of the corridor, I heard Dee Dee coming after me.

'Come on, Ron!' I heard him yell. 'Move it! Get going!'

I glanced over my shoulder and saw Dee Dee running after me. He was still a little unsteady, but he was moving pretty fast. Behind him, Ronnie Bull was on his feet now and coming after me too. He hadn't recovered as well as Dee Dee, and he was stumbling around as he tried to run, but his eyes weren't glazed any more. They were determined and angry.

I carried on running.

The lift was at the end of the corridor, and as I got near to it I could see that the door was open and the lift was waiting. Questions raced through my mind. Should I take the lift or use the stairs? Which was quicker? Could I get in the lift and shut the door before Dee Dee caught up with me?

Come on, think!

Lift or stairs?

I was at the end of the corridor. I had to decide *right* now.

Lift or stairs?

I went for the stairs.

Big mistake.

46

I got down the first flight of steps without any trouble, but as I turned the corner and started heading down to the second floor, that's when it all went wrong. A young couple were coming up the stairs, the woman carrying two babies and the man lugging a pushchair. It was one of those massive twin-buggies, about the size of a small car, and there was no way I could get past the man carrying it. I couldn't understand why they were using the stairs instead of the lift, but then it suddenly struck me that maybe it wasn't just a coincidence that the lift was waiting on the third floor with the doors open, maybe it was there because Dee Dee or Bull had fixed it so it was there – jammed it open or something – in case they needed a quick exit. So the couple with the buggy hadn't had any choice *but* to use the stairs.

'Excuse me,' I said to them, trying to squeeze past, 'I'm sorry, but I *really* need to—'

'Move your arse, kid,' the man growled. 'You'll just have to wait.'

He was obviously pretty fed up with having to carry the buggy all the way up the stairs, and it was clear from the look he gave me that there was no point in trying to reason with him.

Take the stairs, Ron! I heard Dee Dee calling out from above. *I'll take the lift!*

I heard the lift door closing, then Bull's footsteps starting down the stairs.

I moved away from the man with the buggy, backing up the stairs to the landing between the second and third floors, and I looked down over the railings of the stairwell. It was a good three-metre drop to the next flight of steps, and even if I climbed over the railings and lowered myself down, it was still a long way to fall. And there was nowhere safe to land anyway. It was all jutting lumps of concrete and metal railings. I'd be lucky if I didn't break my legs.

It was too late to jump now anyway. Ronnie Bull was coming down the steps towards me.

'Stay right where you are, boy,' he said sternly. 'You're under arrest for assaulting a police officer.'

He was kind of tough-looking, in a grizzly sort of way, and I guessed under normal circumstances he'd be more than capable of looking after himself. But he still looked pretty groggy, and as he came down the steps towards me, he was holding on to the banister to help keep his balance.

'Turn around,' he told me. 'Put your hands on your head.'

I did as I was told.

As he came up behind me, he began cautioning me. 'You do not have to say anything, but it may harm your defence if you do not mention when questioned something which—'

I spun round suddenly and hit him in the belly with a hard right hook. He let out a low groan, the air bursting from his lungs, and as he doubled over, gasping for breath, I stepped round him and began running back up the stairs.

I didn't stop running until I'd reached the fifth floor. The sixth floor, I realised, was a dead end. There was only one way out up there – down – but on the fifth floor I still had the choice of going up *or* down. I went through the door into the car-parking area and started heading across to the other side. I didn't know if there was another lift or more stairs on that side or not, but it was worth having a look. As I went, I took my mobile out of my pocket, intending to call Grandad. But there was no signal. No bars, nothing at all. I tried his number anyway, just in case, but it was a waste of time. I switched to the tracker screen. The green dot was still showing, but it was doing the flickering around thing again, which meant that Dee Dee was either on the stairs or in the lift. I had no way of telling which floor he was on though.

I'd reached the far side of the car park now. There was no sign of any stairs or another lift, and then I saw a sign on the wall that said ALL EXITS THIS WAY, with an arrow pointing back the way I'd just come.

'Great,' I muttered.

I went over and crouched down behind a parked Range Rover and tried to work out what the hell I was going to do.

The first thing I did was put myself in Dee Dee's shoes and try to imagine what I'd be doing if I were him. He had no way of knowing which floor I was on, but he probably knew there was only one way out. So, if I were him, I'd leave Ronnie Bull on the door at the ground floor while I went looking for me. The big advantage I had was that there were plenty of places to hide. Dee Dee had six floors of parked cars to search. On the downside though, I couldn't hide for ever. As the hours passed, the cars would leave, and eventually – I didn't know when – the car park would close. That wouldn't have mattered so much if Dee Dee had been on his own, because the car-park staff would have told him to leave when the car park closed. But he wasn't on his own, he was with a police officer, and all Ronnie Bull would have to do was make up some story about me, and the car-park staff would probably help him look for me.

So hiding wasn't a long-term option. I had to find some way of getting out.

Just then, a Vauxhall Astra started up a few rows away from me, and as it backed out of its parking slot and drove away, I suddenly realised that *that* was my way out. Dee Dee and Bull wouldn't be expecting me to leave in a car. They wouldn't be watching the vehicle exit.

I smiled, quietly pleased with myself, and began to

think that maybe I was going to get out of this situation after all.

All I had to do now was work out how to get into a car.

After thinking about it for a while, I came to the conclusion that there were two basic options. I could either get into a car with or without the driver knowing. To get in with the driver knowing, I'd either have to do it by force or persuasion. Force was out of the question. There was no way I was going to threaten a perfectly innocent person – *drive me out of here or I'll break your nose*. I just couldn't do it. But I didn't think persuasion would work either. I'd have to come up with a believable story, an acceptable reason for needing to get out of the car park in a stranger's car, and I simply couldn't think of anything that anyone would swallow. And besides, who in their right mind was going to let a fourteen-year-old kid who they didn't know into their car?

So that left the other option: getting into a car without the driver's knowledge.

Grandad had taught me the basics of breaking into a car, but I didn't know enough about disabling alarms to feel safe enough trying it. An alarm going off would be a dead giveaway as to where I was. So I was left with just two choices. I could either wander round the car park trying the doors of all the cars, hoping to find one that wasn't locked, then get in the back of the car, hide behind the front seat, and just wait for the driver to return (and hope that they didn't have any back-seat passengers with them). Or I could keep an eye out for a returning driver, follow them to their car, wait for them to open the door, then somehow sneak in the back without being seen.

I decided to go for the first option – wandering around, looking for an unlocked car.

I cautiously straightened up, peering over the bonnet of the Range Rover to make sure there was no sign of Dee Dee or Bull, and when I was satisfied that neither of them were there, I gazed around the car park, trying to work out the best way to set about searching for an unlocked car. I decided to start where I was, go up this row of cars, then down the next row, up the next one, and so on. That way I could keep track of where I'd already searched and not waste time getting lost.

I went over to the first car – a Citröen C3 – and just as I was reaching out for the door handle, something slammed into the back of my head and the world went black.

47

I thought I'd gone blind when I woke up. My eyes were open, but all I could see was a veil of blackness. The back of my head was throbbing like mad, and in a state of panic I began to think that I'd been hit so hard that I'd lost the use of my eyes. I squeezed them shut, held them closed for a few moments, then opened them again. I still couldn't see anything. I automatically tried to rub my eyes, but for some reason I couldn't move my hands. I flexed my arms, and that's when I realised that my hands were tied together behind my back.

What the hell was going on? Where was I? Why couldn't I *see* anything?

Stay calm, I told myself. *Panicking's not going to help. Just keep calm, use your head, try to think things through.*

I breathed out slowly and thought things through.

Where are you? I asked myself.

I was lying on my side, kind of squashed down really uncomfortably in some kind of gap, with something lumpy jutting into my ribs and my head pressed up against a hard vertical surface. I could hear an engine, the sound of a car . . . the sensation of movement . . .

I was moving.

I was in a car.

I tried to sit up, and immediately felt someone pushing me back down again.

Don't move, kid, I heard Dee Dee say. His voice came from above me, and just to my right. *Just stay down there and keep your mouth shut*, he added, *and you won't get hurt*.

Is he awake?

Bull's voice this time, also from above me, but from the other side.

Yeah, he's awake, Dee Dee told him.

I kept still, kept quiet, and gave some more thought to my situation. If I was in a car, I thought, and Dee Dee and Bull were both above me, one to my left and the other to my right, the only place I could be was in the footwell behind the driver's seat. Bull was driving, I guessed, and Dee Dee was in the back with me. It made sense. Sitting in the back meant he could keep an eye on me at the same time as keeping himself relatively out of sight. He was probably keeping his head down as well, unless the car had tinted rear windows, which wouldn't surprise me. The last thing either of them wanted was to be seen together in the same car.

Yeah, I told myself, *that all makes perfect sense*.

And the reason I can't see?

There was something on my head, I realised now, something *over* my head. Something light . . . a cloth. I could feel it on my face too. It was some kind of hood. *That's* why I couldn't see. I had a hood over my head.

Thank God for that, I thought. *I'm not blind after all.*

My sense of relief didn't last very long though. I might not be blind, but I was tied up and hooded in the footwell of a car with Drew Devon and Ronnie Bull. And however you looked at it, that wasn't a good situation.

I moved my head slightly, trying to get my eyes closer to the hood to see if it helped to see through it, but the moment I moved, a bolt of pain shot through my skull like a blunt knife jabbing into my brain, and it was all I could do not to cry out.

Whoever it was who'd hit me – and I guessed it was Dee Dee – he hadn't held back. It felt like he'd smashed my head with a sledgehammer. How the hell had he found me? I wondered. And how had he managed to sneak up behind me without me noticing?

Not that it made the slightest bit of difference now.

He *had* found me, and he *had* sneaked up behind me. How he'd done it was completely irrelevant. All that mattered now was now.

Are you sure this place we're going to is safe? I heard him ask Bull.

It's a safe *house, Dee*, Bull replied, a hint of sarcasm in his voice.

What's it used for?

Witnesses under police protection, informants . . . anyone we need to keep safe, basically. That's why it's called a safe house.

And you're sure it's not being used at the moment?

I'm sure.

How do you know?

I just do, OK? Trust me.

Who else knows about it?

Just a couple of DIs and the DCI. Its location is only given out on a need-to-know basis. Don't worry, Dee. No one's going to know we're there.

Good.

They went quiet for a while then, and I just lay there, listening hard, trying to pick out any telltale sounds from outside that might give me a clue as to where we were, but all I could hear was the soft rumble of the car engine and the unremarkable sounds of streets passing by – heavy traffic, horns beeping, a brief blast of music from a passing shop or a pub . . .

We could be anywhere.

What are you going to do with him? Bull said.

Talk to him, ask him a few questions . . .

Then what?

What do you think?

No, Bull said firmly. *You can't do that.*

Why not?

It's too much, Dee. He's just a kid.

He knows about us, Ron. He heard everything. What do you think's going to happen if he talks?

Well, yeah, but—

We'll both be ruined. You'll lose your job at the very least. You could even end up in prison. And if that happens we'll both probably end up with a knife in our guts.

There must be some other way of keeping his mouth shut.

Yeah? What do you suggest? We just ask him nicely to keep quiet?

Threaten him with something.

I've already threatened him. I've threatened him and his grandad, and I've had the girl who works for them beaten up. But he's still come after me. There's only one way to stop him, Ron. You know that as well as I do.

I don't like it.

You should have thought of that before you started taking my money.

I never thought things would go this far.

You were wrong then, weren't you?

They didn't talk much for the rest of the journey, just the occasional idle remark, and they didn't pay me any attention at all. They hadn't paid me any attention when they were talking about what they were going to do to me either – treating me as if I simply wasn't there – and I wondered if that utter disregard was genuine, or whether it was all part of a ruse to scare me, to soften me up before we got to the house, so that when we got there I'd be so terrified I'd tell Dee Dee everything he wanted to know. As I lay there in the footwell thinking about it, I tried to convince myself that it *was* all talk, and that Dee Dee was only bluffing when he'd told Ronnie Bull that there was 'only one way to stop' me.

The problem with that though, the reason I found it so difficult to accept, no matter how hard I tried, was this: why was Dee Dee taking so many risks – kidnapping a fourteen-year-old kid, being out in the open with a policeman – if all he was going to do when we got to the house was ask me a few questions? He could have stayed in the car park to do that. Why did he feel the need to take me to a place that no one else knew about, a safe house, a safe place? *Safe from what?* I kept asking myself. *Safe* for *what?*

It wasn't easy to put those thoughts from my mind and concentrate on what I *could* do, rather than what *might* be about to happen to me, but I did my best. There was clearly nothing much I could do right now. Even if I could open the car door and throw myself out – which given that my hands were tied and I couldn't see anything was virtually impossible anyway – and even if I survived the fall and didn't get run over by another car, what good would it do me? Bull would just stop the car, and Dee Dee would just jump out and recapture me.

So I had to accept that there was nothing I could do just now, and instead I had to start thinking about what was going to happen when we got to the safe house. Whatever Dee Dee's ultimate intentions were, I was pretty sure he'd want to ask me some questions first, and I guessed one of the things he'd want to know was how I'd found out about him and Bull and how I'd tracked him to the car park. I quickly decided, there and then, that no matter what he did to me, I wasn't going to tell him anything about Jaydie's – or her friends' – involvement in anything. In view of that, I realised, I had to come up with an alternative, and believable, explanation as to how I'd found out about him and Bull and their meeting at the car park.

It took me quite a while, but eventually I worked out what I thought was a good enough story. At least, I hoped it was good enough.

The next thing to think about was how to avoid whatever else Dee Dee might have planned for me. The difficulty with that was that I didn't know what or where I was going to have to escape from, and I wouldn't know until we got to the safe house, by which time it might be too late.

But as it turned out, there wasn't much I could do about that either, because before I had a chance to give it any more thought, I heard Bull say, *That's it, just over there*, and I felt the car slowing down.

Nice-looking place, Dee Dee said.

The car slowed even more, then turned sharply to the right into what sounded like a gravel driveway. We crunched along the driveway for about twenty seconds or so, then finally rolled to a halt.

Here we are then, Bull said, turning off the engine and putting on the handbrake.

Must have cost a bit, Dee Dee commented.

It used to belong to an investment banker. The guy got

busted for bankrolling a massive drug deal, and his assets were seized and handed over to us. We traded in most of them, but this place was perfect for a safe house – private, secluded, easy to guard – so we decided to keep it.

Yeah, I think I remember the guy, Dee Dee said, opening the rear door. *This was about five years ago?*

Something like that.

I remember Joss telling me about some guy with more money than sense who was trying to set up a big deal. Said the guy was an idiot.

Bull laughed, and I heard him getting out of the car, followed by Dee Dee.

Come on, kid, Dee Dee said, grabbing hold of my shoulder. *Time to move your—*

I rolled away from him and quickly lashed out with both feet, but I was fighting blind, and my kicks were futile. I felt Dee Dee take hold of my feet, and then he just yanked me out of the car and started dragging me across the gravel driveway. I struggled for a while, wriggling and writhing around, and when that didn't do any good, I started yelling and screaming as loud as I could.

'*HELP! HELP ME! I'M BEING KIDNAPP—*'

That was as far as I got before something smashed into my face, and once again I was out cold.

48

When I woke up this time, the hood had been taken off my head and I could see exactly where I was. I was in a large, stone-floored kitchen, sitting on a chair at a big wooden table, with my hands tied behind my back and fastened to the chair. There was a window straight ahead of me, but the blinds were closed, so I couldn't see outside. Dee Dee was sitting opposite me, smoking a cigarette, and Ronnie Bull was standing over by the sink. Dee Dee had my mobile in his hands, and from the sound of it he was watching the video I'd made of his meeting with Bull in the car park.

The back of my head was still throbbing, and now my face was hurting too. Dee Dee's punch or kick – or whatever he'd hit me with – had caught me on the cheek under my right eye. It felt bruised and swollen, and it hurt like anything, but I was fairly sure nothing was broken.

Dee Dee looked up at me. 'All right?'

'Never felt better,' I told him.

He grinned, then glanced down at the mobile screen and turned off the video. 'What were you going to do with this then?' he asked me.

I shrugged. 'Post it on YouTube . . . let everyone know you're a grass.'

He nodded. 'That would have made things difficult for me, wouldn't it?'

'Who's to say it still won't?'

'What's that supposed to mean?'

'I emailed the video to my grandad when I was in the car park.'

'Yeah?'

'So if anything happens to me—'

'You didn't email it to anyone.'

'What makes you think that?'

'Well, for a start, the only place you can get a signal in the car park is on the top floor, and you never went there. And secondly . . .' He smirked. 'I've already checked your phone. You haven't emailed the video to anyone.'

There wasn't much I could say to that, so I didn't say anything. I was trying to weigh up my situation now, trying to work out if it really was as bad as it seemed. It certainly didn't look very promising. The only person who knew I'd been to the car park was Jaydie, but she didn't know what had happened there, and she couldn't know where I was now. I didn't even know where I was myself. So even if Grandad knew I was missing – and there was no guarantee that he did – and even if he managed to get in touch with Jaydie, or she got in touch with him, all she'd be able to tell him was that I'd been at the car park spying on Dee Dee and Bull.

But then I suddenly realised something – Jaydie knew about the tracker. She knew that Jazz had put the tracker in Dee Dee's pocket. So if she *was* in contact with Grandad, and she told him about the tracker—

'How did you find out about me and Ronnie?' Dee Dee said, interrupting my thoughts.

I knew what he was doing. He was trying to find out if anyone else knew about him and Bull. I'd already decided that he wasn't going to get any names from me, but the problem was that the story I'd come up with to put him off the scent involved telling him about the tracker. And I'd just realised that the tracker was quite possibly my only chance of getting out of here alive.

'I asked you a question, kid,' Dee Dee said coldly. 'If you don't want to get hurt, I suggest you answer it.'

'Look in the top pocket of your jacket,' I told him.

'What?'

'Your top pocket.'

He frowned, then reached into his top pocket and pulled out the tracker.

'What the hell's this?' he said, studying it closely.

'It's a surveillance device,' I explained. 'It tracks your location and records everything you say. I slipped it into your pocket when you came to our office the other day.'

He stared at the tracker, deep in thought, and I knew he was thinking back to when he was in the office, trying to remember if I'd got close enough to him to put the tracker in his pocket.

'I did it when I gave you the micro memory card,' I told him. 'Remember? It was in an envelope. I got it from my grandad's office and gave it to you. When I handed you the envelope, you took your eyes off me for a second. That's when I put the tracker in your pocket.'

He didn't say anything for a while, he just sat there, thinking hard, trying to picture the moment I gave him the envelope. While he thought about that, I wondered if I'd just given up my only hope of being rescued. Whether Dee Dee believed me or not, he was bound to destroy the tracker, and once it was gone, that was it. No tracker, no way to find me. But at least Jaydie and Jazz should be safe.

'So this records what I'm saying *and* tells you where I am?' Dee Dee said, still examining the tracker.

I nodded. 'I heard you arranging the meeting with Bull, and I tracked you to the car park.'

'How does it work?'

'It's connected to my mobile. If you untie my hands and pass it to me, I'll show you.'

He smiled. 'You think I'm stupid? Just tell me how it works.'

As I told him how to access the tracker screen, I hoped he wasn't going to ask to hear the recording I told him I'd made of his phone call with Bull.

'So this green dot shows where the tracker is, right?'

'Yeah.'

'Who else has access to this screen?'

'My grandad,' I lied. 'It's linked up to his laptop. So right now, he'll know exactly where I am.'

Dee Dee looked at me, trying to work out if I was telling the truth or not. 'Call Delaney's office, Ron,' he said to Bull.

'What for?'

'Just do it.'

'What's the number?' Bull asked me, taking out his mobile.

There wasn't much point in lying, so I told him. He keyed in the number, then turned to Dee Dee. 'What do you want me to say?'

'Just ask to speak to the old man.'

'Then what?'

Dee Dee sighed. 'I just want to know if he's there or not, OK? Put it on speaker.'

Bull called the number and put the phone on speaker. I heard the phone ringing, then the sound of it being answered. 'Delaney & Co, can I help you?'

It was Grandad's voice.

'Is Joseph Delaney there?' Bull said.

'Speaking.'

Bull ended the call.

Dee Dee grinned at me. 'If he knows you're here, he doesn't seem too bothered about it, does he?'

'He probably hasn't checked the tracker screen on his laptop yet,' I said.

'Maybe . . .' Dee Dee said. 'Or it could be that you're lying through your teeth and he doesn't actually *have* the tracker screen on his laptop.'

'That's a possibility,' I admitted. 'But are you willing to take the risk?'

'What risk? The risk that a grouchy old man might turn up here and give me a nasty look?' Dee Dee laughed. 'I think I could just about handle that. Not that it's going to happen anyway. You know why not? I'll tell you why not. Because you're one of those know-it-all kids who think they can do everything on their own, and my guess is that you haven't told anyone else about tracking me and Ronnie. You're keeping it all to your smart-arse little self.'

'I'd have to be pretty stupid to do that, wouldn't I?' I said.

'You'd also have to be pretty stupid to end up tied to a chair, miles from anywhere, with no one knowing where you are. But you seem to have managed that without any trouble. The truth is, kid, you're way out of your league here.'

I hated to admit it, but I couldn't help wondering if he was right. Maybe I *was* completely out of my depth. And maybe if I hadn't been so stupid, I wouldn't be sitting here tied to a chair, miles from anywhere, with no one knowing where I was . . . and not much hope of leaving here alive.

I wasn't going to share my doubts with Dee Dee though, so I forced myself to look him confidently in the eye and let him think that maybe, just maybe, I *did* know what I was doing.

He stared back at me, long and hard, then glanced

down at the tracker in his hand. He tossed it in the air a couple of times, thinking things over, then he got up and started looking through the cupboards and drawers in the kitchen. Eventually he found what he was looking for – a big old cast-iron frying pan. He pulled it out of the cupboard, put the tracker on the stone floor, raised the frying pan over his head, then smashed it down on the tracker, completely destroying it with a single blow. All that was left of it was a small slab of flattened metal and countless tiny fragments of broken plastic and circuitry scattered all over the floor. Dee Dee wasn't finished yet though. He came over to the table, picked up my mobile, and took the back off it. He removed the SIM card and the memory card, put them in his pocket, then dropped the phone to the floor and proceeded to smash it to smithereens with the frying pan. He didn't just hit it once this time, he kept on hammering it over and over again, until he was satisfied that the phone – and everything stored in it – was totally beyond repair.

'Right,' he said, dropping the pan on the floor, 'that should do it. Now I need to make a phone call.' He turned to Bull. 'Where's the nearest phone box?'

'You can use this,' Bull said, offering him his mobile.

'I don't use mobiles. Even if I did, you wouldn't want the number I'm calling listed in your call log.'

A look passed between them then, and it wasn't hard to guess what Dee Dee meant.

'There's a phone box at the end of the street,' Bull

said. 'Just turn left at the bottom of the drive and keep going. You can't miss it.'

Dee Dee glanced at me, then turned back to Bull. 'I'm relying on you, Ron. Do you understand?'

'I've got it, OK? Don't worry.'

Dee Dee stared at him for a moment or two, silently reminding him that they were in this together, and that if anything went wrong they'd both probably end up dead, then he turned away and headed for the door. 'I'll be five minutes,' he said. 'Lock the door after me.'

He went out, and Bull followed him to lock the door, leaving me alone for a few moments. I flexed my arms as hard as I could, twisting my wrists and trying to pull my hands free, but it was useless. From the feel of it, my wrists were bound with police-issue plastic handcuffs, and my tethered hands were securely tied to the back of the chair. I tried to get to my feet, but with my hands fixed to the back of the chair I couldn't straighten up properly.

When the kitchen door opened and Bull came back in, I was kind of half standing up, bent over the table at a right angle, with the chair jammed into my back. Bull didn't say anything, he just came over to me and forcibly sat me back down again.

As he went over and stood beside the sink again, I could see the doubts and concerns in his eyes, and I knew that I had to work on them. He was the weak link. And now that I was alone with him, I had just under five minutes to try and break him.

49

'You know who he's calling, don't you?' I said to Bull.

He didn't answer, didn't even look at me.

'He's calling his hitman,' I went on, 'the guy he uses whenever he needs to dispose of somebody. He's telling him he's got a job for him. You know that, don't you?'

Bull remained silent, just standing at the sink with his back to me, staring blindly at nothing.

'You can't just ignore it,' I told him. 'You're *part* of it. The very least you'll be guilty of is accessory to murder, but the way I see it—'

'Hey, kid,' he said. 'Just shut up, will you?'

'I know you don't *want* to be part of all this—'

'You don't know anything.'

'He's going to *kill* me, for God's sake. Are you really going to just look the other way and pretend it's nothing to do with you? I mean, I know you're a bad cop, and you've got yourself into a bad situation, but underneath it all you're still a police officer. Doesn't that mean *any*thing to you?'

Bull sighed. 'Look,' he said, turning to face me, 'even if I wanted to help you, there's nothing I can do, so you might as well save your breath.'

'All you've got to do is let me go. By the time Dee Dee gets back, we can both be out of here.'

'Yeah? And what good will that do us? What do you think Dee Dee's going to do when he finds us gone? Just forget about us? You think he's going to say to himself, "Oh, well, never mind, I suppose I might as leave them alone now"?' Bull looked at me, slowly shaking his head. 'He'll hunt us and down and kill us both, that's what he'll do.'

'Not if you get him arrested.'

Bull laughed. 'Yeah, that's a good idea. Get him arrested.' He shook his head again, as if it was the most ludicrous suggestion he'd ever heard. 'Do you mind telling me how I'm going to explain *my* involvement in all this if I get Dee Dee arrested?'

'You could try telling the truth.'

'The truth would put me behind bars. I'm a cop, a dirty cop at that. Do you know what happens to cops in prison? I'd be lucky if I made it through the first night.'

'All right,' I said, 'so why not just disappear instead? You must have plenty of money stashed away. If we both leave now, you could be out of the country by tomorrow morning.'

'And then I'd be a fugitive for the rest of my life. Even if Dee Dee didn't find me – and believe me, he'd never stop looking – every police force in the world would be on the lookout for me. I'm not going to live the rest of my life on the run.' He paused, looking away from me. 'I'm sorry, kid, but I've already been through all the possible options, and basically it boils down to a choice between my life or yours.' He sighed again. 'I'm sorry, I just can't help you.'

'You mean you *won't* help me.'

'Whatever.'

'You must be really proud of yourself.'

'I lost all pride in myself a long time ago,' he said emptily. 'I know I'm not a good man.'

'And you can live with that?'

'You can learn to live with anything. In the end it's all about survival. That's all there is. You do what you have to do to stay alive. And then you die.' He smiled humourlessly. 'It's not much of a life, is it?'

'You seem pretty keen to keep hold of it.'

He shrugged. 'I don't know why I bother sometimes.'

'You're pathetic,' I said.

'Maybe so,' he said, glancing at his watch, 'but I'd rather be pathetic than dead.'

It was clear that I was wasting my time with him. He might not have liked what Dee Dee had planned for me, but despite the fact that he thought it was wrong, he'd already made up his mind that the cost to him of making it right was too high a price to pay. Like he'd said, it's all about survival, and the only thing he had left in his life was the primitive desire to hold on to it. In his case, it seemed to be a pretty pointless desire, but that didn't make it any less powerful.

'If I'm going to die,' I said to him, 'you could at least put my mind at rest about my mum and dad.'

'What do you mean?'

'I know you work for Omega, and I know you put them in touch with Dee Dee—'

'Omega?' he said, looking genuinely puzzled. 'Who, or what, is Omega?'

I studied his eyes. 'You really don't know, do you?'

'The only Omega I know is the one that makes expensive watches.'

'Omega is the name of the organisation you put in touch with Dee Dee about the riot in North Walk.'

'Oh, *them*,' he said, suddenly realising what I was talking about. 'So they *do* have a name after all.' He nodded to himself, mildly interested. 'Omega, eh? Well, well . . .'

'They killed my parents,' I said.

He looked at me. 'Your parents' death was an accident. Their car spun off the road. I should know, I supervised the investigation—'

'Why?'

'Why what?'

'You just told me it was an accident, their car just spun off the road.'

'So?'

'So what's a high-ranking CID officer doing investigating a run-of-the-mill road traffic accident?'

Bull hesitated, and I knew then that he was definitely covering something up. 'It was purely a supervisory role,' he said, trying to sound nonchalant about it. 'I wasn't involved in any procedural capacity—'

'Why don't you just tell me the truth?' I said. 'I mean, what harm can it do now? I'm going to be dead before the day's out. All I want is to know the truth about my mum and dad before I go. That's not too much to ask, is it?'

Bull shook his head. 'I'm sorry kid, but I honestly can't tell you anything. I admit that I sometimes do a bit of work for these people you call Omega, but I don't know anything about them. I've never even met any of them. I just get a coded message every now and then from an anonymous contact, asking for information or telling me to do something. I do what I'm told, I get paid, and that's it. But my instructions to supervise the investigation into your parents' death didn't come from Omega, not directly anyway. They came from within the force, from someone a lot higher up than me. I wasn't given any explanation or further details, I was simply told to look over the investigation, check it out thoroughly, and make sure there was nothing suspicious about it.' He looked at me. 'If there *was* any kind of cover-up, it was all taken care of long before I got involved. The only thing I can tell you is that when I went over all the evidence and the accident reports, there was no indication whatsoever that your parents' crash was anything other than a single-vehicle road traffic accident.'

It was possible that he was lying, but if he was, he was one hell of an actor. And I just didn't think he was that good. Every instinct told me he was essentially telling the truth. Of course, that didn't mean that Omega hadn't used the police to cover up their involvement in my parents' death, all it meant was that Bull wasn't their only asset in the local police force. They had people working for them who were much higher up than Bull – higher up, more influential, more powerful. Bull was just a hired hand, a middleman, a go-between. He didn't know anything about Omega. He hadn't even known they were called Omega until I'd told him. I wasn't going to get anything out of him. So I left him to his thoughts – whatever they might be – and I spent the rest of the time before Dee Dee came back trying to figure out a way to stay alive.

50

By the time Dee Dee returned, I still hadn't come up with any ideas as to how I was going to save my skin.

'He'll be here in twenty minutes,' Dee Dee told Bull as they came back into the kitchen.

'I'll leave you to it then,' Bull said. 'You don't need me any more, do you?'

'You stay till he gets here.'

'Why?'

Dee Dee just glared at him. Bull looked back at him for a moment, and I thought he was going to stand up for himself and argue his case, but after a second or two he just let out a weary sigh and went back over to the sink. Dee Dee came over and sat down opposite me at the table. He lit a cigarette and blew out a stream of smoke.

'Scared you can't handle me on your own?' I said to him, glancing at Bull.

'I could handle you with my eyes closed.'

'You think so?'

'I know so.'

'Cut me loose then,' I said. 'Let's see how tough you really are.'

Dee Dee grinned. 'What do you think this is – a James Bond movie?' He shook his head. 'You can try riling me as much as you want, kid. You're staying tied to that chair.'

'If you're so sure of yourself,' I said, trying again, 'how come you need someone else to do your dirty work?'

He shrugged. 'If I need a haircut, I go to the barber's. If I need my flat painted, I call in the decorators . . .'

'Right,' I said, nodding. 'And if you need someone killed, you call in your hitman.'

'Delegation,' Dee Dee said. 'It's the first rule of business. You have to know how to delegate.'

'You're not a *businessman*,' I said scornfully. 'You're just a thug and a bully. You're a small-time gangster, and that's all you'll ever be.'

He shrugged again. 'I've already told you, you're wasting your time. You can insult me, put me down, disrespect me . . . you can say whatever you like about me. It's not going to do you any good.' He glanced at his watch. 'In fifteen minutes' time, a guy who cares even less about you than I do is going to be here, and you're still going to be tied to that chair.'

'What's he going to say when he sees DI Bull and I tell him that you're a grass?'

'Well, firstly he's *not* going to see DI Bull. Secondly, he wouldn't believe you even if you did tell him. And thirdly, you're not going to be able to say anything anyway because by the time he gets here I'll have taped up your mouth.' Dee Dee smiled at me. 'Got any more smart ideas?'

The answer to that, unfortunately, was no. I couldn't think of anything else to say or do. That's not to say that

I'd given up – I was *never* going to give up – but at that moment I simply couldn't see any way out. I was securely bound to the chair. I could barely stand, let alone run anywhere. No one knew where I was. And I didn't have anything to bargain with.

I was, to put it simply, stuffed.

The funny thing was, I didn't actually feel all that scared. I was perfectly aware of the gravity of the situation, and I knew there was a pretty good chance that I wouldn't live to see the end of the day, so it wasn't as if I was trying to kid myself that there was nothing to be frightened of. I suppose I'd just realised – probably subconsciously – that there was simply no point in being afraid. Fear didn't help me. It didn't serve any purpose. All it did was make things worse. So, just for now, I'd bundled it all up into a tight little ball and buried it away in a place deep inside me where it couldn't do any harm.

There'd be plenty of time to let it out later.

Dee Dee had got up from the table now and was talking quietly with Bull over by the sink.

'. . . leave by the back door when he gets here,' I heard Dee Dee tell Bull. 'All you've got to do is keep your mouth shut and everything will be fine.'

'You realise this is going to be massive, don't you?' Bull said. 'Once the media find out that a young kid's gone missing, everything's going to go crazy. TV crews, national newspapers . . . the whole town will be swarming with people. There'll be televised press conferences, cops everywhere . . . I mean, this'll be the biggest investigation we've had for years—'

'And you'll be right in the middle of it, won't you? So if there *are* any problems, you'll be in the perfect position to deal with them.'

'The police are going to be looking everywhere—'

'They won't find anything.'

'But what about—?'

'Listen, Ronnie, there's nothing to worry about, OK? It'll all be forgotten in a couple of weeks anyway. He'll just be another missing kid. Something else will come along that grabs the headlines, the police will start scaling back their operation, and everything will get back to normal. So just sit tight and relax, all right?' Dee Dee looked at his watch. 'He'll be here soon, you'd better get ready to—'

The doorbell sounded then, a loud piercing buzz, and Dee Dee and Bull both froze for a moment.

'Is that him?' Bull said.

Dee Dee leaned over the sink, pulled down one of the slats of the blind, and peered out through the gap. 'What the hell?' he said, sounding confused and surprised. 'What's *she* doing here?'

'Who is it?' Bull said.

'The old woman . . .'

'What old woman?'

'The one from Delaney's.'

'Gloria Nightingale?' Bull said, leaning over and looking for himself.

'You *know* her?'

'Sort of . . .' Bull said, still gazing through the blinds.

The doorbell rang again.

'She's something to do with those people I was telling you about,' Bull told Dee Dee. 'You know, the ones you organised the riot for?'

'She works for them?'

'I don't know if she actually *works* for them, but she's definitely connected in some way.'

'How does she know we're here. Did you tell her?'

'No, of course not. I've only ever spoken to her once, and that was weeks ago.'

'So how does she know?'

'There's only one way to find out, isn't there?'

'Christ,' Dee Dee said angrily, shaking his head. 'I really don't need this.' He looked through the blinds again. 'Is she on her own?'

'I can't see anyone else.'

'All right,' Dee Dee said thoughtfully, moving away from the window. He pulled his knife from his pocket, then came over and stood behind me. He held the knife to my throat, then said to Bull, 'Go and let her in. If she's with anyone else, just shout as loud as you can, OK?'

Bull hesitated for a moment, then headed out of the kitchen.

Dee Dee rested the blade of the knife against my skin.

'You'd better hope she doesn't try anything,' he told me.

I didn't answer, I just sat there, trying to work out what was going on. What *was* Gloria doing here? What was her connection with Bull? Was she just another of Omega's many assets, like Bull, or was she actually part of the organisation? Was she here because of Bull? Or because of me? And how did she know that either of us were here anyway?

I didn't have any answers.

I heard the front door opening, then muffled voices. The voices sounded friendly enough. There was no warning shout from Bull, so I guessed Gloria really was on her own. I could hear footsteps approaching the kitchen now, and as the kitchen door opened, I felt the blade of Dee Dee's knife pressing into my skin.

Bull came in first, followed closely by Gloria.

'It's all right, Dee,' Bull said, 'there's no one with her.'

'Good evening, Mr Devon,' Gloria said calmly, looking at Dee Dee.

He didn't reply.

She looked at me. 'Hello, Travis. Are you all right?'

'Yeah, wonderful, thanks.'

She smiled, then turned her attention back to Dee Dee. 'I strongly suggest you put down your knife, Mr Devon.'

'Or else what?'

She started to reach into her pocket.

Dee Dee immediately grabbed my hair and pulled my

head back, exposing my throat to his knife. 'If you do anything stupid,' he told Gloria, 'I'll cut his throat.'

'There's no need to be alarmed, Mr Devon,' she said, keeping perfectly still. 'I just want to show you something. May I continue?'

Dee Dee nodded. 'Nice and slow.'

Gloria reached slowly into her pocket and – equally slowly – pulled out her mobile phone. She held it up for Dee Dee to see. 'I'm just going to play a video for you, OK? I'm not calling anyone, I promise. Can I go ahead?'

'Go on then,' Dee Dee said.

Still moving very slowly, Gloria pressed a couple of keys on her mobile then held it out again for Dee Dee to see. When the video began, I couldn't make out what I was seeing at first. All it looked like were two dark round lumps on the screen. But then the sound kicked in, and I immediately recognised Dee Dee's voice: *Listen, Ron, I'm getting a bit sick of waiting for you to bust Malik and his boys. Everything's in place with Beacon, the deal's all ready to go ahead. I just need Malik out of the way.*

And then Bull's voice replying: *I'm working on it, Dee. It takes time. I've got to get the go-ahead from my boss, get the warrants sorted out—*

I don't care what you've got to do, I just want it done. I'm paying you good money, and you're going to be getting a ton of gear out of it. I want results.

All at once I realised what I was looking at on the screen. It was a video of Dee Dee and Bull, talking in the corridor at the car park, but it had been shot from directly *above* them. The two dark round lumps were the tops of their heads. I couldn't *believe* it. While I'd been hiding in the maintenance room, recording them through the meshed glass of the door, someone else had somehow been recording them from above.

Gloria stopped the video.

'I have the entire meeting on tape,' she told Dee Dee. 'And there are numerous copies of the video secured in various locations.' She glanced at her watch. 'If I don't send a pre-arranged text within the next sixty seconds, a copy of the tape will be posted on YouTube and texts advertising the posting will be sent to scores of your colleagues. I'm not going to send that text until you drop the knife.' She stared at Dee Dee, and suddenly there was nothing 'old-woman-ish' about her at all. She looked as hard as nails.

'I think you're bluffing,' Dee Dee told her, doing his best to sound confident.

'Forty-five seconds,' Gloria said.

51

It took Dee Dee about fifteen seconds to realise that he couldn't risk calling Gloria's bluff.

'All right,' he said, dropping the knife and holding up his hands. 'Now send your text.'

'Move right away from Travis,' she told him.

'OK, OK,' he said quickly, moving back. 'I'm not going to touch him.'

Gloria kept her eyes on Dee Dee for a moment, then she glanced down at her mobile and pressed a key. 'That's just the first in a series of pre-arranged signals,' she said, looking back up at Dee Dee. 'Each one has to be sent at a specific time. If that doesn't happen, the video *will* be posted and the texts *will* be sent. Do you understand?'

'Yeah.'

'Sit down on the floor over there,' she told him, nodding towards the corner of the room.

Dee Dee did as he was told.

'You too,' Gloria said to Bull. 'Down on the floor.'

'What are you *doing*?' he said, frowning at her. 'I thought you were . . .'

'You thought I was what?'

He glanced sideways at me, then turned back to Gloria. 'I just thought . . . well, you know . . .'

'I told you to sit down,' she said firmly.

He lowered himself to the floor.

'I couldn't care less what you *think*, Detective Inspector,' she said to him. 'All I want you to do is sit there and keep your mouth shut, OK?'

He didn't have anything to say to that, so he just sat there with a sulky look on his face. Gloria stared at him for a few moments, then looked over at me.

'Have they hurt you at all, Travis?' she asked.

I shook my head, desperately trying to work her out. She seemed genuinely concerned for my well-being, and there was no doubt that – for the moment, at least – she was on my side. But I'd *seen* her meeting secretly with Winston and passing him information, and there was no denying that either.

I really didn't know what to think.

What I *did* know though was that if I didn't tell her about Dee Dee's hitman, we were both going to be in serious trouble.

'Dee Dee called someone to come here and finish me off,' I told her. 'He'll be here any minute.'

She looked over at Dee Dee. 'What does he look like?'

Dee Dee didn't answer.

'I'm only going to warn you once more,' Gloria told him, holding up her mobile. 'Unless you do *exactly* as I say, everyone's going to know about your collaboration with the police. Now, what does this hitman of yours look like?'

'He's a scrawny little white guy,' Dee Dee said, with

a resigned sigh. 'About five seven, long straggly hair, bad teeth.'

'How's he getting here?'

'Car.'

'Make and model?'

'He usually drives an old BMW. It's black. I don't know what model it is.'

Gloria hit a key on her phone and put it to her ear. Whoever she was calling answered almost immediately.

'Dee Dee's called in a hitman. He'll be here any minute. White male, five seven, long straggly hair, bad teeth. He's probably driving an old black BMW. Do what you have to do, OK?'

She paused for a moment, listening, then said, 'OK,' and ended the call. She came over to me, picked up Dee Dee's knife from the floor, and began cutting me loose.

'Hold your hands apart if you can,' she said gently. 'That's it . . .'

I could feel the knife slicing through the plastic cuffs round my wrists, and then all at once my hands were free. I immediately began rubbing at my wrists, trying to ease the pain from the cuffs and get my circulation going again.

'Is that better?' Gloria asked me.

I turned round and looked into her eyes, still not knowing what to think of her.

She smiled at me. 'It's all right, Travis. I know you're

confused, but I'll explain everything later. Just trust me for now, OK?'

I nodded, giving her the benefit of the doubt . . . for now.

'Right,' she said, turning to Dee Dee, 'I'm going to tell you what you're going to do now, and you're going to listen very carefully and not say a word until I've finished. Do you understand?'

He nodded.

Gloria turned to Bull. 'The same goes for you, Detective Inspector. Do *you* understand?'

He nodded as well.

'Good,' said Gloria. 'First of all, let me remind both of you that failure to comply with the following instructions *will* result in the video of your recent meeting being made public. Safeguards have already been put in place with a number of third parties to ensure that the video will also be made public if any attempts are made to nullify this threat. That not only includes attempts to destroy or appropriate the tape, but also any attempt to gain access to the video through personal attacks or threats to the staff of Delaney & Co and/or their immediate family and friends.' She paused, looking at Dee Dee and Bull to make sure they understood what she was saying. 'Now I'm sure I don't have to tell you what will happen if the video is made public, but what you *do* need to know is that I'm well aware of the consequences too. I *know* that the revelation of your relationship would be a death sentence for both of you, and you need to know that I'm fully prepared to accept that. In fact, if it was up to me, I'd quite happily have you both taken out right now. But that's by the by. All that matters is that you don't doubt me for a second. This is *not* an empty threat.'

An alert went off on her mobile then, a single quiet *chirp*. She glanced at the screen, reading a text message. She quickly replied to it, her thumb skipping effortlessly across the screen, then she went over to the window by the sink, looked out through the blinds, and closed them again. She then opened a cupboard above the sink and took out a dusty glass. She rinsed it out under the tap, filled it with water, and brought it over to me.

'You probably need that,' she said.

'Thanks,' I told her, suddenly realising how thirsty I was. I drained the glass in one go.

'Do you want some more?' Gloria asked.

I shook my head.

She smiled at me again, then turned back to Dee Dee. 'Right, there's one more thing you need to know about the video before I start telling you what you're going to do. You'll have noticed that it's shot from above, and that in the clip I played you, your faces aren't very clear. Now if you're thinking that's your get-out-of-jail card, because you can deny that it's you on the tape, you're wrong. Firstly, voice analysis will prove that it's you and DI Bull. And secondly, there are a number of occasions on the tape when both of you raise your heads just enough to make identification unquestionable. You don't have to take my word for it. I've already had a copy of the tape emailed to DI Bull's mobile, so you can watch it at your leisure and see for yourself. Now, if we're all clear on that, I think it's time to get down to business.' She went over to Dee Dee, stood in front of him, and stared down into his eyes. 'Listen very carefully, Mr Devon. This is what you're going to do.'

52

Although I still had serious doubts about Gloria, and I was only temporarily putting them on hold because I didn't have any choice, I couldn't help but admire the way she commanded the situation. She was totally in control of everything. Armed only with a mobile phone and a series of calmly spoken threats, she had Dee Dee and Ronnie Bull exactly where she wanted them. All they could do was sit on the floor like naughty children and listen to her while she reeled off a string of demands.

'First of all,' she told Dee Dee, 'you're going to write off Lisa Yusuf's debt and let her keep her job in Tanga Tans if she wants it. You'll employ her on a completely legitimate basis, and you'll pay her twice the minimum wage. If she doesn't want the job, you'll let her go with a one-off cash-in-hand redundancy payment of £5,000. Whether or not she wants her job, you'll stop laundering drug money through Tanga Tans. Is that understood?'

Dee Dee looked as if he was about to protest, but when Gloria glared at him, he changed his mind and just nodded instead.

'Secondly,' Gloria went on, 'you'll make a £25,000 donation to a charity called Parkinson's UK. Agreed?'

Dee Dee shook his head. 'I don't have that kind of money.'

'You'll have to take out a loan then, won't you? I'm sure you know plenty of people who are willing to lend you money at very reasonable rates. Now, I'll ask you again, is that agreed?'

'Yeah,' he said sourly.

'Thirdly,' Gloria continued, 'you'll have no further contact of any kind whatsoever, either directly or indirectly, with the staff of Delaney & Co or their families and friends. You will not approach them, talk to them, go anywhere near them. You will not threaten them. You will not harm them. You will not touch a single hair on their heads. Is *that* understood?'

Dee Dee nodded again.

'All right,' Gloria said. 'Well, that's just about it.'

Dee Dee looked surprised. 'You're not going to turn me in?'

'As long as you comply with our demands, you're free to carry on doing whatever it is you do. It's not my job to clear the streets of dog mess like you. Just make sure you keep your stink away from us, that's all.'

'What about me?' Bull said.

'What *about* you?' Gloria replied.

'Do you have any demands for me?'

Gloria laughed. 'What could I possibly want from *you*? You know that I hold your life in my hands, and you're not going to do anything to jeopardise that, are you? I'd *like* to report you to your superiors and let them deal with you, but for one thing I don't trust your superiors, and for another, any action taken against you would necessarily implicate Mr Devon, and unfortunately, at the moment, it's easier for everyone if he remains a free man. So, no, I'm not going to do anything with you, Detective Inspector Bull. You can carry on as you are, living your dirty little life, taking the devil's gold.' She smiled coldly. 'That's if he still wants you on his payroll, of course. It's quite possible that he doesn't require your services any more. But I'll leave that to you to sort out between yourselves. I'm sure it'll all work out very nicely for you.'

The doorbell rang then.

'Ah,' Gloria said, turning back to Dee Dee, 'I almost forgot. There's someone else who wants a quick word with you.' She looked at me. 'Would you mind getting the door, Travis?'

'Who is it?' I asked, wondering what on earth was going on.

'Why don't you go and see?' she said, smiling.

I got to my feet, hesitated for a moment, then headed out of the kitchen. The doorway led through into a spacious hallway with a stone-tiled floor and a high ceiling. The front door was on my right. I wondered briefly if Gloria was setting me up for an unpleasant surprise, making me think that everything was OK and then – BAM! – I open the door and it's Winston or Lance Borstlap or somebody else from Omega. But then I realised that it didn't really matter whether I opened the door or not, because whoever was there was going to get in anyway. So I just took a breath, unlatched the security chain and unlocked the door, and opened it.

'Hey, Travis,' Courtney said, beaming at me. 'I bet you didn't expect to see me here, did you?'

I felt so relieved I couldn't speak for a moment, I just threw my arms around her and squeezed her tight.

'Whoa!' she said, wincing. 'Not so hard, Trav. My ribs aren't quite up to it yet.'

'Sorry,' I said, letting her go and ushering her into the house. 'God, am I glad to see you. How are you? How's your head? Do you know what's going on? I haven't got a clue—'

'Just calm down a second, Travis,' she said. 'Everything's OK. I'll explain it all when we get out of here. Where is everybody?'

'Through there,' I said, indicating the kitchen doorway. It was only then that I noticed she was carrying a baseball bat. 'What's that for?' I asked her.

'Retribution,' she said simply, heading for the doorway.

53

'Is everything taken care of?' Gloria asked Courtney as we entered the kitchen.

'No problem,' Courtney said, glancing around at Dee Dee and Bull. 'The guy in the black BMW showed up about a minute after you called me.' She slapped the baseball bat into the palm of her hand. 'He's having a little nap in his car at the moment. And when he wakes up he'll find that he's cuffed to his steering wheel.'

'Has Joseph turned up yet?'

'No. I tried calling him but his mobile's turned off. He's probably stuck in traffic or something.' She looked at Bull. 'You must be Dee Dee's pet cop.'

Bull didn't reply, he just sat there looking sorry for himself.

Courtney turned to Dee Dee. 'And you, of course, are the mighty Drew Devon. Mr Big. The tough guy who gets his goons to do his dirty work for him.' She went over and stood in front of Dee Dee, her eyes fixed on his like laser beams. 'I'm Courtney Lane,' she told him. 'You're responsible for putting me in hospital. Do you enjoy getting women beaten up? Does it make you feel good?'

Dee Dee shrugged. 'It's just business.'

'Just business?' Courtney said quietly.

'You want me to apologise?' he said, sneering at her. 'All right, I'm sorry you got hurt, OK? But you can't say I didn't warn you. I *told* you to keep out of it, didn't I? You've only got yourself to blame.'

'Get up,' she said.

'What?'

'Stand up.'

Dee Dee hesitated. 'What are you going to do?'

'If you don't stand up, right now, I'm going to crack you in the head with this baseball bat. That's what I'm going to do.'

He slowly got to his feet. He didn't look quite so defiant now. He'd seen the look in Courtney's eyes, and he'd realised there was a lot more to her than he'd thought.

'Hey, listen,' he said, holding up his hands. 'I understand how you must feel—'

'Turn around.'

'What?'

'Turn. Around.'

The uncertainty in his eyes had changed to a look of genuine fear now. He knew that Courtney wasn't just messing around with him. She meant business.

'You can't do this . . .' he muttered. 'You can't just—'

She raised the baseball bat over her shoulder. 'If you don't turn around in the next three seconds, I'm going to smash open your skull. Do you understand?'

'What are you going to—?'

'One . . .'

'No, *please*—'

'Two . . .'

'OK! OK!' he spluttered, turning round.

'Now put your hands against the wall,' Courtney told him.

He did as he was told.

'Spread your legs.'

'*Please* don't do this,' he begged. 'I promise I'll make it up to you. I'll do anything—'

'I said, spread your legs.'

As he hesitantly spread his legs, he was literally shaking with fear. He was standing there with his hands against the wall and his legs wide apart, and he was absolutely terrified of what Courtney might do to him.

She was just standing there now, staring murderously at the back of his head, the baseball bat gripped tightly in her hands. I wanted to reach out to her, to tell her to stop, don't do it, don't sink to his level, but I couldn't even breathe, let alone speak. I was frozen to the spot, petrified by the look in Courtney's eyes.

'How does it feel, big man?' she said calmly. 'How does it feel, knowing that you're about to die?'

'*Please*,' he sobbed. 'Please don't—'

'It's not very nice, is it?' she said, stepping softly towards him.

'No . . .'

She moved right up close to him, paused for a second,

then leaned forward and whispered in his ear. 'If I ever see you or any of your thugs again, I won't just make you wet your pants, I'll make you wish you'd never been born. Nod your head if you understand.'

As Dee Dee desperately nodded his head, I noticed a dark stain on his trousers. Courtney really had made him wet his pants.

She stepped away from him, turned round, and for a second or two she just stood there, breathing quietly, staring at the floor. Then she let out a long sigh and looked up. The violence had gone from her eyes.

'Right,' she said, 'I think it's about time we got out of here, don't you?'

54

As we left the house and headed down a long, hedge-lined gravel driveway, Gloria tried ringing Grandad again. There was no reply from his mobile, and as she tried the office number, I looked around at the tall privet hedges and the rooftops of neighbouring houses in the distance.

'Where are we?' I asked Courtney.

'Birch Grove,' she said, 'home to the wealthy and privileged.'

She was right. Birch Grove is easily the most well-to-do suburb in Barton, the kind of place where houses start at around a million pounds. The only locals you're likely to see around the Grove, as it's known, are the people who come here to work – nannies, cleaners, gardeners. I'd only ever been to Birch Grove once before, and after everything I'd just been through, I'd be perfectly happy if I never had to come here again.

'Any luck?' Courtney asked Gloria.

'No . . . no answer. It's a bit strange, don't you think?'

'Is Grandad supposed to be here?' I asked.

'That was the plan, yeah,' Courtney said. 'I'm sure there's no need to worry,' she told Gloria. 'Like I said, he's probably caught up in traffic somewhere. There's a lot of black spots between here and town where the mobile reception isn't that good.'

Gloria nodded, but she didn't look reassured.

We'd reached the end of the driveway now and were coming out into a broad residential avenue lined with bare-branched birch trees and large detached houses. The houses were all set back from the street behind well-tended hedges and long winding driveways.

'We're parked over there,' Courtney told me, pointing along the street. 'Come on, there's someone in the car who wants to see you.'

We passed the old black BMW on the way to Courtney's car. Dee Dee's hitman was slumped in the driver's seat, still unconscious, his left hand secured to the steering wheel with a plastic cuff. An egg-sized bump was clearly visible on the side of his head, and a thin stream of blood was oozing down his face.

'Baseball bat?' I said to Courtney.

She nodded. 'I didn't hit him all that hard. He'll probably be all right.'

He didn't look like much – just a stringy little guy, kind of ratty-looking, with grubby skin and dirty fingernails, wearing an old blue anorak and a sweat-stained baseball cap. I don't know what I expected a hitman to look like – maybe a chisel-jawed guy with a scar on his face, dressed in a black suit and gloves – but whatever I was expecting, this scrawny little guy certainly wasn't it.

But then it suddenly struck me what he'd come here to do, and despite his underwhelming appearance, the sight of him made me shudder. I looked away and carried on walking, trying not to think about what could have happened.

I could see Courtney's car up ahead now, and just as I spotted it, the door swung open and a familiar figure jumped out. It was Jaydie, and from the way she was smiling and running towards me, her eyes lit up like neon lights, I guessed she was pleased to see me. I had to admit that my heart was beating pretty quickly too.

'Travis!' she yelled, throwing herself at me. 'Thank *God* you're all right! I was *so* worried about you!'

I held her tightly for a moment or two, surprised at how good it felt to be back in her arms, and then I remembered that we weren't alone. I gently put her down, not feeling *too* embarrassed, and just stood there grinning at her like a fool.

'It was you, wasn't it?' I said. 'You made the video of Dee Dee and Bull.'

She nodded. 'I thought you might need a bit of help.'

'I should have asked you to help me in the first place,' I said. 'I wanted to . . . I just didn't want you to get hurt.'

'I know . . . it's all right, Trav. Everything's OK now, that's the main thing.'

Gloria interrupted us then. 'Excuse me, you two,' she said, 'but we really ought to get going. There'll be plenty of time to talk in the car.'

*

Once we were in the car and on our way back to Barton – Jaydie and Courtney in the back, me in the passenger seat, Gloria driving – I finally began getting some answers. Jaydie explained how she'd got the bus into town and gone to the car park after calling me about the meeting between Dee Dee and Bull.

'I was pretty annoyed with you, Travis,' she admitted. 'I mean, I'd done all the work – bugging the phone box and getting the tracker planted on Dee Dee – and now you were telling me to keep out of it.'

'I didn't mean it like that,' I told her. 'I tried calling you back to explain—'

'I didn't want to talk to you,' she said, grinning. 'So I turned off my phone.'

When she got to the third floor of the car park, she explained, she did exactly the same as I'd done when I got there – looked around for somewhere to hide.

'I tried all the doors, but they were locked, as you know. So I kept looking, and that's when I spotted the hatch in the ceiling. I guessed there must be some kind of crawl space or something up there, otherwise what was the point of the hatch? And I knew it was a good place to hide, because people never look up, do they?'

'She's right,' Gloria said. 'People hardly ever look upwards, whatever they're doing. You ought to try it one day, when you're in a really familiar place, like walking along the High Street or something. Just stop and take a look upwards. You'll suddenly see things that you've never seen, even though you've been there hundreds of times before.' She smiled. 'Sorry, Jaydie, I didn't mean to interrupt. Carry on with your story.'

'Well,' Jaydie said, 'it wasn't hard to get up to the hatch, I just climbed onto one of those metal unit things against the wall, gave the hatch a quick shove, and it opened straight away. All I had to do then was pull myself up. There was a massive space up there, like a six-foot-high gap between the whole of the third and fourth floors. It was filled with wires and cables and all sorts of stuff. Anyway, I got myself into a reasonably comfortable position, kind of lying down on my front with my head over the hatchway, and I put the hatch back so there was just enough of a gap to see through, and then I just had to wait.'

'So you were there when I arrived?' I said.

'Yep. I was up there watching you. I nearly called down to you at one point, but I was still really angry with you, and it kind of made me feel good that you didn't know I was there, you know, like I was getting one over on you.' She shrugged. 'It sounds a bit childish, I suppose . . .'

'Hell hath no fury like a woman scorned,' Courtney said, smiling.

'Yeah,' Jaydie agreed. 'Something like that.'

'So you saw me picking the lock and going into the maintenance room,' I said.

Jaydie nodded. 'I have to admit that was pretty

impressive. You only just made it in time though, didn't you?'

'It was close, yeah.'

'So, anyway, while you were in the maintenance room recording Bull and Dee Dee, I was looking down through the hatchway doing the same thing on my phone. The only difference was that I was smart enough to put mine on silent.'

Courtney laughed, and I saw Gloria grinning.

'Yeah, I know,' I said, embarrassed by my own stupidity. 'It's the first rule of surveillance. Make sure your phone's either turned off or on silent. I just forgot, OK? I was in a hurry—'

'That's no excuse, Trav,' Courtney said. 'You should have put it on silent before you even got there.'

'I *know*. It won't happen again. I've learned my lesson the hard way.' I turned to Jaydie. 'So what did you do when it all kicked off with Dee Dee and Bull?'

'I waited to see what happened first. I didn't think there was any point in me getting involved in any physical stuff. I mean, I can look after myself, but I wouldn't stand a chance against two full-grown men, and there was no point in both of us getting caught. I thought you'd got away once you'd taken out Bull and got past Dee Dee, so then I decided to call your grandad to let him know what was happening. But I couldn't get a signal. By the time I'd got down from the hatch and gone looking for you, I couldn't find you anywhere. But when I went down to the ground floor and saw Ronnie Bull guarding the exit, I guessed you hadn't got away after all. So I went out into the street, Googled your office number, and called it.'

'I answered the phone,' Courtney said, taking up the story. 'I'm not supposed to be back at work yet, but Mum's carer wouldn't let me do anything to help out around the house, and I just got so bored sitting around doing nothing, so I popped into the office to see what was happening. I took Jaydie's call, and she quickly told me everything about Dee Dee and Bull and what had just happened at the car park. I told her to stay where she was and I'd be there as soon as possible. I explained everything to Gloria and your grandad before I left, and while I went to get Jaydie and see if I could find you, your grandad and Gloria got working on a plan.'

I looked across at Gloria.

'I'm not what you think I am, Travis,' she said, glancing sideways at me. 'I'm not working for Omega.'

'I *saw* you meeting with Winston,' I told her. 'I followed you to the castle and I saw you giving him something.'

'I know you did. You were *supposed* to follow me and see me with him. That was all part of the plan.'

'Plan?' I said, confused. 'What plan?'

'To bring Omega out into the open.' She glanced at me again. 'They've been keeping you and your grandad under surveillance ever since that night at the warehouse. That's how they knew that your grandad had hired me.

They've been blackmailing me from the day I agreed to work for Delaney & Co.'

'Blackmailing you?'

She sighed. 'It started with a phone call from the man who calls himself Winston.'

55

'I was married for a short while in the late 1980s,' Gloria explained. 'It didn't work out, unfortunately, but the one good thing that did come out of it was my son, David. I was doing a lot of deep undercover work for the security services while he was growing up, and the truth is I wasn't a very good mother. I should have spent more time with him, but I was so obsessed with my work at the time . . .' She shook her head. 'I had my priorities all wrong. I know that now, but at the time I just couldn't see it. Anyway, my relationship with David suffered as a result, and it wasn't really until he was in his late teens that we finally managed to patch things up and get to know one another as mother and son.' She smiled sadly. 'Everything's fine now. We're not *just* mother and son, we're really good friends, and I'm doing my best to make up for lost time. David's doing really well for himself. He seems to have inherited my aptitude for information analysis and communication technology, and after getting a first-class degree in computer science at Cambridge, he now works in research and development for one of the big US technology corporations. It's a great job – good money, excellent prospects – and he really loves it. So when Winston phoned me and threatened to ruin David's career unless I did what he told me . . . well, as you can imagine, it put me in something of a quandary.'

'How was he going to ruin David's career?' I asked.

'He didn't go into any specific details, he just told me to go to my computer and open up a certain email. When I did what he asked, I found pages and pages of personal information about David. They basically knew absolutely everything about him – email addresses, passwords, phone numbers. There were copies of his emails, both private and work-related, copies of texts, copies of document files, details of supposedly secret projects he was working on . . . there was even a video taken from the webcam of his own laptop, showing him typing away in his laboratory. Winston was letting me know that Omega had complete access to David's phones, computers, everything.' She sighed. 'It wasn't hard to guess what that meant. With that level of access, they could put whatever they wanted *into* his phones and computers – false information, incriminating information, information that, if it got out – which Winston promised it would if I didn't do what I was told – would ruin both his career and his life.'

'What did Winston want you to do?'

'Work for him, basically. Take the job at Delaney & Co, keep track of your investigation into Omega, and keep him informed of your progress. If I did that, Winston assured me that David would be left alone.'

'So what did you do?'

'I told your grandad. On my first day at Delaney's,

I passed him a note telling him that we needed to talk privately, and that the office might be bugged. We arranged to meet in that little cafe at the end of North Walk, and I told him everything. That's when we realised that if I pretended to go along with Winston's demands, it would not only keep David safe, but we could actually use it to our advantage.'

'How?'

'By letting Omega know that we were getting close to proving they were responsible for your parents' death. Once they knew that, we knew they'd have to do something about it. And they could only do that by coming out of hiding, which is exactly what your grandad wanted. By bringing them out into the open, that would give him the chance to go after them.'

I remembered then what Grandad had said to me a few days ago. *Whatever happens*, he'd told me, *right or wrong, never forget that there's more than one way to catch a rat.*

I didn't know what he meant at the time, but now I understood.

'Why didn't you let me in on all this?' I asked Gloria.

'I'm sorry, Travis, but we had to make it look as if I really *was* working for Omega. We swept the office for bugs, and we got rid of the ones we found, but we still couldn't be 100% sure that Omega weren't listening in. If you and Courtney knew what we were doing, we'd all have to have been so careful about what we said all the

348

time . . . it would have been almost impossible not to let it slip.'

I looked at Courtney. 'You didn't know either?'

She shook her head. 'I only found out a few hours ago.'

Gloria went on. 'We also realised that if you or Courtney suspected me, you'd probably start watching and following me, and that would make my betrayal look even more believable.'

'Is that why Grandad showed me the trackers?' I asked. 'Because he guessed I'd try to follow you?'

'He thought you might,' Gloria admitted.

'So you knew I was following you when you went to the castle?'

She nodded. 'Winston spotted you too. And it worked. He genuinely thought that because you were following me, that had to mean that I was doing my job for him.'

Although I finally knew the truth now, I was still just as confused as ever. There was no doubt that Grandad and Gloria's plan made perfect sense. If it did work, if it did bring Winston and Omega out into the open, that in itself was further proof that Omega were responsible for the car crash that killed my mum and dad. Why would they come after us if they weren't? And there was no question that proving Omega's involvement in Mum and Dad's death took precedence over everything else, and in that sense it didn't matter that Grandad and Gloria had not only used me, they'd used Nan and Courtney too.

But at the same time I couldn't help feeling that it just wasn't right to have put Nan and me through so much suffering, even if it was for a good cause.

But then I remembered again what Winston had once said – *sometimes we have to make short-term sacrifices for the sake of potential long-term benefits* – and I wondered if maybe Grandad was right after all.

It also suddenly struck me that perhaps Grandad had been just as confused and conflicted about the rights and wrongs of the plan as I was, and that was the reason behind the flicker of embarrassment and guilt I'd seen in his eyes that day in the office when he'd told me there was more than one way to catch a rat. He knew what he was doing was the right thing to do, but at the same time he couldn't help feeling ashamed of himself for doing it.

I couldn't think about it any more. Not now. It was too confusing, and I was too tired. I'd talk to Grandad about it later on.

I put it from my mind and turned to Gloria. 'You knew Jaydie had planted one of the trackers on Dee Dee, didn't you?' I said. 'That's how you knew where Dee Dee and Bull had taken me.'

She nodded. 'I'd already connected both trackers to my laptop and my mobile before your grandad showed them to you. I guessed you might use one on me, and rather than having to keep looking through all my pockets and my handbag all the time to see if you'd planted one somewhere, all I had to do was periodically check the tracker screens to see where they were. So when Jaydie told us how you'd put a tracker on Dee Dee, it was a piece of cake to find out where you were. We just had to work out the best way of getting you out of there. That's why your grandad stayed in the office while we set off after you. We guessed Dee Dee might want to double-check that no one else knew where you were, and that the simplest way for him to do that was to call the office and make sure someone was there. And besides, I knew that if I turned up at the house in Birch Grove on my own, Ronnie Bull would be more likely to let me in.'

'Because he thought you were working for Omega.'

She nodded. 'I'd worked out that it was Bull who'd put Omega in touch with Dee Dee about the riot, and when I met up with him a few weeks ago – ostensibly to ask him what he knew about Omega and Dee Dee – I dropped a few fairly heavy hints that my loyalties lay with Omega rather than Delaney & Co.' She paused then, looking up at the rear-view mirror. 'We're coming into town now, Jaydie. Do you want me to drop you off at the Slade?'

'Yes, please. As long as it's not any trouble.'

'No trouble at all.'

I turned to Jaydie. 'Are you going to tell Mason or your mum about any of this?'

'I think it's probably best if Mason doesn't know anything. I don't know about Mum though. What do you think?'

'She's going to wonder why Dee Dee's written off her debt and given her a pay rise,' I said. 'That's if he does, of course.'

'He will,' Gloria said. 'He can't afford to let anyone see that video. It'll bury him if it gets out. He won't risk that.'

'If I were you,' Courtney said to Jaydie, 'I'd just tell your mum that we managed to get something on Dee Dee and we used that to punish him for what he did to me, and that one of the conditions of his punishment was that he started treating your mum properly. You don't have to go into any details, and it's probably best if she doesn't know that you were involved either. Just tell her that you heard from Travis what happened. Does that sound OK? I mean, I know it means lying to your mum a little bit, but that's better than worrying her to death.'

'I think I can live with a few little lies,' Jaydie said, smiling. She looked out of the car window. We were on Slade Lane now, approaching the estate. 'You can drop me off here,' she told Gloria.

'Are you sure? I don't mind taking you all the way to your place.'

'It's probably best if you don't.'

'Of course,' Gloria said, slowing down and pulling up at the side of the road.

Before the car had stopped moving, Jaydie leaned forward and put her arms round my neck. 'Promise you'll call me soon, Trav, OK?'

'Yeah, I promise. And thanks for saving my life.'

She kissed me on the cheek. 'You're welcome.'

'And I'm sorry I messed you about.'

'I'll forgive you this time,' she said. 'But if you ever do it again . . . well, Courtney's not the only one round here who can kick ass.' She playfully squeezed my neck. 'Do you understand?'

'Yes . . .' I said, choking. 'You're strangling me, Jay.'

'Oops,' she said, grinning. 'Sorry about that.'

She gave me another quick peck on the cheek, then said her goodbyes to everyone and got out of the car. As Gloria drove off, I looked back and saw her waving both hands and doing a dopey little dance on the pavement.

'She's nice,' Courtney said. 'I like her a lot.'

I smiled to myself.

I liked her a lot too.

56

As we drove back to the office, Gloria was getting more and more concerned about Grandad. She was obviously very fond of him, which was nice, but also kind of unsettling. I liked the fact that she cared for him, but at the same I hoped – for Nan's sake – that she didn't care for him *too* much.

Courtney tried calling him again, but she got no reply from his mobile or the office phone, and when she called Nan, she hadn't seen or heard from him either.

'When was he supposed to leave the office?' I asked.

'As soon as Dee Dee or Bull had called to check he was there,' Gloria said. She glanced at her watch. 'What time did they call?'

'What's the time now?'

'Ten to nine.'

I thought back to when Bull had called the office, but I realised that I had no idea what time it had been. 'It was at least an hour ago,' I said. 'Maybe an hour and a half.'

'There's no way he could have been stuck in traffic for that long,' Gloria said.

'Maybe he was called out on an urgent job or something,' Courtney suggested.

'He would have let us know.'

'Maybe the battery in his mobile ran out.'

Gloria shook her head. 'He would have found a way to contact us. Joe always finds a way.'

We lapsed into silence for a while then, the three of us just sitting there in the car, lost in our thoughts. My head was still throbbing, and the side of my face where Dee Dee had hit me felt swollen and raw to the touch. I suddenly felt very tired, and as I leaned my head against the cool glass of the window and closed my eyes, I found myself thinking over everything that had happened in the house at Birch Grove, wondering what could have happened, what might have happened, replaying in my mind what did happen. I remembered the murderous look in Courtney's eyes as she stood behind Dee Dee with the baseball bat in her hands, and I wondered how close she'd come to actually using it. I tried to work out how I would have felt if she had. Would I have felt that Dee Dee deserved it? Does *anyone* deserve getting badly hurt or killed, even if they are cruel and vicious and totally lacking in mercy themselves? An eye for an eye, a tooth for a tooth . . . is that the way it should be?

I didn't know.

All I knew was that I was glad Courtney hadn't killed him.

'There's a light on in the office,' Gloria said.

I opened my eyes and looked out of the car window. We were just turning off the North Road roundabout, heading for the back street where Grandad usually parked, and the office wasn't in sight any more.

'You saw a light?' I asked Gloria.

She nodded, suddenly looking much more positive. 'It wasn't bright enough to be the main office light, so it must have been the light in Joe's office. Did you see it, Courtney?'

'Yeah, I think so,' she said, allowing herself a tentative smile. 'He probably fell asleep in there, forgot all about us.'

Gloria smiled too, but I could tell she didn't think Grandad would fall asleep in a situation like this, no matter how tired he was.

We entered the back street and Gloria drove along until she found a parking space. She pulled in, turned off the engine, and we all got out of the car. It was a cold starless night, the street empty and quiet, and as we headed off towards North Walk, our footsteps echoed dully around the brick walls of the office buildings that backed onto the street.

'You know all that stuff you told Dee Dee about a series of signals you'd worked out with Grandad?' I said to Gloria. 'Was that true?'

She half smiled. 'It didn't have to be. As long as there was a possibility it was true, Dee Dee was never going to take the chance that it wasn't.'

'Do you really think he'll leave us alone now?'

'He's not stupid. He'll hate us for getting the better of him, and he'll despise Courtney for humiliating him, and for a day or so all he'll be able to think about is how to get revenge. But in the end he'll realise it's just not worth it. He'll also realise that the only witness to his humiliation was Bull, and he's not going to say anything, so his reputation is still intact. And reputation is all that counts to people like Dee Dee.' Gloria put her hand on my shoulder. 'We don't have to worry about Mr Devon any more.'

We were walking along North Walk now, approaching the door to the office building. Gloria had been constantly on the alert as she was talking to me – looking around, checking behind us, keeping her eyes open for anything out of place – and as Courtney took out her keys to open the door, I could sense the rising tension in Gloria. She was concentrating intensely – looking, listening, thinking – every sense in her body on the highest alert.

Courtney opened the door. The hallway was dark, a faint light showing through the glass panel of the office door at the end of the corridor. As Courtney went to go through the doorway, Gloria put a hand on her arm.

'Let me go first,' she said.

She stepped past Courtney into the hallway and then stopped. For a moment or two she just stood there, staring at the office door, listening hard. The building was silent. All I could hear was the quiet hum of water pipes from somewhere upstairs, and the distant sound of traffic on the streets outside.

'Stay behind me,' Gloria said quietly, moving off down the hallway.

We followed her to the office door, where she stopped and listened again, staring through the glass of the door. The main office was dark, and it was quite obvious now that the light was coming from Grandad's office. It wasn't strong enough to be the ceiling light, and so it could only be from the lamp on his desk.

Gloria slowly reached for the door handle. The door was unlocked. She opened it cautiously, pushing it gently with her hand, staying exactly where she was. The door to Grandad's office was open, but his desk wasn't visible from here.

'Joe?' Gloria called out quietly. 'Are you in there, Joe?'

There was no reply.

'Stay there,' Gloria said to us, stepping softly through the doorway.

'Joseph?' she said. 'Is everything OK?'

Still no reply.

I saw Gloria take a deep breath, and then she walked slowly but confidently across the room to Grandad's office. She paused again outside it and called out to him again.

'Joseph?'

She waited a second, then took another breath and went in.

I heard a low voice then, a man's voice. It wasn't Grandad's. I couldn't hear what the man was saying, but I recognised his voice. The sound of it made my heart sink.

The voice said something else, and a moment later Gloria appeared in the doorway and beckoned us over. There was a look of calm, but profound, resignation on her face.

I went over to the doorway, and Courtney followed me. I already knew who I was going to see when I went into the office, but when I walked in and saw him sitting on a chair in the corner of the room, his steel-grey eyes watching me from the shadows, the sight of him still made my blood run cold.

It was Winston.

Sitting in a chair in the opposite corner was Lance Borstlap. Both men had pistols in their hands.

Grandad was sitting dejectedly at his desk. In the light of his lamp, I could see a nasty gash just above his right eye. It looked like he'd been hit with the barrel of a pistol.

'Sorry, Trav,' he said sadly, looking up at me. 'They took me by surprise.'

I stared hatefully at Winston.

'Hello, Travis,' he said casually. 'It's good to see you again.' He turned to Courtney. 'You too, Ms Lane. I hear you've had a spot of trouble recently. How are you feeling now?'

'I was feeling fine until I saw you,' she said.

Winston gave her a tight-lipped smile. 'Right, well, now that we're done with the pleasantries, why don't you all come in and take a seat. I think it's time we had a little chat.'

There was no doubt in my mind now that this was the man who was responsible for the death of my parents, and as I stood there that night, staring into his cold grey eyes, I promised myself that whatever it took, however long it took, I was going to make him pay for what he'd done.

About the Author

Kevin Brooks is the critically acclaimed, prize-winning author of eleven books for young adults, including the 2014 CILIP Carnegie Medal-winning *The Bunker Diary*. These have been translated into many different languages and published with great success around the world. He has also written thrillers for adults. The Travis Delaney series is Kevin's first foray into fiction for younger readers. Having worked in places as diverse as a zoo and a crematorium, Kevin now writes full-time. He lives in Richmond, Yorkshire, with his wife.